Before
BEN

New York Times & *USA Today* Bestselling Author

CYNTHIA EDEN

This book is a work of fiction. Any similarities to real people, places, or events are not intentional and are purely the result of coincidence. The characters, places, and events in this story are fictional.

Published by Cynthia Eden.

Copyright ©2019 by Cynthia Eden

All rights reserved. This publication may not be reproduced, distributed, or transmitted in any form without the express written consent of the author except for the use of small quotes or excerpts used in book reviews.

Copy-editing by: J. R. T. Editing

CHAPTER ONE

"You ever had a hate fuck?" His voice was low and rumbling and, dammit, *sexy*. "Because I have heard they're incredible. You get out all of that rage...all of that desire. And the only thing left is pure pleasure."

Courtney McKenna slowly lowered her appletini. The bright green liquid jostled a bit, spilling over the edge of the martini glass and dribbling onto her wrist. What a waste of a good drink. She eased out a slow breath before she glanced at the cocky SOB who'd sidled up beside her.

Ben Wilde flashed his killer grin. The absolutely *killer* one. The one that made the twin dimples he possessed dig gorgeous groves into his cheeks as the smile revealed his perfect, white teeth.

That was the thing about Ben. Physically, the guy was perfect. Tall, built, with shoulders that stretched and stretched. Dark blond hair, deep blue eyes. Golden skin. A straight nose, square jaw, lips that were—

"Come on, Court," he said, shortening her name to the dreaded *Court* that she hated. "Is that a yes…or a no?"

"It's a *hell no*." Time for another calm-down breath. She had to take a lot of those when Ben was near. She blew this deep breath out very, very slowly. "Besides, you aren't serious."

His eyebrows rose. "Of course, I am."

"No, you're not. I've known you since law school. You're an arrogant prick who thinks it's fun to mock me." Her eyes narrowed on him and his stupid, too well-fitting suit. "There are plenty of women in this bar who would be happy to jump your bones. Go find one of them. Leave me alone. I've got better things to do."

Instead of backing away—like a *normal* man would do when he'd been shot down so hard—Ben laughed. And, not shockingly at all, Ben's laugh was as sexy as the rest of him. Deep and warm. And designed to get right under her skin.

I totally hate him.

"Better things?" He put his hand on the bar and leaned in close to her. So close that she caught the crisp scent of his cologne. It was a lickably good scent, not that she would *ever* tell Ben that fact. "Court—"

"Court-*ney*. Court-*ney*. My name has two syllables. Use them both."

Those dimples came again. "Courtney."

Wow. He'd just said her name all deep and rough and sexy-like. The way he'd probably say it if he was, in fact, in bed with her. Having the hate fuck he'd just mentioned…

Maybe she should have stuck with Court. Why did the nickname irritate her so much? And why had he *always* gotten under her skin so easily?

His warm gaze slid over her face. "There is no one *better* when it comes to sex. Come with me, and I will give you a night you will never forget."

"You have been hitting on me since the first year of law school." She could only shake her head. "Doesn't the routine get old?"

"Trust me, nothing about you gets old to me."

Courtney sighed. "You didn't mean it back then. You don't mean it now. You're just messing around with me, and I don't have time to waste." Her gaze slid over his shoulder.

His brow furrowed. "Are you looking for someone else?"

"Uh, yeah. I'm not here to meet *you*." Her stare shifted back to him.

He put a hand to his heart, as if she'd grievously wounded him. Bull. "And all this time," Ben said dramatically, "I thought you were mine."

The bartender frowned at them.

"Ben," she gritted out.

He winked. "I love it when you say my name." He hopped onto the bar stool next to her. Didn't even seem to notice the admiring stares coming his way from the ladies who were close by. "I'll love it even more when you—"

"Do *not* say scream it," she snapped at him. "I am so over your crap—"

With a wave of his hand, he motioned to the bartender. "I wasn't going to say scream." He seemed to consider the matter a moment. "Do you *want* me to say scream? Do you want to scream my name? Is that a fantasy?"

Her cheeks were flushing. Good thing the lighting in the place was so bad.

"I was just going to say…" He cleared his throat. "I love it even more when you get all pissed with me in court and you kind of…snarl my name. Snarl, not scream. There's a distinct difference there."

She wanted to put her head down. He wasn't being serious. Had he *ever* been serious? "Everything in this world comes easy to you, doesn't it?" The question slipped out. Hell, the bartender had already brought him a beer. Instant service. Meanwhile, she'd had to wait twenty minutes on her drink. "You flew through law school and opened up your own firm immediately. You have every woman you want begging for you—"

"Not everything is easy." His voice wasn't mocking. It *seemed* dead serious. "I've never had you."

She reached for her drink again. "And you never—"

"Why?"

Her fingers tightened around the stem of her glass.

"I'm a reasonably attractive guy."

Uh, no, he was drop-dead gorgeous.

"I have a successful practice. I pay my taxes. I hold the door open for ladies and children, and, hell, everyone. But you…you just don't like me."

She lifted her drink. And downed it too fast.

When she choked, he helpfully patted her on the back.

Only…when she stopped choking, his fingers lingered. Her head turned toward him. When she'd started to choke, he'd bounded off the bar stool and crowded in all close to her. Oh, damn. His scent was teasing her again.

"Have you ever wondered, Courtney? Come on, tell me. Have you ever thought about what would it be like between us?"

Only a time or twelve.

"Maybe we should start with something simple." His gaze dropped to her mouth. "Like a kiss."

They were in the busiest bar in Atlanta. One that was packed to the brim on a Friday night. Normally, bars weren't really her scene, but she'd decided to swipe right and give the date tonight a try. Only…

I've been here for thirty minutes and my swipe right is a no show. That would teach her to try and hook up with a guy online.

Courtney realized that her gaze was on Ben's mouth. That delectable mouth of his. Her stare whipped up so that she focused on his eyes. Did he know that he had flecks of gold in the depths of his eyes? The gold could get all warm when he was arguing a case. Almost blazing. And it probably blazed when he was making love to a woman, too. *Not* that she was going to find out.

His powerful shoulders rolled in a shrug. "We're two mature, consenting adults. A kiss wouldn't hurt anything."

He was so tempting. Too tempting. She dug some money from her bag so she could pay her tab and run out of there. "I have to see you in court almost every single day. And, usually, we're fighting each other."

"No, our *clients* are fighting. Not us."

"Getting involved personally would be a mistake." Because she'd sleep with him and then have to see him move on to the next woman in line. That wasn't how she worked. She didn't do one-night stands.

Or at least, she'd never done one before.

"It could be a mistake," he agreed. "Or it could be the best sex of your life."

Laughter came from her. She simply could not help it. "You are so cocky."

He shrugged again. "You can be the judge."

"No, not happening." Just like her date for that night wasn't happening. Time to go home, ditch her heels, find some chocolate ice cream, and slip into some comfy PJs. Ben could romance someone else.

She ignored the pang in her heart. The pang that had been there for a very long time.

Too long, at least as far as Ben was concerned. She could bluff a good game, but the truth was when it came to Ben…

He's always tempted me a bit. Tall, strong, and gorgeous with a mind that was freaking insane...

Walk out slowly and casually. Ben never needs to know that you've had a ridiculous crush on him for years. He never needed to know just how hard it was to say no.

When she really, really wanted to say yes.

She brushed past him.

"He's one lucky bastard."

Ben's voice was...different. Rougher.

Not quite so perfect and charming any longer. Very *un*-Ben. She looked back at him.

His eyes were different, too. The gold had started to blaze in his blue depths. "The guy you're looking for tonight." A muscle jerked in his jaw. "He's one lucky bastard to be meeting up with you."

It actually sounded like he meant those words. That was—

She didn't know what it was. Courtney turned away from him and pushed her way through the crowd. Her date wasn't coming, and she needed to get out of there before Ben realized she'd been stood up. How humiliating would that be?

But...

She risked a glance back at him. *You ever had a hate fuck?*

She didn't hate Ben. Never had, never—

Oh. A blonde had already taken Courtney's spot at the bar. A blonde who was sliding a well-manicured hand up Ben's arm. Courtney's back teeth ground together. She whipped her head back around and stormed for the door. Moments later, she was outside, and the hot, Atlanta night air slammed into her.

Her heels clicked over the pavement as she hurried for the parking garage. The sooner she got home, the better. The sooner she —

Footsteps rushed behind her.

Courtney automatically glanced back, but a woman was just running toward a man, with her arms outstretched for him.

Couples were everywhere. Like she was in the mood to see *everyone* else being happy. Once more, Courtney marched forward, picking up her pace, and soon she was entering the garage. The security guard gave her a friendly wave, and she smiled back. A horn echoed in the distance. Her car was on the next level up. Getting a spot in downtown Atlanta required some serious maneuvering, but she'd done it.

She entered the stairwell. Automatically, her hand shoved into her purse because a woman learned early on to be careful. And dark stairwells? Um, yeah. Not fun. Courtney gripped her keys between her knuckles just like she'd been taught in self-defense class, and she rushed up the stairs. *Hello, cardio.* Soon she was on the next level and heading for her car and —

"You fucking bitch!" A man in a black hoodie launched at her.

Courtney screamed even as she yanked her hand — and her make-shift weapon — out of her bag.

***

He'd struck out again. At this point, Ben couldn't remember the number of times that Courtney McKenna had shot him down.

Straight down in a blaze of glory.

He took another long pull from his beer.

"I like dancing," the blonde next to him said as she trailed her fingers up his arm. "And I like beaches. But I don't like the water because you know, there are *things* in the water. I like country music. And some rock. I like dogs. Like, really big dogs that are super fluffy."

Okay. He slanted a glance toward her.

And that was when he noticed that Courtney had left her ID on the bar. Hell, yes. The excuse he needed. "Sorry." He swiped up the ID. "My friend left this. Got to give it back to her." Then, yes, he hauled ass out of the bar. So he looked desperate. He was. Mostly because he always tended to say the wrong stupid shit to Courtney.

He bounded after her as fast as he could. He saw her as she ducked into the parking garage, and, damn, the lady was moving at a clip. An impressive feat considering the heels she wore. Courtney usually stuck to sensible shoes, but tonight, when he'd spotted her in the bar, he'd realized she was wearing three-inch, spike, black heels.

On another woman, he might have called them fuck-me shoes. On Courtney…

Those shoes just made him want to drool. *Make men beg* shoes.

When he ran into the parking garage, the guard surged toward Ben. "You following that woman?" The fellow was immediately suspicious probably because, yes, indeed, Ben was following her.

Ben held up the ID he still clutched. Courtney was out of his sight. "I'm trying to return this to my friend."

The guard looked at him with even more suspicion.

"We *know* each other," Ben muttered. "She left her ID at the bar, and I wanted to give it back to her."

The guard's eyes were narrowed and his beefy body was tight with tension. Obviously, he wasn't buying the story that Ben was trying to sell.

"What the hell, man?" Ben finally threw out in disgust. "I park here every week. I know you've seen me before."

The guard grunted.

"I even brought you coffee once. On that really cold-ass night."

Finally, the guard relented with a long exhale and a wave of his hand. He also stepped back. Ben didn't waste more time. He was pretty sure Courtney had gone up to the next level. He lunged for the stairs. Tried to get a less desperate look on his face as he bounded up, and when he reached the second level and shoved open the door—

Courtney.

The sight that greeted Ben made red-hot fury fire through every cell of his body.

Courtney was fighting with some asshole in a black hoodie. The bastard had his fist drawn back to hit her, and even as a bellow of rage exploded from Ben, he saw Courtney pound her fist—and her keys—into the guy's stomach.

Her attacker staggered back. He reached down even as Ben bounded forward. The piece of shit was digging into his boot—and pulling up a knife. "Courtney!" Her name escaped Ben as a roar of absolute fury. He grabbed her arm and yanked her back, hauling her behind him as he faced off with the SOB.

The attacker swung his knife. Because Ben's father had dragged him to martial arts classes for far too many years—and because Ben's older brother owned *the* best security company in Atlanta, no, on the whole East Coast—Ben was ready for the attack. He kicked out, sending the knife clattering to the pavement, and then he launched at the jerk. He hit him hard and low, plowing his shoulder into the guy, and Ben took that dumbass down.

But the punk was a fighter. He drove his fists into Ben, twisted and heaved, and he managed to get in a vicious blow to Ben's ribs.

Heels clattered close to them. Courtney's heels. Shit. "*Get back!*" Ben blasted. The last thing he wanted was for her to get hurt.

He saw her bend to scoop up the knife.

Ben lunged to his feet and put his body in front of hers. And the sonofabitch in the hoodie—he turned and ran. *Oh, hell, no.* Ben leapt forward.

"*Freeze!*"

That somewhat shaky command came from behind him. Behind him *and* Courtney. Ben risked a glance back to see the security guard emerging from the stairwell. The guy had a taser in his hand, and he was closing in fast on Ben.

"I'm not the attacker!" Ben snarled.

The guard barked, "Drop the knife, lady!"

Courtney dropped the knife.

Ben moved, making sure he was between her and that taser. No way was the guard about to send bolts of electricity through her delicate body. "You're letting the bad guy get away!"

"I'm getting the cops here," the guard snapped right back. "They can sort this out. They can—"

An engine growled. A black motorcycle came speeding toward them. The driver wore a black hoodie, tattered jeans, and a black helmet that completely concealed his identity. And he was driving *straight* for them.

Ben grabbed Courtney and yanked her into his arms, pulling her out of the way. Her body shoved hard against him, every single perfect inch of her feeling like heaven.

Her eyes stared into his. Her dark chocolate eyes were wide and huge. Her lips were parted. Her full lower lip trembled a moment as the growl of the motorcycle echoed in the garage.

"Ben?" Courtney whispered.

He shook his head. Managed to drag his fool gaze *off* her and onto the motorcycle. "Told you he was getting away!" Ben fired at the guard who was gaping.

There was no tag on the motorcycle. Nothing to stop the guy. He zoomed down the exit ramp even as they all gave chase. But it wasn't like they could catch a motorcycle. By the time they reached the gate, he was long gone.

Fucking sonofabitch.

***

"I'm following you home." Ben's voice came out rough and angry. A side effect of the situation. A situation that made him *feel* rough and angry.

Courtney turned her head toward him. She'd been talking to a uniformed cop, giving her statement, and looking so gorgeous that she made Ben ache.

She could have been hurt tonight. He kept seeing the image of that jerk with his fist drawn back, ready to hit her in the face. Ready to attack her.

"He didn't take anything, ma'am?" the cop asked. "You're sure?"

She shook her head. "No. I-I think he was going for my purse, but I hit him with my keys. Punched him in the stomach." She lifted her hand, and Ben saw that she had her keys arranged so that the sharp points slid through the lines between her fingers. A nice weapon.

One that had saved her ass.

Ben edged closer to her.

"We'll check the security feeds here," the uniform assured her. "There have been some snatch and grabs in the area. Probably the same guy."

Was that supposed to make it *better* somehow?

"It would have helped if you'd gotten a better description of the guy…"

"Sorry," she bit out. "I was busy fighting him. His hood was up, it was dark, and everything happened so fast."

"You're not *getting on to her* because she couldn't get the guy's ID?" Ben's voice held barely banked rage. "I didn't get a look at the jackass, either. His hood covered him, just like she said, and the asshole was sticking to the shadows. Courtney fought him. She's okay. You need to be telling her what a fucking awesome job she did."

"You're safe." The cop nodded. He didn't follow Ben's order and tell her that she was *fucking awesome.* Loser.

The cop caught Ben's glare, winced, and quickly added, "That's what matters."

Damn straight it was what mattered. Ben cleared his throat. "I'm going to follow you home," he said again to Courtney.

The cop wandered away. He'd bagged the knife as evidence, but hadn't seemed to think any usable prints would be recovered. *Way to be optimistic.*

Courtney's gaze slid to Ben. "Following me home is not necessary."

Uh, yeah. It was. His hand lifted, and he brushed back a lock of her hair that had fallen forward. He loved her hair. A mix between red and brown. Most times, her hair *would* look totally brown, but when the light hit it just right, the red shone through. Burned so deep and rich.

His fingers lingered against her cheek. Her skin was silky soft. So delicate. "If he'd punched you, I would have killed him."

Her eyes widened.

Whoops. Had he just said that part out loud? He needed to dial back the rage, but that was hard. Because this was *Courtney.*

"I didn't expect you to be a white knight." Her voice was low. Husky. He thought Courtney pretty much had the sexiest voice in the world. Sometimes, when they were in court…

Focus, dumbass. He cleared his throat and dropped his hand. She'd called him a white knight. She was way wrong on that score. "I wanted to beat the shit out of him."

Her lips—plump, red—curved just a bit. "You did." Her fingers reached for his. Courtney winced as she caught his hand and lifted it up. "Your knuckles are already bruising."

When she touched him, his body reacted. Every muscle tensed, and he *wanted.* Typical Courtney McKenna response. He was usually in hyper drive where she was concerned. Not that she ever seemed to notice.

Her fingertips slid over his knuckles. "I'm glad you were there."

He raised a brow. "Careful, or I'll think you actually like me."

Her hand immediately jerked back from his. Shit, he'd said the wrong thing. For a guy who was normally so smooth with the ladies, he sucked when he was one-on-one with Courtney.

"I, um, I should get home."

His eyes narrowed. "I thought you had a date."

"Canceled." Her dark gaze darted around the garage. "So I need to head home, climb into a shower, and forget this mess."

He would *not* think of Courtney in the shower. If she wanted a white knight, he'd give her one. For the night, anyway. "I'll be right behind you."

Her breath expelled in a long rush. "You don't need to do that."

"I want to. Look, if I don't see you home safely, I'll worry about you all night. I won't be able to sleep. I'll just be thinking about you." Like he hadn't spent other nights doing the same thing. "Save me some misery and let me tail you, okay?"

The ghost of a smile slid across her lips. "Thank you."

His chest burned. He didn't want her gratitude. "It's what any friend would do for another."

He headed for her car. She still had her keys — keys that had proven to be a very fine weapon. She unlocked her ride with a press on the key fob, and Ben opened the door for her. But Courtney didn't slide inside. Instead, she paused, tilted back her head, and stared up at him. "I didn't think we were friends."

"No? Colleagues, then?"

"Enemies. Isn't that what you said back at the bar?"

"No, ba—" He caught himself before he let *baby* slip out. "No, ah, Courtney, I said hate fucks were great." He flashed his smile, deliberately using dimples because they often worked when he needed to get out of a sticky situation. "But when I was talking about hate, I wasn't talking about how I feel for you."

Her brow furrowed. Her delicious scent teased him. And when her tongue snaked across her lower lip...

Ben swallowed.

"*I* don't hate you," she said, voice even huskier.

Huh. That was progress. Not friends, but she didn't *hate* him. "Then how do you feel about me?"

She didn't answer. The little furrow between her dark brows deepened, and she slid inside the car. He slammed the door. Headed for his Benz. A few moments later, they were out of the garage. Heading through the streets of Atlanta. He kept her vehicle in sight, and when they parked at her building, he was out and at her side before she could even open her door.

She slid out of the vehicle, those sexy shoes of hers and that short dress putting her legs on perfect display. But he didn't let his gaze linger on the heels or her legs. *White knight.* He offered his hand to her and helped ease Courtney out of the vehicle. He was being on his best behavior because this was so important—

"I want you."

Ben blinked when she said those words, certain that he'd just straight-up imagined them. *Hello, auditory hallucination.*

"You asked me how I felt about you." She inched her body closer to his. "That's how I feel. I want you. I've wanted you for years and hated *myself* because I did."

His heart thundered in his chest, and the pants he was wearing became even more uncomfortable as they stretched over his dick.

"I thought the desire would go away eventually. It hasn't. So maybe I just need to work it out of my system." She stared straight into his eyes. "Will you come upstairs with me, Ben?"

What the ever-loving — "Hell yes."

CHAPTER TWO

The elevator doors closed. Her apartment was on the top floor of the building, and as soon as those doors closed—

Ben pulled her against him. "I'm going to kiss you."

Um, okay, that was—

"Are you fucking sure about this?"

No, she was absolutely *not* fucking sure about this. She was scared and shaking and Courtney feared adrenaline was boiling her blood. Having sex with Ben was probably the worst idea ever. But the truth was—

I do want him. She'd wanted him for a very long time. They were both adults. Why not take this one time and go after what she wanted?

Besides, she could work him out of her system this way. Finally end the Ben madness.

"Courtney?"

Her toes curled. "I'm going to kiss *you*." And she did. She surged up, wrapped her hands around his shoulders, and hauled him toward her. Their mouths met, and she was expecting him to be a good kisser. This was Ben Wilde, after all. But…

He wasn't good.

His lips parted beneath hers. His tongue stroked out. Slid into her mouth. Teased. Caressed. Thrust. Ben was taking his time and seeming to savor her.

No, he wasn't a *good* kisser. The man was fantastic.

He kissed her like he was tasting her. Like she was some kind of delicious wine. He wasn't too rough or dominating. Didn't slam his lips into hers. He seduced. He tempted. He had a moan building in her throat as her nails sank into—

He moved in a flash. Caged her between his body and the wall of the elevator. And he'd lifted her up as he'd moved her. His hands were around her waist, and her legs curled around his hips, an instinctive response. She'd known he was built, but the way he'd just lifted her—*he's strong.* Way stronger than she'd given him credit for being.

She'd seen his strength, though, when he'd pounded her attacker. When he'd attacked with such dangerous and fast force.

Her heart gave a little squeeze.

"It's okay, Courtney, I've got you." His lips took hers again, and the fear that had stirred for just a moment within her vanished.

It vanished as—

Ding.

Her whole body froze because right after that ding, she heard—

"Ahem."

Someone was there.

She tore her mouth from Ben's and risked a horrified glance over his shoulder. They weren't on her floor. She recognized the dark-haired, tattooed guy who smirked at her.

"Fuck off," Ben growled at him. "Elevator is full." He reached over and pressed the button to close the door.

And, sure enough, those doors slid closed and blocked her neighbor's hard stare.

Courtney felt her cheeks burn. No, not burn. *Blaze.* "OhmyGod." She unwound her legs from his waist and realized it had probably looked like they were fucking. Right there. Her heels clattered to the floor and she almost fell as—

Ding.

The doors opened again. Finally, on *her* floor. She rushed past Ben and headed straight for her apartment. Hers was the only one on that floor, and her fingers fumbled as she reached for the lock.

"Courtney."

Ben was right behind her. The thick carpeting in the hallway had swallowed the sound of his steps, but she'd known he was closing in. She'd managed to open the door. Her alarm was beeping, so she stepped inside and quickly tapped on the keypad to shut it off.

Then she turned back to face Ben. He looked so normal. So completely and totally in control. As if caging a woman on an elevator and kissing her like crazy was a normal experience for him.

Maybe it was. Probably a typical Friday night in his world.

"Change your mind?" He hadn't entered her apartment. He stood just beyond the threshold.

This was her chance. She could easily say that, yes, she'd changed her mind. Made a total mistake because she'd been shaken by the attack. She *was* shaken.

But she also just wanted Ben. One night. One stupid night. She could have this. She played by the rules every single day. Why not take one small walk on the wild side? And who better to take that walk with than Ben Wilde?

Her hand flew out. Her fingers fisted in his shirt-front. He glanced down, and she saw the wink of his dimples. "Is that a yes…or a no?"

The same question he'd asked her at the bar. She yanked on his shirt, and he came forward. "It's a *hell yes.*" What she'd really wanted to say at the bar, but fear had held her back. Insecurity. Worry. "I haven't changed my mind. I want you, Ben Wilde."

He kicked the door shut. "Then you've got me."

***

Cole locked his apartment door. He raked a hand over his face, and he reached for the phone he'd left on his nightstand. It wasn't a call that he particularly wanted to make, but he had a job to do.

Watching Courtney McKenna had been an easy enough task. The woman pretty much only lived for her job. But tonight, well…

His fingers slid over the screen. The call was answered on the second ring. "We've got a…problem," Cole announced. Tension knotted along the back of his neck. "She didn't come home alone."

***

"Strip."

Courtney blinked at the curt order from Ben. They were in her bedroom, faint light spilled from the nightstand lamp, and Ben filled the doorway.

"Um…" She reached for the zipper on the back of her dress. He was probably used to women who seduced and tempted like it was second nature. That was so very much not the case for her. She felt awkward and nervous and about a million miles out of her element. But she fumbled and stretched and by some miracle, Courtney actually got the zipper undone. Then she shimmied and the dress pooled at her feet.

She stood before him, wearing a black bra and black panties. And her heels. She should ditch those, too. Courtney bent down—

"Oh, no, baby, those *definitely* need to stay on." He stalked toward her. His gaze raked over her, and Courtney's body seemed to heat. Her breasts ached, her sex quivered, and when he reached out his hand to trail his fingers over her arm, Courtney jerked.

Ben frowned. "You okay?"

No. Yes. "Let me turn the lamp off." This would be so much easier in the dark.

Ben shook his head. "Then I can't see you."

Exactly. That would be why she wanted the lamp—

"And I want to see every single inch of you." His hand slid around her back. With a little flick of his wrist, he had her bra dropping to the floor. The cool air teased her breasts, and her nipples were already hard and pointing right at him.

"Fucking gorgeous." He curled his hand around her waist and lifted her up. "I'm going to make you *go crazy.*"

Her life was controlled. She was controlled. Sex with lovers was good, yes, but not *go crazy* intense. She wasn't the screaming, moaning type. She should warn him. No, he should've figured that fact out about her by now. He'd seen how she lived her life and—

"Baby…" He feathered a kiss over her lips. "Do me a favor?"

"Y-yes?"

"Stop thinking. Just feel."

Then she was on the bed. He was on top of her. He'd lifted onto his arms so his weight didn't crush her, and he was kissing her with sensual intensity. His legs were between hers, the fabric of his pants brushing along her sensitive thighs. He moved down, down, kissing her neck, sending a shocked rush of lust pounding through her because she'd never thought her neck was particularly sensitive before. And maybe he was just very—

His lips closed over her nipple. He licked and sucked and her hips rocked up against him. Her breath panted out. That was good. He kept licking. Kissing. Sucking.

She felt her panties get wet.

Better than good.

"We'll start with moans," he rasped. "Then work our way up to screams."

No, not happening. She was *not* the type to—

He was kissing a path down her stomach. Her belly quivered. Oh, wait, was he *already* heading straight for the finish line? No, he couldn't. He wasn't going to just jump right in and—

His fingers slid along the crotch of her panties. Her teeth sank into her lower lip as she rode his hand. It was an instinctive move because she wanted more of his touch. Wanted it firmer, harder. Wanted the panties out of the way. "Ben!" Not a moan. Not a scream. Just his name. Just a frantic whisper.

His broad fingers moved under the edge of her panties. He stroked her sex, teasing her clit and then dipping into her core. Courtney's neck arched as pleasure pierced through her.

"Always wondered how you would taste…"

Her eyes locked on him.

He smiled at her. Then he eased away from her.

Away? Um, no. Her whole body was quivering. She needed him back!

He slowly pulled the panties down her legs. Eased them off the high heels that she was still wearing. He dropped the panties, and she didn't care where they went. She swallowed, twice, because her throat had gone dry.

He pushed her legs apart. Locked his stare on her exposed sex.

His dimples weren't flashing. He didn't look charming. Didn't look like the poised lawyer. He looked wild and rough and sexy.

And…hungry.

His head lowered toward her. Her hands flew out and clamped around the sheets even before his mouth pressed to her. She was just getting ready. Kind of bracing herself. She normally didn't even really like it when—

His mouth touched her. His lips caressed. His tongue licked. His fingers stroked.

He knew *exactly* how to touch her. He acted as if he'd done it a thousand times before. He worked her with his mouth. He licked her clit. He stroked his fingers into her, and he had her *moaning* out his name as the pleasure built and built. Her whole body had gone bow tight. She was pushed closer and closer to the edge with every lick of his tongue. Her hips arched, her body tensed, and she *wanted.*

His tongue thrust into her.

She came. The pleasure crashed through her as Courtney lost her breath and damn near her mind. It wasn't some easy, gentle pop of pleasure. It was a full-on avalanche that rolled through her again and again.

"So fucking beautiful."

His gravel-rough voice barely registered, but a moment later, she felt his hips settling between her thighs. Her eyes opened, and she saw him pulling on a condom. He still wore his shirt, but he'd ditched his suit coat at some point. He'd yanked open his pants. Her body quivered with pleasure, and he hadn't even thrust his cock into her yet.

She licked her lips. "Ben—" *Take off your shirt. Get naked.*

"Just getting started." His cock lodged at the entrance to her body. His burning blue gaze pinned her. "Just." A hard thrust.

Her breath caught.

"Getting."

He withdrew.

Her legs locked around his hips as she fought to pull him back inside of her.

"*Started.*"

He sank deep, and the aftershocks of pleasure stopped being little ripples. As he withdrew and thrust, he started a rhythm that drove her absolutely insane. Her hands flew up. Her nails dug into his shoulders, pressing into the fabric of his shirt. She wanted his clothes gone. Wanted to be completely naked with him, but her second orgasm was building too fast. She couldn't slow down. Her body had ignited, and there was no going back.

"Hell, yes," Ben urged her as his thrusts quickened. "Let me feel you, let me feel you come around me."

Her lips parted. A wild cry broke from her. The pleasure slammed into her again, and her sex clamped around his cock as she erupted. And he was right there with her. Courtney felt the shudder that ran the length of his body, and Ben held onto her so tightly, his hands locked around her hips as he seemed to seal her to him.

Her heart thundered. Her breath heaved. The whole world spun.

Had she screamed his name? Courtney had no clue. She had to wet her parched lips. Clear her throat. And then she managed to open her eyes, too.

He was staring down at her.

Weren't guys supposed to look all sated and relaxed after sex? She was pretty sure that was typically the case. Only Ben didn't appear that way.

His eyes were darker than normal. His hair tousled. His jaw locked. His whole expression was just—dangerous. Intense.

"We'll be going again," he told her.

Oh, yes, please. She didn't say that. She could try to play this whole thing cool. *Try.*

He withdrew from her. She hated that. Missed him almost instantly.

He stalked to her bathroom, and since she didn't normally just hang out in bed, totally naked as she waited for her lover—well, naked except for the high heels—she immediately grabbed for the cover and yanked it over herself.

She heard water running in the bathroom.

I had sex with Ben. With Ben. And it had been as incredible as she'd always both feared and hoped it would be. Her hands raked through her hair. It was a long and tousled mess, and she needed it get it looking better so—

Her phone was ringing. Courtney frowned. Where in the hell was the phone? She'd come inside, and she'd had her bag on her shoulder. Had she dropped it on the desk in the corner? Right before Ben had stalked toward her and things had gotten hot, way fast?

She slid from the bed and made sure to pull a sheet with her. The phone rang again, the peal guiding her to the corner. She wrapped the sheet around her so her ass wasn't flashing, and Courtney snaked her hand in her purse. The number on the screen wasn't one she recognized, but she *had* given the cop at the scene her contact information. Maybe he was calling to tell her that he'd already made an arrest? Her finger slid over the phone and then she put it to her ear. "Hello?"

"You lying bitch."

The voice was so angry and filled with hate that it took the actual words a moment to register.

"You will fucking pay, you understand me?"

No, she didn't understand. "Who the hell is this?" Courtney demanded.

He hung up.

She immediately tried to call the number back. It just rang and rang—

"Everything okay?"

Courtney spun around. Ben stood a few feet away, his head tilted. Still wearing the shirt and pants. She clutched the phone with one hand and pressed the sheet to her chest with the other.

His eyes narrowed. "Who's on the phone?"

"I have no idea." She swallowed. "Just a prank call."

He took a step toward her. "You sounded…stressed."

Because someone had called her a "lying bitch" and said that she would "fucking pay"—yes, that would make a person stressed. "It's nothing." Just an asshole who wanted to ruin her already crazy night. She slid her fingers over the screen of her phone and selected the option to block that particular caller. He wouldn't be spewing his hate at her again.

Courtney dropped the phone.

But she kept holding her sheet as she faced off with Ben.

After sex talk. *Um, extreme awkwardness.*

His gaze was hard, and the gold was still showing in the blue. "I don't like it when you're scared."

His words surprised her. "I—I'm not." Okay, yes, that crazy caller had made her a little afraid for like…two minutes, but it had really been one hell of a night already. She should be entitled to stress or fear or anything else she wanted.

He advanced slowly.

Before he'd headed to the bathroom, he'd told her they'd be going for another round. In the heat of the moment, that had been an awesome plan, but now she was getting nervous again. Because—*Ben.* It was Ben. And they were crossing lines left and right. Like, all of the lines. Every single one out there.

His hand lifted, and his fingers trailed over her shoulder. "You're beautiful."

She sucked in a gulping breath. "You're still dressed." The words blurted out.

He blinked. Then slowly, that killer smile of his curled his lips. She waited, almost holding her breath, until she saw his dimples wink at her.

Some of the tension slid from her body. *Fuck that prank caller.*

He wasn't going to take the rest of the night away from her.

"I am still dressed," Ben agreed. "Want to help a guy out with that problem?"

In order to help him, she'd need to let her sheet go.

If you're doing this thing…

Her hand slid away from her chest. The sheet immediately slithered to the floor — near her heels.

If you're doing this thing, then do it right. After all, she only had the one night with him. One night to live out every single fantasy she had. Why hold back? There would be no second chance at this thing. Not like you got a do-over on a wild sex night with your sworn enemy.

The same enemy who'd come rushing to your rescue.

"Holy fuck, Courtney."

She smiled at him, feeling sexy, feeling bold, and feeling determined to make the rest of this night work. Screw the guy on the phone. Screw the asshole in the garage. She was taking the power. She was taking her pleasure. She'd have the night she wanted.

Her fingers trailed over his shirt. Slowly, enjoying every second, she began to unhook the buttons. The fabric parted, and, oh, yes, he had abs. So many abs. A six pack. A twelve pack? A whole lot of working out must be on the man's daily schedule. Courtney leaned forward. Her lips skimmed over his chest even as her fingers slid down to the front of his pants.

He'd buttoned up. Zipped up while in the bathroom.

That just wasn't going to work.

Down, down she slowly went. She reached for the top of his pants. The button there gave way beneath her fingers. The zipper hissed down.

Her knees touched the floor.

A moment later, that thick cock of his was in her hands. Her heart thundered, and part of her could not believe she was about to do this. She was going to go down on Ben Wilde. *Ben Wilde.* Seriously, what was she—

"I'll go insane if you put your mouth on me." He pulled her up. Lifted her in his arms and held her with the strength that she was finding so stupid sexy. "Save it for next time because I have to make you come *first.*"

She'd already come. Twice. And she'd wanted—

"I need in you. *Now.* The first time barely took the edge off. I want to be balls deep, and I want you moaning beneath me. On top of me. Wherever the fuck you want to be."

He carried her to the bed. Put her down. Used so much care. Then he grabbed his wallet. "One condom left." A muscle flexed along his jaw. "Tell me you have more here."

"I have more here." A woman liked to be prepared, right? Not that she'd needed the condoms lately. The box might even be a wee bit dusty. A fact she would *not* share with him.

"Fucking fabulous." He rolled on the condom. Climbed on the bed. She reached for him, so ready, so eager. Turned on more for him than she could ever remember being for any other lover.

When he sank into her, her whole body trembled.

The bed shook beneath his thrusts. She held onto him as tightly as she could. He was thick and long, and the man knew exactly how to move every single inch of his body. They rolled over the bed. He pulled her on top of him. One of his broad hands gripped her hip as she rose and fell, and his other angled to stroke her clit.

"Want to watch," he growled. "Every single second."

The tension that had gathered within her exploded. She came, her knees shoving against the mattress as she fell forward and slammed her hands onto his chest. Courtney called out his name. She may have screamed it.

Only fair, because a few moments later, Ben roared hers.

CHAPTER THREE

Her alarm sounded—immediately blasting her favorite song because that was how she had the helpful device set up. The pounding music filled the air and brought her to instant wakefulness and to the realization that she was so not alone.

Because a naked Ben Wilde was growling next to her.

She snatched up the covers. Light had just begun to trickle through the blinds, and seeing him first thing in the morning—all that tanned skin, those flexing muscles, his—

Her gaze whipped away from his crotch. Someone woke up happy in the morning.

"Why, *why* would you have your alarm set for 6 a.m. on a Saturday?" His voice *wasn't* happy.

She sat up in bed, tugging the covers with her. He didn't even try to conceal his body. "Because I…" *Do not look down again.* "I run on Saturdays."

Crap. Her gaze had darted down.

No, no, no. Courtney snatched her gaze back up.

"Every Saturday? Like, is that a Courtney McKenna rule?"

She nodded. Kept her gaze on his. A line of stubble covered his jaw. Jeez. He looked even sexier first thing in the morning. All rough and gorgeous.

Oh, damn. She was in trouble. They'd had awesome sex last night. Amazing sex. The toe-curling, and, heaven help her, screaming kind. But it was supposed to just be for one night. Ben wasn't the kind of guy who looked for a commitment.

And *she* wasn't looking for commitment. Especially not with him.

One and done. That was what it should have been. Right?

"Why are you giving me that look?"

She cleared her throat. "What look?"

His head tilted. "And why are you trying to pull the covers over your head?"

She inched the covers back down. "I was not."

He leaned toward her. His eyes narrowed. "You are the most confident, determined attorney that I have ever faced in a courtroom. But right now, you are blushing like hell and trying to sink into the bedding." He smiled and flashed his dimples. "You are so fucking cute."

This was a nightmare. "It's time for you to leave."

He nodded. "Sure. Because you have to go on your run." Ben climbed from the bed and presented her with one delicious view of his ass.

Then he glanced back, caught her looking, and winked.

Her flush burned even more.

"Want company?" he asked as his hand scraped over the stubble on his jaw.

"What?"

He'd pulled on his pants. Good. Very good. *Bad, very bad.*

"On your run." He motioned one hand vaguely in the air. "You want company?"

"You...don't have running clothes here."

Ben just shrugged one powerful shoulder.

She sidled from the bed. As fast as she could, Courtney jerked on her exercise clothes. And he kind of...watched.

And whistled.

Her hair flew around her shoulders as she spun back toward him. "Shouldn't you be rushing for the door?"

His gaze darted to her bedroom door, then back to her. "Why?" Ben seemed genuinely confused.

"Isn't that how your one-night stands end?"

His brows climbed. "You do a lot of research on my love life?"

"No." Yes. *OhmyGod.*

He stepped toward her. Ben had lost his smile. "That what you think I do? Just hook up and move on?"

"*Don't* you?" Courtney had no idea what else to say.

Ben shook his head. His hand rose, and he tucked a lock of her hair behind her ear.

A shiver slid over her body. And when she found herself leaning toward him, when her lips parted as if she'd go in for a kiss again...

Courtney snapped her spine straight. "This was a mistake." Such a mistake. A huge, colossal, life-altering mistake.

He frowned at her.

Her chin lifted. "Mark me off your list. You had sex with the woman you've been facing off with since law school. Done. Challenge met. One and done. Now just move on to the next lucky lady on your list."

His hand fell away from her. His fingers fisted at his side. "You have a really bad fucking opinion of me." His voice vibrated with anger.

With rage?

She blinked. "I…I thought you'd want an easy out."

"Nothing about you has ever been easy. And no, I don't want an out." A muscle flexed along his jaw. "And I wouldn't call it a mistake. I would call the sex fucking awesome. Phenomenal, even."

He'd call it what now?

"Whoever the fuck you were supposed to meet at that bar last night?"

Uh, yeah, about that—

"Forget him. I can *make* you forget him."

He already had.

"But you want space? You got it." He pulled on his shirt. And she caught a glance at the wicked scars on his side. She hadn't seen the scars last night, and her breath sucked in, but before she could talk to him, he fired out, "If you change your mind, you know where to find me."

In court, fighting against her.

But he was grabbing his things and heading for her den, and she rushed to follow him. He stopped at the front door and spared a glance over his shoulder at her. There was still rage on his face, but his voice was more controlled when he said, "I don't like it when bad things happen to you."

Courtney swallowed. "Neither do I."

"When I saw that bastard trying to hit you, I swear something snapped inside of me."

She realized she was holding her breath. Courtney let it go in a quick exhale. "Thank you for rushing to the rescue last night."

He took her hand in his. Brought her fingers to his lips. Pressed a tender kiss to her knuckles.

His knuckles were sporting bruises.

"You were driving your keys into his stomach. From where I stood, you were saving yourself. Just hate that you had to do that. I want you to always be safe." Another kiss. "Thanks for one hell of a night, Courtney." His left dimple winked.

She didn't smile back. She didn't *do* this. One-night stands weren't casual or easy for her. What in the heck had she been thinking?

I wasn't thinking. I was scared and shaky from adrenaline. He was there, and I'd wanted him for so long.

Line crossed.

No going back. They could only go forward. She could—would—put this behind her. They would go back to being professionals. To being enemies. To being—

"When you want to scream again, like I said before, you know where to find me."

He was so arrogant — and, fine, dammit, she *had* screamed for him last night but —

His face sobered. "Or if you ever get scared, if trouble should come your way again, call me, baby, and I'd be there in an instant."

What? "Why?"

A shrug. "You'll figure it out eventually."

He opened the door. Headed out. The guy was leaving at 6 a.m., walking away with rumpled hair, a serious line of stubble on his sexy jaw, and wrinkled clothes. There was no hint of a shame walk. Just a slow, satisfied prowl.

Men.

She shut the door. *One and done. One and done. One and…*

Done?

***

Her scent was on him. A sweet strawberry scent. And Courtney's beautiful image was in Ben's head as he strode into the elevator and pressed the button for the bottom floor. As the elevator descended, he reached down to hook another button on his shirt.

The doors opened. *Not* the ground floor.

The dark-haired, tattooed guy from the night before stood there. The fellow was wearing jogging shorts and running shoes, but no shirt. He had a bottle of water clutched in one hand. When he saw Ben, his expression tightened. "Kicked your ass out, huh?" The tightness gave way to a smirk as the fellow marched onto the elevator.

Ben didn't like the guy, and he sure as shit hadn't liked the way the fellow had looked last night when he'd caught sight of Ben and Courtney in the elevator. Shock. Then…anger. An anger that had looked far too personal.

"Just so you know, I'm a friend of Courtney's," the man drawled.

A friend who was wearing jogging shorts and running shoes at 6 a.m. Oh, hell, no. They'd better *not* have a habit of running together first thing on Saturdays. That was not cool. Not. Ben grunted. "I'm the same thing. Her friend."

The guy stabbed the elevator's control panel.

Ben's gaze scanned over him. Some of those tats were military.

"You didn't look like a friend last night."

Friend with fucking benefits, asshole. Ben's stare rose to pin the man. "What I do with Courtney isn't your concern."

The elevator dinged. When the doors opened, Ben marched forward.

"You won't be back."

Ben stopped. Then he turned his head to flash a slow smile at the fool. "Of course, I will be." He threw up a hand so the doors wouldn't close. "Stop worrying so much about Courtney. I've got *her*." The words were possessive as they slid from his mouth. And he realized…

Hell. Maybe he *didn't* have Courtney. But she sure had him. Because one night with the woman he'd fantasized about for so long just wasn't going to cut it.

He wanted more. A whole lot *more.*

***

"I was starting to think you weren't going to make it."

Courtney straightened her spine when she heard Cole's deep voice. She'd just slipped outside of her building, and it was about ten minutes later than her *normal* Saturday morning running time.

Cole raised one dark brow as he stared back at her. "I waited a bit, just in case."

Because sometimes they would run together. It had become a routine they'd followed since he'd moved in a few months ago. And, truth be told, she preferred not to run alone. Having a partner helped to push her to run faster, to make new goals. To keep shit going.

But she'd dreaded like hell seeing him today.

Especially after what he'd seen *last* night.

"Thought you might be too…you know…*tired* from your Friday night fun."

"Shut the hell up," she muttered as she bent into a stretch.

He laughed. "Saw the boyfriend leaving a few minutes ago. Guy seems like a real dick. Why the hell would you hook up with him?"

She leaned forward, letting her ponytail slide over her face so she didn't have to see him right then. "He's not my boyfriend."

"No? Sure looked like he was last night. I mean, the way his hands were on you and the way your legs were wrapped around him—"

"He was a mistake." She'd been repeating that same thing to herself over and over—ever since Ben had walked out. "Not gonna be a repeat performance."

"Oh." A world of knowledge was in that one word. "So he sucked in bed. I get it. Figured he would. Douchebag with his fancy clothes and—"

She whipped up. "He didn't suck."

Cole blinked at her.

I so wish I could take those words back. But, no way, *no way* on earth had Ben Wilde sucked in bed. He'd been the best lover—hands down—that she'd ever had. Her body ached in the best possible ways. They'd had sex over and over again, and each time it had just been *better.*

"You're blushing."

And he was gaping. What was worse?

"You're not…do you *like* the guy? I mean, I didn't even know you were dating anyone and then you—"

She stopped hearing what he was saying because Ben was walking toward her. Courtney had to blink twice to make certain she wasn't imagining him, but, yes, Ben was really there. Looking incredibly gorgeous with his sleeves rolled up, a wide grin showcasing his dimples, and a bouquet of flowers in his hand. It was like…six fifteen in the morning. Where in the hell had he gotten those flowers?

"Fucking hell," Cole muttered.

She ignored him. Her hand swiped over her shorts. Ben's gaze had just darted down her body, and when it rose again, there was a decided heat in his blue stare.

Ben stopped in front of her. "I realized I left without telling you something."

Those flowers were gorgeous.

He held them out to her. "Thank you for an incredible night, Courtney McKenna." He leaned forward and brushed his lips over her cheek. Then, his head turned and his lips feathered over her ear as he said, "You were more than worth the wait."

Her fingers curled around the flowers as he eased back.

Ben inclined his blond head. "See you in court, sweetheart."

Then he turned and headed away. She was pretty sure he was whistling.

Cole was swearing. The guy needed to chill the hell out. Courtney lifted the flowers to her nose. She couldn't remember the last time that someone had given her flowers. Wait..._had_ she gotten flowers before?

Cole tugged the flowers from her hand. "Dude is a player." He glowered. "Don't fall for that shit. He'll use you up and spit you out."

She snatched the flowers back. They were hers, after all. Because she couldn't very well take them on her run, she turned back for the building. "Go on without me." Her gaze slid to him. "I'll put these in water and then I'll take my run."

"What the hell ever." He gave her a little salute and took off.

Courtney smelled the flowers again.

You were more than worth the wait.

***

Her feet pounded over the pavement as Courtney ran along the trail in the nearby park. She'd put Ben's flowers in water. There had been no vase at her place, so she'd just taken the biggest glass she could find to house the present.

Flowers.

Okay, yes, maybe it was silly for her to be so excited about them, but…

Her life hadn't exactly been filled with flowers and presents. She'd spent her youth bouncing in and out of foster homes because her mother had died and then her "father" had abandoned her. She'd been quiet and reserved and too afraid to get close to anyone. Why make friends when you were just going to be shipped to another house — and another school — far too soon? She'd barely dated. She'd spent all of her time focusing on her school because one older girl in the same foster house had once told her…

If you want out, you're gonna have to do it yourself.

So she'd done it. Graduated from high school as the valedictorian. No one had been there to cheer for her. Just like no one had been there when she moved into a college dorm. And she'd gotten into law school *on her own*. She'd worked side jobs, she'd worked assisting any professor who needed help. She'd busted ass.

There had been no time for playing or partying. She'd gotten the job done. Now she was a lawyer in demand, with plans to open her own firm very, very soon. The sky was the limit. It was—

She rounded the corner and saw him.

Black sweatshirt. Ski mask.

What the fuck?

Her hand shoved into her pocket.

Oh, hell, no.

It looked like he was waiting for her. She didn't waste time screaming—it was too early and no one else was there. She just turned and she ran. Her feet pounded over the earth and the wild beat of her heart filled Courtney's ears. Her fingers curled around the pepper spray in her pocket. She always ran with pepper spray, just as a precaution. And after last night, she'd been feeling way on edge—

She risked a quick glance over her shoulder. But he wasn't there. She'd snaked back down the path, so maybe he was just out of sight for the moment. Maybe he was—

A twig snapped.

She whipped her head back around. She lifted up the pepper spray with a wild cry.

"*Jesus!*" Cole threw up his hand. "What the hell?"

Her breath sawed in and out. "Guy was there... He was..." Another glance back. No one was behind her.

"Some punk messing with you?" Cole demanded.

"He was there." He *had* been there. She was sure of it.

"Where?" Cole's voice was angry. Flat.

Her fingers stayed curled around the pepper spray. "Around the bend. Near the pine tree that splits in two—"

He ran past her.

"Cole, Cole, *wait!*" She surged after him, running quickly because did it *look* like she wanted to be left alone?

But when they got to the split pine tree, no one was there. Cole searched the area, and she stayed close to him, only there was no sign of the man in the ski mask.

He'd vanished.

***

"You had quite a scare last night, didn't you, miss?" The police officer glanced down at his notes. "You said someone in a black hoodie tried to steal your purse in a garage."

"Yes, but—"

"And now you *thought* you saw someone in a black sweatshirt and ski mask in the park? Waiting for you?" The cop, a young guy with bright red hair, gave her a sympathetic glance. "It's normal for victims to be on edge after an attack."

Cole sidled closer. "Wish you'd told me about that attack sooner."

When? When would she have told him? When he caught her and Ben in the elevator?

"Sometimes, victims can even relive their attacks." A delicate pause. A little cough from the cop. "Even see things that might not be there."

Her eyes narrowed. Was the cop shitting her? Or was he seriously standing there saying that she'd imagined the guy in the ski mask?

The cop winced, as if realizing he'd pissed her off. "Or, you know, it's possible you saw another jogger. Someone who just happened to be wearing a sweatshirt—"

"*And* a ski mask?" In the Atlanta heat?

"You told me that he didn't say anything to you and there's no sign he tried to follow you—"

"Because I hauled ass away!"

The cop glanced over at his waiting patrol car. "I'll do a sweep of the area."

That was all she was going to get. The officer didn't believe her. Even Cole looked doubtful.

She hadn't imagined the guy in the park. No way.

The cop talked a little more, told her to call the authorities if she saw anything else suspicious. Blah, blah. His words held no emotion, and she got the feeling he was just feeding her a line. Standard procedure.

He was gone moments later, and she turned for her apartment building.

"Courtney…you okay?" Cole asked.

"Fine." She tossed a brittle smile his way. "Just going to head upstairs and shower."

"I...I didn't see him." Cole's voice was halting. "I'm sorry."

Didn't see him... "You believe I saw him, though, don't you?"

He hesitated. Just for a second. Well, damn. She and Cole had become...friends, of a sort, since he'd moved in the building. Friends were supposed to trust you, weren't they?

"I need to get upstairs." She kept her fake smile in place. "See you later."

"Courtney! Courtney, yeah, shit, I believe you!" He grabbed her arm. "But it was probably just some dumbass messing around. Nothing for you to worry about."

She was worried. The guy in the garage, the phone call last night, and now the creep who'd seemed to be *waiting* for her? All of that was bad. Very bad. She muttered something to Cole. One of those vague things people said when they just wanted to escape, and a few moments later, she was riding the elevator back to her place. It took her a moment to realize she'd put her hand against the back wall. The same wall that Ben had pinned her against the night before. Her hand pressed to it, as if she was trying to touch the memory.

Would Ben believe me?

The thought snaked through her mind. She had zero proof about the guy in the park. No one else had seen him. She and Cole had come across a few other joggers, they'd questioned them, but those women hadn't noticed anything out of the ordinary. They definitely hadn't seen a man in a ski mask.

Courtney headed to her home. Unlocked the door. Walked inside. She marched straight for the kitchen, wanting to get a drink from the fridge, but she stopped near the counter, her body absolutely frozen in place.

Her flowers had been ripped apart. Thrown onto the floor. The glass — the one she'd tried to use as a vase — had rolled toward the fridge, and the water pooled near her feet.

Someone had been in her apartment.

Oh, God, someone could still be in there...

CHAPTER FOUR

Something was wrong.

Ben knew it the minute that Courtney stepped into the conference room on Monday morning. He rose, his body going on high alert.

She wore a long, black pencil skirt and a loose black top. Her hair had been pulled back and tamed in a sleek ponytail. She carried a briefcase in one hand, but her grip was too tight. White-knuckled.

And dark shadows lined her eyes. As if she'd had trouble sleeping.

When she approached her client, Courtney inclined her head to Hayden Laslow. No smile softened her lips. Courtney was usually all business in the courtroom, so the lack of a smile was no surprise, but the way her fingers trembled when she put her briefcase on the table…

Yeah, hell, he was noticing minute details about Courtney. That was his thing. He always noticed too much about her. Story of his life. In law school, she'd always liked to wear black converse shoes. Flowing tunic tops. Tight jeans. He'd been able to predict the outfit she'd wear by the time they were—

She caught her lower lip between her teeth. Slanted him a quick glance, then looked away.

But not in time. Not before he saw the flash of fear in her eyes.

Ben took a step toward her.

"She was late." His client's hand flew out and curled around his wrist. "Is that good for us? Or bad?"

He glanced back at Kadi Laslow. He hadn't wanted this early morning meeting, but she'd insisted on it. Divorce wasn't what she desired, and Kadi was hoping her husband would change his mind about the proceedings. Thus, the little meet and greet to supposedly talk over mediation options.

But, judging by the hard set of Hayden Laslow's jaw...that wasn't happening. Mediation didn't look like the guy's master plan, and Ben knew why. Hayden hadn't been particularly thrilled to find out that his wife had cheated on him.

Three times.

Three times that Hayden knew about, anyway. Because there had been more. Fidelity wasn't Kadi's strong suit.

"Let me find out why she was delayed," he murmured to Kadi. Her blonde hair fell loosely to her shoulders. The scent of her perfume surrounded him, a heavy scent that made his nose a bit twitchy. She'd deliberately dressed for this meeting—wearing her tightest and shortest skirt, her highest heels, and a blouse that plunged to reveal the breast increase that Hayden had been only too happy to purchase three months ago.

Unfortunately, Hayden wasn't happy with anything about his wife these days.

Kadi released Ben's hand. His head turned toward Courtney. Her gaze was on him. Or rather, on him and Kadi. A little frown pulled at Courtney's lips.

Her client had stood up, and now Hayden crowded in close to Courtney. "Why the hell were you late?"

Ben stiffened at Hayden's tone. *Watch it, buddy.*

"I don't *pay* you to be late," Hayden seethed. "Your firm said you were the best they had, but I am seriously doubting that sh—"

"*Excuse* me," Ben cut in. His voice came out hard and growling, but he'd bitten back the *fuck off* that had wanted to spring from his lips so he figured he was being polite enough.

Hayden frowned at him. The guy's distaste was plain to see. "You fucking her, too?"

Her? Ben's gaze automatically cut right back to Courtney—

"Of course, he's not fucking me, Hay!" Kadi cried out. "You're the only man I want! You know that." She'd risen to her feet and her hands pressed dramatically to her chest.

The better to push up her assets.

Ben felt a throb in his left temple. It was too early in the day for this. "I'm not involved with your wife, Laslow." *But I did fuck your lawyer.* Yeah, no, not a tactful thing to say at the moment. *And I want to fuck Courtney again and again.* Again, not the right words. Ben inclined his head to Courtney. "I'd like to have a word outside with you, counselor."

He heard Kadi's excited inhale. She'd already told him that she wanted time alone with her husband. Time that Ben had advised *against.* Not that she'd listened. He hadn't planned on giving her that time, not until he'd realized that Courtney was afraid.

Now Kadi could have her five minutes to try and work a miracle with the enraged ex. And Ben would take his time to find out why Courtney wasn't looking him in the eyes.

Courtney's lashes fluttered. "I don't really think speaking outside is necessary."

Oh, it was. Unless she wanted to tell everyone why she was afraid, and he didn't think she did. Courtney had always been reserved. Private.

Prim and proper to his "Wilde" ways...hell, there had even been a running joke about that back in their law school days. Only he didn't think Courtney had found it funny. And, truth be fucking told, neither had he. He'd never found anything funny that made her uncomfortable. He'd told the others to cut that shit out, but he doubted Courtney knew about his intervention attempts.

"We are just here as a courtesy," Courtney continued, clearing her throat. "My client and I are quite ready to proceed with the divorce proceedings."

She wasn't going to talk privately outside with him. Or at least, she wasn't talking yet. They'd wrap up this talk and *then* he'd get her alone.

But before he went back to business...Ben leaned in close. "You okay?" His voice was a rasp meant for her alone.

Courtney gave a jerky nod.

Lips thinning, Ben stepped back. He returned to his client. A pout had pulled down Kadi's lips. "I wanted alone time," she muttered.

Then maybe you shouldn't have screwed around on the guy. He'd agreed to take her on as a client because he owed a friend a favor. She'd been the favor, but Kadi was driving him crazy.

Courtney eased into her seat. Hayden brought his own chair a bit too close to her. He glowered at Kadi and at Ben.

Courtney folded her hands on top of her briefcase. "Why did you want this meeting today?"

"Because I don't want the divorce!" Kadi exclaimed.

Ben tapped her hand. It probably looked like a consoling gesture, but it was really his way of saying...*Dammit, let me handle this.* "Mediation is always a good idea." His voice was perfectly bland and easy. "Especially in situations like this one. When you have two people who care so very much for one another, every option should be explored."

Courtney slowly lifted one eyebrow. She looked at him. At Kadi. A faint smile curved her lips.

"My client..." He pulled his hand away from Kadi. "She still loves her husband. I would suggest marriage counseling for them. Before we see the dissolution of this two-year marriage, we need—"

"*You screwed around on me, Kadi!*" Hayden blasted. "With three friggin' guys. We're done, and you're not getting a dime from me!"

Kadi let out a dramatic sob.

"Not three." Courtney unfolded her hands. Reached into her briefcase and pulled out a manila file. She pushed it toward Ben.

He opened it and wasn't particularly surprised to see the photos inside.

"Four," Courtney politely corrected. "My investigator recovered these photos from the phone of a Mark Santos. The photos were taken *one month* after Courtney married Hayden. That's why I was delayed this morning. I had to pick up the photos on my way to this meeting."

The ache in Ben's temple got worse. He couldn't say he was surprised by the photos. Courtney was always thorough as hell, so it was no wonder she'd been able to get her investigator to dig deep but...

Ben sighed. He reached into his bag. Pulled out his own files and slid them across the table. Two could play at this game. A lick of excitement fired in his blood, as it always did when he faced off with Courtney.

Neither Mr. nor Mrs. Laslow had believed in fidelity or in marriage vows. "One month, huh? My photos date back to one *week* after the marriage."

Kadi let out another dramatic cry. This one held a surge of shock. "How could you, Hay? How could you?"

Ben kept his face expressionless. Kadi had known about the photos. He'd talked to her about them, but the woman was acting like she was stunned by the revelation.

Hayden's face turned red. "Meant *nothing*."

Kadi jumped to her feet. "And the men meant nothing to me! You're the only one who matters. It was always you!"

Him...and *maybe* the five million that was up for grabs as part of the divorce proceedings. Hayden Laslow had a giant import/export business, and Kadi wanted her share of the loot.

There had been no pre-nup. Amateur mistake.

"I don't want this divorce." Kadi hurried to Hayden's side. She batted her lashes. They weren't wet. No tears marred her cheeks. "Let's try to make this work."

Hayden stared at her.

"Counseling," Ben suggested coolly. It was what his client wanted. It was what he'd say. "Continue the separation until you see how the therapy works, and we can proceed from there."

Hayden's hands fisted. "I'll think about it." He shoved to his feet. "I'm done here."

Without another word, the guy stormed out of the office.

Kadi tossed Ben a satisfied smile. She took her time gathering her things and strolling out. He heard his assistant talking to her outside. They were in Ben's conference room. *His* firm. After graduating from law school, he'd gotten rich clients, damn fast. And he'd made some killer deals for those clients. Maybe this wasn't the way he'd thought his life would go...bleeding rich assholes dry for their wives but...

Courtney's gaze was on the photos. There was something about her expression...a hint of recognition.

Hmm...Did she know the blonde? Because he didn't, not yet. The photos had been sent to his investigator, and he was working to track down the mystery lady's identity.

"You know her?" Ben pushed.

Courtney's attention shifted to him. That dark stare of hers...gorgeous. "I know when I see a stall tactic. Their marriage is over. Those two are toxic together."

Yes, they were. And—

And Courtney was heading for the door.

He lunged after her. "Stop!"

She stilled. Glanced back at him. "I don't think there's more to discuss right now. I need to meet with my client again—"

He shut the door to the conference room. Kadi had left it open, and he wanted privacy. "You're scared." He gave a hard shake of his head. "Of me? Because of what happened between us, you're scared of me now?" He'd called her over the weekend. Only gotten her voice mail. He hadn't wanted to pull stalker shit, so he hadn't tried again or gone back to her place. He'd known he'd see her at his office for this meeting. He'd just needed to wait. Unfortunately, patience had never been his strength. Not when he wanted something very badly.

He couldn't remember wanting anything as badly as he wanted her.

"Of course, I'm not scared of you. I'm *annoyed* that you thought you could blindside me today." She rolled her eyes. "I knew about the one-night stand Hayden had with the woman in your photographs." She pinned him with her dark chocolate gaze. "Did your client tell you *everything*?"

No, she hadn't. He'd suspected Kadi had been holding back on him. He'd deal with her secrets later because he had other priorities right then. Or, one main priority. Courtney. "If you aren't afraid of me, then what's wrong?"

Her lips parted.

He leaned toward her.

But Courtney shook her head. "Nothing. I've just had a few jumpy days." She headed for the door once more.

He stayed in her path. "You're the least jumpy person I know." She was all business, through and through. He crossed his arms over his chest and glowered at her. "Talk."

"Ben, I have other appointments. I have things to do. Get out of my way. *Now.*"

He was being a dick. He was also worried. "You didn't sleep this weekend. Not well, anyway."

Her lashes fluttered. "You know this because...?"

"I can see the shadows under your eyes. You tried to hide them with makeup—did a good job, but I see them."

"Aren't you observant." She didn't sound impressed.

He shrugged. "You're holding your briefcase too tightly right now. You did that when you came in, too. It's an old habit you have. Used to do the same thing with your laptop case right before a big presentation in law school. You'd grip it too tightly because you were nervous."

Now she took a step back. "You—you didn't notice stuff like that when we were at Emory."

"I noticed everything when we were at Emory." *Everything about you.*

She laughed, but the sound held no real humor. "Bull. You noticed every pretty girl you could seduce into your bed. You didn't notice me, except when I was in your way. I was the competition that you had to eliminate so you could be in charge of the Law Review and I was—"

"You were the hottest girl in class. The smartest one. The one who drove me crazy when she'd show up in her black converse shoes wearing those skin-tight jeans. You'd have your hair loose and long, and sometimes, you'd even have on those glasses with the black frames..."

Her mouth dropped open.

"I noticed you." And maybe he'd antagonized her a bit. Because...hell, he'd been a dumbass. And he'd wanted her attention. He *still* antagonized her for the same reason.

And I'm still a dumbass where she is concerned. But this was different. "Tell me why you didn't sleep this weekend."

"I have an active imagination."

"Huh?"

Her hold on the briefcase tightened even more. "Fine. You truly want to know? When I went jogging Saturday, I-I thought someone was waiting for me in the park."

His heart thudded fast in his chest.

"A guy in a black sweatshirt and wearing a ski mask."

What the fuck?

"I ran from him, and when I looked back, he was gone. Cole didn't see him. Cole, ah, he's the neighbor who saw us in the elevator."

The jackass. Check.

"None of the other joggers saw him, and the cop I called said I must have just been stressed from the attempted mugging on Friday."

He didn't move. But rage sure grew inside of him.

"When I got back to my apartment, I, um…" She looked away. "I'd put your flowers in a glass of water on my kitchen counter. I guess I didn't put it far enough from the edge or something because they'd fallen over. The water was across the floor, and at first, it even looked as if someone had torn the flowers apart." The last was said softly. She squared her shoulders and glanced back at him.

"But I searched my apartment. No one was in there. The place was *locked*. The security system turned on. There was no way anyone could have gotten inside, so I was imagining stuff."

Every muscle had tightened. "You should have called me."

"Why?" A quick, nervous laugh. "Because I was imagining things—"

"I've never known you to make anything up."

Once again, her gaze cut away from his. "Was I supposed to call you because we had a one-night stand? We're not exactly *friends,* Ben. Calling you would have been a mistake."

As much of a mistake as fucking me? He waited until her gaze came back to him. "You should have called me," he said again. "Because I will help you. Because I would do anything to keep you safe."

A little furrow appeared between her brows. "Why?"

"Because I'm not a total dick?"

Her lips parted.

"Because I don't like to see someone in trouble, and you *are* in trouble. The bastard in the parking garage was attacking you. And now you say that you think someone was waiting on your jogging trail for you? That someone might have been in your home? That's like a million red flags—"

"Or just a few," she whispered.

"You need me."

Her shoulders stiffened.

"My connections," he corrected smoothly, though, in truth, he'd meant those exact words. *You need me, baby. You'll figure that out soon enough.* "My brother owns Wilde Securities. It's the best security business on the East Coast."

Her tongue slid over her lower lip. "I know about Wilde. They handle celebrities. Billionaires. They're not exactly going to care about my mugging."

Wrong. "They'll care."

"Why?"

Because I care. He glanced down at his watch. "My schedule is clear for the rest of the morning." It wasn't, but he'd make it clear. "I'll take you over there right now. If someone was in your home, we need Wilde Securities to do a major system upgrade for you. No way can you keep staying in that place."

"Ben…I don't understand you."

"Well, what can I say? I'm a man of mystery." He turned away. Hurried outside the conference room. His assistant wasn't at his desk, so Ben sent a quick text to the guy.

Reschedule all morning meetings. Heading out of the office.

He heard Courtney following him—slowly. He waited for her at the elevator. Then he motioned for her to proceed him inside. As the doors slid closed, she sighed.

And he tried not to pounce. But the last time he'd had her in an elevator…

"You're a shark in court," she murmured. "You attack, and you never back down. We fight all the time."

A nod. "That's court. What happens in there, it's separate from what happens…" He motioned between them. "Right here."

She was still holding too tightly to her briefcase. "You're saying the sex is separate. That we can keep being adversaries in court, but we're something else…outside?"

"We can be whatever you want in court." But out of court, he wanted to be her lover. He wanted to take her in a hundred different ways…and then a hundred more. First, though, the thing he wanted most—it was for her to be safe. "By the way, your client is an asshole." And a guy who—Ben suspected—was involved in some seriously shady business dealings.

Her lips twitched, but she caught the movement before a full smile could form. "And yours is one real prize."

A laugh slipped from him. "Maybe their therapy will work. They kind of deserve each other."

She stared at him a moment. The elevator dinged. Already at the ground floor. Courtney squared her delicate shoulders. "Why are you helping me? Why do you believe me so easily?"

"Because it's *you*, sweetheart. You're Courtney McKenna. Lawyer most likely to succeed. Most ethical. *Least* likely to get caught in a sex scandal."

She winced at the last one. "You won the prize on that one. The *most* likely."

Actually, he had been the recipient of that unfortunate moniker. The "titles" had been given out at a party right before they'd graduated. He held the elevator doors so she could slip outside. Then he wanted to set the record straight. "I was also most likely to kick ass."

Her dark gaze lingered on him. She didn't laugh. He'd wanted to at least make her smile. Her smiles always made his chest feel a little warmer.

"So trust me to help you." He wasn't kidding. He wasn't just the playboy that the world saw. Playboys didn't work twenty-hour days so that they could build a firm. They didn't fight dirty and rough. They didn't get their hands bloody when need be.

He did.

For her…he would do just about *anything*.

CHAPTER FIVE

"You have a new client," Ben announced as he strode right into his brother Eric's office. He didn't bother knocking. He never knocked. But he kept his hold on Courtney—his fingers were twined with hers—as he pulled her inside after him.

"I tried to stop him!" Dennis, Eric's assistant, blared. "But he ran right past me."

"Dennis, please, you know you have to try a whole lot harder with me." Ben focused on his brother. Eric was seated behind his desk, a faint frown pulling at his face. It was a familiar expression to Ben. He referred to it as Annoyed, Level One.

"This is a mistake," Courtney whispered as she sidled closer to Ben. "He doesn't look happy, and I think we were supposed to wait in the lobby."

"I never wait in the lobby," Ben threw back. As far as he was concerned, that was a brother privilege.

Eric sighed. "No, he doesn't." He motioned to Dennis. "I've got this."

After a glower at Ben, Dennis yanked the door shut on his way out. Eric leaned back in his chair.

His curious gaze swept over Ben…then down to Ben's left hand. The hand that still held Courtney's. Then his gaze flickered to her. Sharpened.

"This is Courtney McKenna." Ben figured he should do introductions. "Courtney, that's my brother Eric. He's going to give you a brand new security system."

"I am?" Eric raised his eyebrows.

"Absolutely." He pulled Courtney forward and guided her to one of the chairs near Eric's desk. He took the other chair. Scooted it a little closer to her. "Some piece of crap attacked Courtney in a parking garage on Friday night. She thinks that she saw the same jerk in the park when she went running on Saturday *and* someone was in her house."

Eric's expression immediately hardened. "You've gone to the cops?"

"Y-yes," Courtney responded. She seemed flustered. Nervous. Very un-Courtney-like. "But they didn't seem optimistic about catching the mugger. And, um, I don't think they believed me about the man in the park."

"They're idiots." Ben immediately dismissed them. "Of course, she's telling the truth." He nodded toward Eric. "Got to put the new system in her apartment right away. And we need to figure out who this jerkoff is and why he's targeting her. Sounds to me like a stalker escalating, and we both know that shit isn't good." No, it wasn't. The last thing Ben wanted was for Courtney to be put in any additional jeopardy.

Eric blinked. "Uh, how about you come with me for a minute, *bro?*" He rose. Motioned to Courtney. "Please, just relax until we return. I'll have Dennis bring in coffee for you, and he can get some general info for a Wilde investigation dossier."

Eric wanted him to leave Courtney? Why? "I'm good right here." He waved his hand vaguely in the air. "Come on, let's get down to business." They didn't need to waste time.

Eric shook his head. "We need to talk, now." His voice had gone even softer. Always a bad sign from his too-controlled older bro.

Great. Now he had his Annoyed, Level Two face *and* voice happening.

Ben sighed and glanced at Courtney. He gave her a reassuring smile. "I'll be back before you can miss me."

She had a little furrow between her brows. Cute as hell. Part of him wanted to lean forward and kiss that little furrow — a very big part of him, but they weren't at that stage yet so…yeah, he just rose and stalked toward the door. He yanked it open and spared Dennis a menacing glance. "You take care of her until I'm back."

Dennis opened his mouth. Closed it. Opened it again. "I…will?"

Behind him, Eric swore. "Just give her some coffee and start getting basic case file information. We'll be right back." Then he hurried around Ben and led the way to the conference room. One of the conference rooms, anyway, because Wilde

Securities was huge. Even though Eric was leading the way, it wasn't as if Ben needed an escort. He knew every inch of the facility.

As soon as they entered the conference room, Eric slammed the door shut. "What in the hell are you doing?"

Ben shoved his hands into the pockets of his pants. "Trying to help out a woman in trouble?" Was this supposed to be a pop quiz? He tended to ace those.

Eric growled. "Don't bullshit me. You never succeeded at that crap as a kid, and you are not succeeding now."

Ben shrugged. Fine. He'd be as honest as possible. "I don't like what's happening with Courtney. She's scared. You specialize in this kind of thing so I figured bringing her here was a good idea."

Eric crossed his arms over his chest. "You aren't going to use my company to get that woman in your bed."

Oh, hell, no. Hell, *no*, Eric had not just said that. Ben's shoulders stiffened. "First...I don't need to use anyone or anything to get a woman in my bed. I'm Ben Fucking Wilde, okay? Getting sexual partners isn't a problem for me."

Eric shook his head in clear exasperation.

"And, second, she's already been in my bed."

Now his brother squeezed his eyes tightly shut.

"Though in the interest of full disclosure, I'd like to get her back there as soon as possible."

Eric's eyelids flew open. "That's why you're using me! You're here because—"

"And let's go back to my *first* point," Ben snapped. "I don't need help getting a lover. Can handle that all on my own, thanks so much. Of the two of us, I *am* the one who is more charming."

"Who the hell says that?"

"Everyone." He started to pace. "I want a new system at her home. I want to know what the hell is happening. I want her safe."

"You keep talking like that, and I'll start to think you care about this one."

This one? He whirled. "Why do you think I'm an asshole? Huh? I don't toss away any lover. That's not who the fuck I am. Piper knows the truth about me. You'd think my own brother would, too. But then again, you did think I was having sex with Piper for years so..." He let the sentence trail off.

Since Eric had married Ben's best friend Piper, it wasn't any surprise that Eric's face immediately flushed. "I was wrong about that."

"About a lot of things." Ben nodded. "Like you're wrong right now. I'm here because I want Courtney safe." He rubbed a hand over his jaw. "On Friday night, *I* was the one who found her in the parking garage. The asshole had his fist drawn back to punch her. The cops say it was just a snatch and grab robbery, but if that's the case, then why did she see him in the park the next day?"

"Are you *sure* it was the same guy?"

"Can't be sure. Courtney said he had on a ski mask in the park. And in the garage, he had his hoodie up, mostly covering his face and it was dark and everything happened so fast…"

Eric's gaze turned considering. "You're saying she never got a good look at her attacker. And in the garage, neither did you."

"I'll foot the bill," Ben said immediately. "All of this will come to me. She's scared, Eric, and I can't have that."

What could have been surprise flashed on Eric's face, but then the emotion was quickly masked. "You want full-service protection? Are you asking for a bodyguard, too?"

Now Ben stiffened. "Look…you acted as a bodyguard for Piper, and you married her."

One shoulder rolled in a shrug.

"Then Simon hooked up with Gwen Soloman when he was put on her protection detail." Simon Forrest was one of Ben's closest friends, and a guy that Ben considered to be one lucky bastard. Why? Because Simon was now deeply involved with the gorgeous Hollywood actress he'd risked his life to protect. From what he could tell, there would soon be wedding bells in Simon and Gwen's future.

Two bodyguard situations. Two marriage endings. Um…there might be a pattern. "If Courtney gets a bodyguard, how about we assign Julia? She's smart and capable and—"

Not likely to marry Courtney.

Eric sighed. "You are so messed up in the head."

No, but he was realizing he was a jealous SOB when it came to Courtney, and the idea of some bodyguard moving in and watching her twenty-four, seven...*New idea. Better protection plan.* "Courtney can stay with me."

"You're not a bodyguard."

"No, I'm not. But *you* installed the security system at my place." After Ben had been attacked by the creep who'd been obsessed with Piper. Another story, another day. "And we both know it's probably one of the best systems in the world."

"Uh, try *the* best. You think I was going to risk your safety ever again? Your place is like Fort Knox. Better."

"Exactly. So while you are giving Courtney's place an upgrade and figuring out what's happening with her case, she should stay with me." Obviously, it was the perfect solution. "I'll keep her safe."

"How long have you been involved with this woman?"

"Seriously, you want me to kiss and tell?" Ben whirled and strode for the door. "Tacky."

"*Ben.*"

He looked back. Fine. "Friday night."

Eric's eyes widened. "You slept with her the night she was attacked?"

"Yeah. I did." His voice roughened. "I've wanted her for a very, very long time, and I wasn't going to be dumb enough to walk away from her. I was with her at the bar right before the attack. I let her leave on her own, even though every instinct I had screamed for me to follow her. I was at the fucking bar with some blonde I didn't know while

Courtney was being attacked. How the hell do you think that shit makes me feel?"

Eric's expression sobered. "Ben?"

"She'll move in with me until her place is secure." As far as he was concerned, it was a done deal. "Now let's get back to Courtney. I want to get moving on her case."

A done deal.

***

"Absolutely not." Courtney gaped at Ben. "You think I'm moving into your place? No way. *No.*"

She was still in Eric Wilde's office. Ben and his brother had returned a few moments before, and they'd brought in a new guy with them, Simon Forrest. Simon was tall and fit, built much like Ben and Eric. But Simon had a darker, dangerous air that made her feel a bit uncomfortable.

What made her feel *majorly* uncomfortable? The idea of moving into Ben's home. His bed.

She shook her head. "If the security upgrades are going to take a while, I can always stay at a hotel. I'm sure the security there is—"

"Security at most hotels is shit," Simon cut in with his rumbly voice. A voice that reminded her a lot of her favorite actor. "Far too easy to swipe a key from a maid or to shimmy a cheap lock. That's the last place you want to go."

"Um…" She rubbed her hands against the top of her thighs. "The cops didn't seem to think I was in any real danger. And I don't have *proof* that anyone was inside my home." Her stomach twisted into knots. "Look, maybe I should—"

"Courtney," Ben said her name softly and with no emotion.

Her head swung toward him.

"Are you afraid?"

She knew the tone of voice he was using. Knew the look in his eyes. He pulled this routine in the courtroom. Looked all unthreatening and easy, but the truth was that Ben was moving in for the kill.

"Courtney?" Ben prompted.

Her back teeth clenched. "Yes, I'm afraid."

"Do *you* think the same guy was in the park?"

"I believe it was him, yes, but I don't have any proof. And the police said—"

"Wouldn't you rather be safe?" Ben pushed. "Don't you want to be cautious? I can give you a secure place to stay for the night. And it's probably only going to be a night or two before—"

"I am *not* staying at your home." That would be a serious mistake. Because…she didn't trust herself around him. Getting him out of her system—well, that plan had been absolute crap. If anything, she wanted him more now than ever before. Mostly due to the fact that she now knew just how incredible sex with Ben actually was.

His sexy lips thinned. "Fine," Ben seemed to bite out that retort. "Then I'll just move into your place."

Uh, no. That wasn't an option, either.

"I'm not leaving you on your own," Ben added darkly. "Not until we figure out what's happening.

Simon and Eric can both attest to the fact that these sorts of situations go south, fast. I'm not going to turn away and have something happen to you." He shook his head. "Bad enough that I can't get that image of you in the garage out of my head. You think I'll just stand by and let you be put at risk again? Let you be alone if some predator is coming after you?"

He couldn't get the garage image out of his mind? That was…surprising. Courtney faltered as she stared up at him.

Simon cleared his throat. "Ben's place is safe. I can vouch for that. I helped to oversee the installation of his system. And I mean, sure, I get not wanting to stay with him because the guy can be an ass some days—"

Her lips parted in surprise.

Ben turned his head toward Simon. Glowered. "Thanks, *buddy*."

Simon shrugged. His lips twisted a little as a faint light appeared in his gaze. "But he's also a good guy. The kind of guy you can count on when shit hits the fan. And Ben's right, I have seen situations like this go south, faster than you can blink. Until we know the full details, I would always advise caution. If you have a safer place to stay while we get your apartment secured, then take it."

Ben looked back at Courtney. He flashed his dimples. "See? I'm the *good* guy. You can count on me."

She didn't think he was good. More like dangerous trouble. But she was also afraid and not sure what to do at all.

"We can put a bodyguard on you," Eric offered. He was leaning his hip against the edge of his desk. "Offer you twenty-four, seven protection with one of our best agents…"

Ben's dimples disappeared. "You'd better be talking about Julia," he muttered.

She didn't know who Julia was but… "That sounds expensive." Getting the new security system at her place sounded expensive, too. Just like hiring Wilde Securities to investigate the things that had been happening was *expensive.* The firm catered to high-end clients, so, of course, the price tag was going to be huge. The problem, though, was that she didn't have a huge budget.

She'd been saving every dime because she wanted to open her *own* firm. She didn't want to be forced to take certain clients by the higher ups — like she'd been forced to do with Laslow. She didn't want to play political office games. She wanted to be her own boss. To have the independence that she'd always craved. And she was *almost* there.

To pay for the security services, she'd be dipping into her savings. The bodyguard, oh, jeez, she was sure the bodyguard would put her way over her budget. "No bodyguard," she said, shaking her head before anyone else could comment. "I, um…" Her stare darted back to Ben. "I need to talk to Ben alone."

Ben blinked.

"Can we go outside, Ben?" Courtney asked quietly. Before she made any sort of decision, she wanted to discuss a few things, without an audience.

"Why?" He seemed genuinely perplexed. "Eric is in charge of your case. I trust my brother completely. We don't have secrets." A roll of one shoulder. "At least, not anymore." He waved toward his brother...and Simon. "Whatever you need to say, speak freely. It's okay."

Well, if he thought so...Fine with her. "I'm not sleeping with you again."

Simon seemed to choke.

She spared him a frown. "You okay?"

"Great." His face flushed. He flashed her a shark's smile. "Never better. Please continue. *Please.*"

She peered back at Ben. "I'll take the couch if I stay at your place. *Not* your bed."

"Sweetheart..." Dammit, why had his voice gone all soft and tender? She'd thought he would be mad. If anything, he was staring tenderly at her. Like she'd just said the sweetest thing ever. "As far as the couch...Not happening."

She sucked in a breath. "Ben—"

"I have a guest room. You can use that. No couch needed."

Her mouth closed.

"And I promise..." He eased in close. His voice was low, just for her now. "I will keep my hands off you. Unless you should decide that you want them *on* you."

Her chin notched up.

"Protection doesn't come with a price." He leaned back. Stared in her eyes. "Not from me. I truly want you safe, and I'll play by any rules that you put out for me." Another shrug. "Didn't you hear Simon? I'm the good guy, you can count on me."

Bullshit. He was wild and rough and he played by his own rules. He flashed his smile, and the guy got whatever he wanted.

And he'd decided he wanted her.

***

"I like her."

Ben paused at Simon's announcement. Courtney was right outside of the office, chatting with Eric and Dennis, and Ben had been intent on following her out. But at Simon's words, he glanced back.

And found his friend grinning at him. "Your charm isn't going to work on her."

Ben straightened his shoulders. "My charm works on everyone."

"She's different from the others. You know it. That's why you're so quick to rush after her."

Hell, yes, he knew Courtney was different. She'd always been different. Just out of his reach. She'd never responded to his flirtations. Never laughed at his jokes back in the day. He'd had her in his bed, but the woman still seemed a million miles out of his reach.

Why?

But now it would be different. For the night, at least, he'd have her close. In his home. In his bed…his guest bed, anyway.

And he would keep his hands off, just like he'd told her. Until Courtney asked him to put his hands *on* her. Then it would be a whole new game. They could fight in the courtroom all day long. He rather enjoyed those battles. But when they were alone, it wasn't a fight he wanted.

It was just her.

"You know what it's like when we take one of these cases." Simon advanced slowly toward him. "We have to explore all aspects of our client's life. She going to be okay with that?"

So far, she'd agreed to getting an updated security system and to spending the night with him. Eric was going to talk with his contacts at the PD and see what he could find out about the attack at the parking garage. Courtney had answered all the questions asked of her, but as far as shoving into her life? No, she hadn't agreed to go down that road, not yet.

"Huh. That's what I thought." Simon rubbed a hand over his jaw. "People have secrets, Ben. Sometimes, those secrets can be pretty dark. You sure you'd be up for handling that?"

Did he look scared? "I can handle anything that comes my way." Simon was his friend, but his buddy didn't get it. Simon only saw what was on the surface. Like the rest of the world, he saw what

Ben wanted him to see. The image he presented to the world.

Good guy, my ass.

He could fight dirty. He could play hard. He could be the sonofabitch you never wanted to face in the dark.

CHAPTER SIX

"I just want to get a few things, and then I'll be ready to go." Courtney's body was way too stiff as she stood in the elevator with Ben. After the meeting at Wilde Securities, she'd gone back to her office to meet with clients. The day had dragged — minute by slow minute — until she'd finished up just after six p.m. To her surprise, Ben had been waiting outside for her.

He'd followed her back to her place, and now he was heading up with her as some sort of — she didn't know…security? Bodyguard? *Friend?*

"You're tense."

And his voice was gravel rough. Sexy. Her dang toes had curled.

"Do I make you nervous, Courtney?"

He'd kept a very careful distance between them. At his question, she turned toward him and laughed. "Of course not." *Yes, yes, a thousand times yes.* "The situation is just insane, and it's making me a little flustered."

The elevator had reached the top floor. The doors opened with a ding.

"You have a right to be flustered. You have a right to be any fucking thing you want to be."

She slipped from the elevator and glanced back at him. He stalked after her. He'd taken off his suit coat and rolled up the sleeves of his blue dress shirt. A fancy, crisp shirt that she was sure had cost several hundred dollars. The guy had always looked like money, even when he'd been running around in faded jeans and tight-fitting t-shirts that stretched across his chest.

That blue shirt, though, it made his eyes gleam. Contrasted with his golden skin. Made him just look...

Lickable.

I shall not lick.

She hurried toward her place. She wasn't surprised to see the men near her doorway. Eric and Simon had said they'd meet her after work.

Courtney would bet a month's pay that they didn't give every client this personal attention. The CEO and VP of the company coming out for a security inspection? No way. Ben had pulled strings. The good old family connection, and, honestly, she was grateful for that connection right then.

Eric lounged near her door. Simon stood at attention, his hands loose at his sides as he glanced to the left and the right. "We need security cameras out here. One that focuses on the elevator. One that aims for the stairs. And we need them downstairs, too. We should be able to see every single person that enters and leaves the building."

Ben slid closer to Courtney. But when he spoke, his words were directed at Simon. "Hello to you, too, buddy. My day was good. Thanks. So was Courtney's. And how was yours?"

Simon glowered.

Ben tossed Courtney a smile. "He's never been big on the chit chat, but the man can get some serious security business handled."

Courtney glanced between them. "Um, we should check with the building manager to make sure it's okay to install cameras out here."

"It'll be okay." Eric seemed absolutely confident.

Too confident. Her eyes narrowed on him.

He shrugged. "I know the owner. Consider it a done deal."

Uneasy suspicion cut through her. "Tell me you aren't the owner."

A laugh slipped from Eric. "I'm not the owner. If this was my building, trust me, security would be one hell of a lot better."

Her shoulders sagged a little as she stepped forward and unlocked the door. Her security system beeped when she went inside, and Courtney quickly tapped in her code. The men followed her inside, and the apartment that she'd always considered spacious and open suddenly felt absolutely tiny. Or maybe they were all just too big.

"Nothing looks disturbed," Simon noted as he began to prowl around her den.

No, nothing looked out of place. The apartment seemed totally normal. Did he doubt her now? Was that—

Ben nodded toward her bedroom. "Why don't you go get the things you'll need for tonight?"

His voice was so careful. *He* was being careful. She didn't quite know how to respond to Ben this way. She was used to the sparring, slightly sarcastic Ben. Courtney could handle him. This guy—this careful gentleman made her nervous.

She muttered something—something vague and semi-polite as she hurried into her room. She flipped on the lights and—

Stay away from him.

For a moment, Courtney couldn't move at all. She stared at the words in bright red that had been left on her bedroom wall. Right over her bed. The letters—*God, that had better just be paint, red paint and not blood*—had dripped into long streaks that trailed down the white wall. "Ben." At first, his name came out of her as a rough gasp because the shock was like a punch straight into her gut.

She had to shake her head, had to take a step back, had to suck in a breath.

Maybe it's not there. It can't be there. It's— "Ben!" Now she yelled his name as she got her breath, and he responded in a flash. She heard the pounding of his footsteps as he ran to her, felt his hands curl tightly around her shoulders and then—

"Fucking son of a fucking bitch!"

Then she heard his rage.

He pulled her back. Pushed her behind him.

Simon and Eric were there, crowding in close.

"Don't touch a damn thing," Simon barked.

Her hands were shaking so Courtney balled them into fists. Touching wasn't on the agenda. Getting the hell out of there? *Yes, please.* Suddenly spending the night at Ben's place seemed like the best idea ever.

"We need to search and make sure the perp isn't still here," Simon added grimly.

She gaped. "Still…here?"

"Stay with her, Ben," Simon directed. And she saw that he'd shoved back his fancy suit coat to reveal a holster. He pulled a gun out of the holster like it was a totally normal thing to do. Maybe it was normal for him.

But *not* normal in her world.

"Take a breath, Court." Her hated nickname came from Ben, but right then, she didn't even mind. She was busy taking a breath and trying not to flip the hell out.

Trying—*failing.* "He was in my home." Even though the front door had been locked. Her security system armed.

Ben's hands curled around her shoulders. "Look at me."

She couldn't. She was too busy staring at the wall. At the paint—*better be paint, had to be paint*—that looked far too much like blood as it dripped down her bedroom wall. Some of the paint had even reached her bed covers.

She and Ben—they'd had sex in that bed. And now—

Stay away from him.

"Courtney."

Her stare whipped to Ben. "He knows about you."

The creep knew that she had spent a wild night with Ben.

Ben's brow furrowed.

"You're the only man I've been with in six months." The truth hurtled from her.

His blue eyes widened.

"There isn't anyone else. He *has* to be talking about you." But why would anyone care whether or not she was sleeping with Ben?

"Clear," Eric announced as he and Simon came back toward her. "The guy is gone."

"There was no sign of a break-in," Simon added. "Not so much as a scratch on the locks."

Eric rubbed the back of his neck. "The security system wasn't triggered. He knows the code or he's good enough to bypass."

Chill bumps covered her arms.

Ben pulled her against him and eased her back into the den.

Stay away from him.

"Who has a key, Courtney?" Ben questioned carefully. "People always give backup keys to neighbors or friends. Who has your key? And does the same person know your security code?"

"Uh...Yes." Her heart raced too quickly. "I had to go out of town for a conference last month. I needed someone to water my plants so, um, so Cole said he'd do it for me."

Ben's gaze changed. Went hard and cold. "The asshole who lives on the floor below you? The one who saw us together?"

The knots in her stomach were getting worse. "Yes. Cole Trevor. But he gave me the key back when I got home—"

"Could have made a copy," Simon noted. "And if you didn't change your code when you returned, it would be simple as hell for him to get inside."

Cole wouldn't do that...would he? He'd always seemed like such a stand-up guy. She'd even seen him bringing in groceries for Mr. Jamison on the second floor. Jamison was pushing ninety and not nearly as spry as he wanted the world to think he was and—

"We need to call the cops." Eric was stalking around her apartment, but being very careful not to touch anything. "Right now. We've got a physical attack on you. We've got a break-in at your place. This has to stop, before anything worse happens."

She didn't want to think about "worse" options.

A sharp rap sounded at her door. Courtney's head whipped to the right.

"You expecting someone?" Ben rumbled. He was already heading for the door.

Expecting someone? Seriously? "No." She rushed to follow him.

He grunted and glanced through the peephole. "Speak of the friggin' devil."

What?

Ben yanked open the door. "Hello, asshole," he greeted a surprised-looking Cole. "What the hell do you want?"

"Courtney," was his flat answer. And, apparently, a very wrong answer. Because in the next instant, Ben had grabbed her downstairs neighbor and hauled Cole inside the apartment. Ben had moved lightning-fast, and, once again, his fierce strength surprised her.

Ben was the fancy suit guy, the calm and poised guy, the charmer, he was—

He was about to punch Cole.

"Stop!" Simon grabbed Ben's hand. "Easy, man. Easy."

Her breath heaved in and out. She didn't think there was anything "easy" about the situation.

Cole's narrowed gaze swept to Ben. To Simon. To a glowering Eric. And then back to her. "Courtney..." Cole rasped. "What in the hell is happening here?"

"Someone broke into my home." Her voice sounded hollow to her own ears.

His brow wrinkled. Voice doubting, he began, "Is this like the other day, when you thought some guy was in the park and he wasn't—"

"*Asshole*, watch your tone with her," Ben snapped back. He yanked his hand from Simon. "She didn't *think* some douchebag was in her house. He was here. Just like he was in the park the other day. When Courtney says something, take it as straight gospel, you got me? She doesn't lie. She doesn't make shit up. That's not who she is."

Her gaze flew to him, but Ben's stare was locked on Cole. And Ben looked—he looked like he wanted to tear the other man apart. She'd never seen that look of savagery on Ben's face. Come to think of it, she'd never seen *any* look of savagery on him.

Maybe she didn't know the man as well as she'd thought.

Maybe…maybe she didn't know him at all.

"You have a key to her place?" Simon demanded as he crossed his arms over his chest and seemed to size up Cole.

"Ah…" Cole's gaze darted to Courtney. "She gave me a key a while back, but I returned it to her."

Eric strode closer. His face was just as savage as Ben's. "And you didn't make a copy while you had the key?"

"What?" Cole's jaw dropped, but a moment later, a sneer twisted his face. "Oh, shit, you really think you are going to pin this on me? Sure, right, has to be me, huh? The ex-con downstairs, so you just assume that I'm the one—"

"You're an ex-con?" Courtney blurted. She hadn't known. *Because I don't know anything about his past.*

"I liked fast rides when I was a kid." A shrug. "Ancient history."

Her head was spinning.

"Courtney's break-in doesn't happen to be ancient history," Ben snarled right back.

Was Simon *holding* Ben back? It looked like he was. Simon's hand had clamped tightly around

Ben's shoulder, and he appeared to be restraining Ben from an attack on Cole.

His face etched with fury, Ben blasted, "Some dick broke into her place, and you're the dick I see with access. You know her security code. You could've copied her key. And now, you just showed up on her doorstep saying you wanted *her*."

She realized that while Ben had been firing his accusations, Eric had texted someone. The cops?

"I wanted to *apologize* to Courtney," Cole gritted out. A muscle flexed along his jaw. "She was jumpy the other day, and I felt like I should have listened to her more. I wanted to talk with her, all right? I didn't break into her place! Didn't—"

Ben cut in, "Leave a warning spray painted on the side of her bedroom wall?"

Cole blinked. "Hell, no, I didn't do that shit!"

"But you just happened to appear at her doorstep. And you're the guy with the means to get inside." Ben's face twisted with his fury. "So excuse the hell out of me if I don't take you at your word."

Cole's stare immediately locked on Courtney. "You know me better than this."

Did she? They'd gone for runs. Had a few coffees and lunches. Chatted at the tenant meetings. He'd seemed like a good guy, but she knew appearances were deceiving.

"She had no clue you were an ex-con," Simon pointed out. "So, I'm guessing there is plenty she doesn't know about you."

Cole's lashes flickered. "That was juvie stuff. I wouldn't hurt Courtney. That's not why I am here."

Eric shoved his phone into his pocket. "We'll let you explain to the cops. I'm sure they will want to know all about you. They'll also be sending a tech team to wipe down the scene as they look for fingerprints."

It obviously paid to have Wilde pull. When Eric Wilde said jump, the local authorities hurtled into the sky.

"They'll find my prints here." Cole's breath heaved out. "I've been in her apartment before. Of course, my prints will be at her place."

Ben's head turned. His gaze met Courtney's. "But they shouldn't find your prints in her bedroom. Because you have no fucking reason to be in there."

Courtney shook her head. No, he shouldn't have been in there. They hadn't been involved.

Ben gave a slight nod, and his focus returned to Cole.

"I...might have gone in there when I was watching her place," Cole muttered. "Just, uh, looking around. It's what people do, you know, it's what—"

A growl escaped Ben. "It's not what people fucking do. You don't go into Courtney's bedroom when she's not there."

"Look, I can—"

Ben broke free of Simon and drove his fist into Cole's jaw. "And you don't fucking *lie* when you're confronted, asshole."

Cole barrelled straight into Ben's stomach. His arms locked around Ben and the two men slammed into the floor.

Courtney screamed because seriously — what in the hell? They were brawling in her home! And everything was crazy. Insane. It was —

Ben threw Cole off him. Leapt to his feet. Cole rushed at him again, but Ben struck out fast and hard, and Cole staggered back.

"Stop them!" Courtney shouted at Simon and Eric. They were just standing there, watching.

Simon shrugged. "I'd kind of like to see how this plays out."

Eric made no move to stop anything. "Ben has this."

Men. They could be such idiots. She leapt forward and grabbed Ben's arm before he could punch Cole again. "Stop it!"

Ben whirled toward her. His eyes blazed and pure fury marked his face.

He looked...intense. Scary. Very un-Ben-like.

Her breath shuddered out. "You can't beat the shit out of him in my home."

"I think I can."

"Not without getting arrested!" He was a lawyer, she shouldn't have to remind him of things like this.

Cole groaned. "Pretty-boy...won't beat me in a fight. I've got him. I've — "

"Consider yourself fucking evicted!" Ben moved his body, putting himself in a protective position before Courtney. "You lied on your rental application. You said you had no criminal history. You also said that you were former Army, only when my brother started digging into your past today, he found out that line was BS."

Consider yourself fucking evicted? Ben couldn't evict anyone. Not unless he—

Oh, hell. She was still holding onto his arm. Now her fingers clutched him even tighter. "You own my building?"

A quick nod.

"When were you going to tell me that fact?"

But Cole spoke before Ben could respond. "You're digging into my background?" He leapt toward Eric. "What gives you that right?"

Eric smiled. A very cold smile. "Courtney hired me to find out who might want to hurt her. It's standard procedure to investigate neighbors and friends. Let's just say that when my people started their digging on you, we noticed some inconsistencies."

Cole's hands were fists. "This is BS."

"Explain it to the cops," Eric urged him. "They'll be here soon, and it's an explanation I'd love to hear. I'm sure they would, too."

Cole whirled toward Courtney and Ben. He pointed at Ben and asked, "Want me to explain that you assaulted me? Is that the shit you want the cops to hear?"

Ben lifted his hands in a whatever-gesture. "Do I look scared?"

Cole jutted out his chin. "Maybe you should be. Maybe you don't know who the hell you're dealing with."

Both Simon and Eric closed in while Ben put his body directly in front of Courtney's. She could practically feel the tension pouring from Ben as he demanded, "Why don't you just tell me *exactly* who you are—because I have the feeling you've been lying for a while now. Lying your way into this building. Lying to Courtney. Lying to get close to her."

No, no, that couldn't be right...could it?

"And I'll be damned if I let you hurt her," Ben continued in a low and lethal voice that she'd never heard from him before. "Because from now on, in order to get to her, you'll have to tear through me."

CHAPTER SEVEN

"You own my building?"

Ben reset the alarm at his place even as a low chuckle slid from him. "After everything that's happened tonight…" He turned to face her and crossed his arms over his chest. "*That's* the first question you have as soon as we're alone?"

Alone…in his home.

She stood a few feet away, still wearing the pencil skirt and black top. Looking gorgeous and sexy and completely untouchable. She gripped her briefcase a bit too tightly, and her high heels tapped on the floor when she advanced toward him. A quick flurry of steps—then she stopped. Courtney hadn't come close enough to touch. And he very much wanted to put his hands on her.

Her overnight bag was near his feet. She'd gotten it together while the cops had been at her place. He knew that Eric had pulled strings to get such a fast response, and he hoped like hell that his brother's connections would pay off for them.

Cole had clammed up. The cops had been eager to question the guy, but Ben wasn't sure how much the uniforms would be able to get from the man.

No, Ben figured that Eric and Simon would learn far more about Cole Trevor when they got the Wilde agents to tear deeper into his past.

"You own my building." This time, her words weren't a question.

He shrugged as his hands fell to his sides. "I might." Ben scooped up her bag. "Come this way. I'll show you to the guest room."

She stepped into his path. *Still* didn't come close enough to touch. "There is no *might* about it. Either you own the building or you don't. Answer the question, counselor."

Damn but she was cute when she got that hard, demanding lawyer tone. But it probably wasn't the time to tell her the tone seriously turned him on. "In that case, yes, I do own it."

Her dark eyes glittered. "I've lived there for a year. A *year*. And you never mentioned to me that you were my landlord?"

Tread carefully. "You didn't ask."

"Ben!"

"What? Shit. So I have some investments in town. I own the building, I have a manager who runs things, and I didn't even know you were *thinking* about moving in until the manager told me that you'd been offered a lease."

"You should have told me."

"You liked the building, didn't you? I mean, you got the best apartment there." Something he'd made sure had happened once he'd realized that Courtney wanted to move in. "You got your own floor. The biggest apartment! Total privacy. No one else in the building has that option. And I gave you a super deal on—" *Uh, oh. Shut up, Ben. Shut up, now.*

"I knew the rent was too low. Stupid low." She sucked in a deep breath. "You did that."

"Sue me. Yes, I gave you a deal on the rent. I knew you were saving to open your own firm, and I wanted to help—"

But her burning gaze said she didn't appreciate his help. "I don't need your pity." She grabbed for her bag. "I'll find the guest room myself." She tried to yank the bag from him.

He tightened his hold.

And she wound up jerking *against* him as her body fell forward. For an instant, her body pressed to his. All of those wonderful curves. All of that sexy skin. All of that rage.

She had a lot of it.

Before she went in for an attack, he needed her to know… "Pity is the last thing I would ever feel for you."

"Bullshit." And her eyes gleamed with…tears?

Oh, no. Oh, hell, no. He didn't know if those were rage tears or sad tears, but the sight made his chest feel like someone had taken a sledge hammer to his heart.

"I know pity because I'm the girl who grew up with nothing. With a mom who died when I was five and a so-called father who didn't want me. I'm the one who was shoved into foster care and left there until I was eighteen. I'm the one who had to work three jobs even *with* a scholarship just so I could afford the room and board in college and then in law school. I'm the one who always had second-hand shit while everyone else was wearing designer clothes. I'm the one who never went to the parties you liked to throw because I knew I wasn't going to fit in. I couldn't afford your crowd, and I didn't want them staring down their noses at me. I'm the one who rode a freaking bike everywhere because I couldn't afford a car back then."

Every muscle in his body had locked down.

"But you know what?" Courtney continued grimly. "I'm the one who graduated at the top of the class. I'm the one who did all of that on my own, without my family's wealth giving me an easy ride that I didn't deserve. I'm the one who works hard every day, and I'm the one who is making a life that I will be proud of." She yanked on the bag again. This time, he let go immediately. "So, keep your pity. Because *I'm* the one who doesn't need it." Courtney turned on her heel and marched off, heading down the hallway.

It took him a moment to move. A moment to break straight through the shock that held him immobile. *Baby, I am so sorry.* "You were the one girl *everyone* wanted."

She froze.

"You didn't know that? Fuck, first day of law school, I walked in, and there you were. With your hair in that long braid, sliding over your shoulder, those jeans that fit you like a glove, and a loose, red shirt that slid off one of your shoulders. You were reading the syllabus, with your head down, and you didn't realize that every dumbass guy there had already taken the seats around you. They were all just waiting for you to look up." He'd even kicked one of the dumbasses out of a chair so Ben could get close to her.

Her laugh was brittle. "Those jerks just wanted a fast screw. They didn't care anything about me."

Like he hadn't punched the shit out of one of the jerks in question because the fool had bragged about what he'd supposedly done with her. Not that Ben had ever told Courtney about that fight. Why bother her with BS? "You were the one…I competed with."

Now she looked back, a faint frown on her face.

"Because you were—*are*—so fucking smart. You challenged me. You worked your ass off—yeah, I saw it. In class and out. You made me want to be better. You could drive me insane when you'd argue with me, when you'd go toe-to-toe with me in mock trial or in debate, but I loved it. Because I knew I was going against the best. You didn't take crap from me or anyone else."

Her frown deepened.

"You didn't go to parties because you thought people would look down on you? Oh, baby, you have that so wrong. You were the one who should have looked down on the drunk dumbasses. *On me.* Because I'll tell you right now, no one is better than you. *You* are the one." *The one I always wanted, and never, ever thought I could have.*

She hadn't moved.

"And for what it's worth, I liked your damn bike with the white basket and that crazy-ass bell.

I'd smile every single time when you came rolling through campus ringing the bell at everyone so they'd get out of your way. I thought you were cute as hell."

Now she blinked. "You were…laughing *at* me. I remember—"

He closed the distance between them. Had to do it. His hand rose as he brushed away the tear drop that had fallen on her cheek. Courtney shouldn't cry. Not ever. And maybe his new job would be to make sure she didn't cry again. "Never. You made me smile because you made me happy. But sometimes, dumbasses don't know how to convey things the correct way. With you, I never seem to do things the right way." He wanted to kiss her. Wanted to hold tight and never, ever let go. And because he wanted that so badly…

Ben stepped back. "My life has been easy." He knew it. Fuck, yes. He'd had easy street, and she'd struggled, and it pissed him off. "My family has money. Shit, my brother made a killing with his tech security devices, and I have always had the support and protection that he and my whole family gave to me. I was lucky, and I know it. A roll of the freaking dice, and I could've had a different life. That's the thing, isn't it? We don't get to choose where we're born or who we get for family. Shit happens. Then we live that life. *You,* Courtney, have been incredible."

"Stop. Don't tell me lies that you think I want to hear, don't—"

He hadn't known about her parents. Hadn't known...*Sweetheart, I'm so sorry.* "I'm not lying to you. I won't lie to you." He needed her to believe him. "I knew you'd be pissed if you found out I owned your building—you've made it pretty clear I'm not on a top ten favorite list for you. But the apartment was good. The rental price I could offer you was probably the best in the city. I *wanted* you to keep saving so you could open your own firm. I wanted you to get every dream you had. I didn't do it out of pity. I did it because I respect the hell out of you."

Her lower lip trembled. "And not because you wanted to get in my pants?"

"Hell, baby, I wanted that from day one." Again, he wouldn't lie to her. "But you staying in my building had nothing to do with sex. You'd turned me down over a dozen times before you moved in. And I'm sure you turned me down a dozen more times after that, too." Tenderness pushed through him. "You'll see, one day, I'm really not the enemy."

"Then what are you?"

"I'm whatever—whoever—you need me to be."

Her gaze searched his. She seemed to lean toward him, and he wanted her to make that move. He'd chased her for too long. What happened next—everything that came—he wanted Courtney to make the first move. He wanted her to reach out to him.

But she pulled in a quick breath and stepped back. "I'm tired." Her long lashes shielded her gaze. "I think…I think I'll go to bed." She turned and headed for the nearest door.

"Okay, sweet—Courtney." He cleared his throat. "But that's my bedroom." And as much as he'd love to have her in there… "The guest room is on the right."

She stopped. Immediately angled her body to the right. But didn't go in that bedroom. "I didn't want to be another in line."

He didn't see any line.

"You always had girls lined up around you. And you *never* stayed with them. Except…except for Piper."

Piper Lane. The name pierced through him. Well, now she was Piper Wilde—his brother's wife.

"I figured you loved her. She'd pop in and out of your life, and you'd always seem so happy with her."

"I do love Piper." He would always love her. "She's my best friend. She has been, since Pre-K."

"You were hurt a while back…" Courtney's voice was halting. "Because of…her?"

"Because of a dumbass with a knife." A bastard who'd thought Ben was involved with Piper. "He was obsessed with her. That's one of the reasons I know just how dangerous obsessions can be. Why this mess with you scares the hell out of me."

He saw a tremble slide over her body. "I saw the scars on you." Her low confession. "On your side."

"I have more scars than that." Because the knife had cut deep. And the attack had been long. He'd been in the hospital for days. Courtney had sent him flowers. A balloon. Even a card. *Get well so I can kick your ass again in court.* She hadn't come by, though. He'd wanted her there. Hadn't he always wanted her?

"She married your brother." Again, Courtney's voice was slow and hesitant. "Did that…I'm sorry if that hurt you."

He laughed.

Courtney's head swung toward him.

"I love her. I'm not *in love* with her. Never have been. I'm glad that Piper married Eric because I know he freaking worships the ground that she walks on. He will always take care of her, and that's exactly what I wanted for my best friend." The fact that Eric and Piper had tried to keep their relationship secret from him? Uh, hell, no, that part had pissed him off.

Courtney gave a slow shake of her head. "I don't think I understand you."

"That's because you don't know the real me yet. You've just seen the surface. I think it's time we both go way past that."

She bit her lower lip.

He'd be happy to bite it for her. "I'm a cold-hearted bastard. I'm arrogant and demanding. I fight dirty in and out of court. I can use my charm to get most things in this world—and believe me, I've done it. I'm a terrible enemy to have, and I will do just about anything to get what I want." So, yes, she'd been right to think he was a prick. To most people, he was. To her… "I can be more. I can be better." It took all of his self-control not to close the distance between them. "I saw how terrified Piper was when that psycho was after her. I *don't* want you feeling the same fear. I can keep you safe. I can help you. I can stand between you and any danger that comes."

"Why?" The question tore from her. One hand clutched her briefcase and one seemed to hold a death grip on her overnight bag. "Why do you want to do this for me?"

She'd asked him before if he'd wanted to get in her pants. Hell, yes, he did. But helping her, protecting her, had nothing to do with the white-hot lust that stirred in him every time he looked at her. "Because the idea of anyone hurting you drives me insane." When it came to her, he wasn't quite rational.

It was a truth he'd known for a long time. Ever since their days at Emory Law, when Gavin Donally had told a straight-up lie about Courtney going down on him…

Gavin had been the one to go down—he'd fallen hard when Ben had launched at him.

On that day, Ben had realized that when it came to Courtney, he had a problem. Maybe his own obsession. So, he'd started to play a role around her. Sure, he'd still asked her out every now and again—because he couldn't fucking help that—but he'd been pushing her away at the same time. Wanting her to see the dark parts of him. Wanting her to get away because if she ever did get too close, if he ever got a real taste of her…

I'm not sure I can walk away. And signing over his soul to a woman wasn't a good idea. He saw how badly marriages ended every single day. Saw the wreck left after love turned sour.

"Get some sleep, Courtney," he urged her because he was already nearing the limits of his self-control. "If you need me, I'll be here. All you have to do is call out my name."

She put down the overnight bag long enough to open the door. But then she asked, "Call your name and what? You'll come running?"

For her? "Yes."

He heard her quick inhale, as if his answer had caught her by surprise, but then she hurried into the guest room and didn't look back. The door closed softly behind her.

Ben scraped his hand over his face. How long had he thought about getting Courtney in his home? Now she was finally here, but he had to keep his hands off her. Hands off, dick zipped up, gentleman role in place. He could do this.

For her, maybe he'd do just about anything.

***

Cole's fingers clenched around his phone. "She's at his place." His voice was low and rough. "And the plan is shot to hell. Wilde Securities is tearing into my background. They're going to learn the truth."

He listened intently, then laughed. "No, they *are* that good. That shit isn't just speculation. They'll find out the truth, and then I'll be screwed. Hell, the cops already spent an hour questioning me tonight."

The response was fast and angry.

"I'm not going to jail for you," Cole snarled right back. "Forget that shit. The truth is going to come out. I will name you because I am not going down for you or anyone else." He had one rule that he followed in this twisted world.

Look out for yourself.

Because no one else was going to do it.

"I can't get to her any longer. Ben Wilde is acting like he's her freaking protector." Talk about a total lie. He'd done his research on Ben. Rich boy. Playboy. General smooth-talking jackass.

Only...that jackass had surprised him with one hell of a punch. He'd like to see just what other surprises Ben might be hiding.

"He owns the building we live in. I didn't know that. He had his name hidden behind some corporation. Yeah, yeah, he *owns* her place, and now he's got her in his home." Talk about danger signals. "He was in her bed the other night. And from the way he's acting, Ben doesn't plan to let her go anytime soon."

He waited for his boss to speak. And he didn't like the order he was given. So... "Screw off," Cole snapped. "I'm done. You want Courtney McKenna? Go after her yourself." He hung up when the guy's snarl filled his ears.

It was time to cut out of this town. His cover was about to be blown, and the last thing he wanted was to be pulled in for another chat with the cops. He'd never quite managed to get along well with cops. He stepped onto the street, knowing he had to get back to his apartment and clear out of there. As fast as freaking possible.

But when he'd taken just a few steps, he heard the sudden, fierce growl of a vehicle's engine.

Bright lights hit him, and Cole instinctively threw up his hand. "What in the hell?"

The driver was coming straight at him. Cole tried to lunge out of the way, but the headlights turned toward him—the vehicle aimed for him even as that engine growled harder, louder.

The impact tossed Cole into the air. For a second there, he was flying and the world was spinning and he didn't even feel the pain.

The pain came when he landed. When he slammed hard into the pavement and felt something snap. His whole body shuddered, and he knew that he should get his ass up. Especially when the driver braked.

And then backed up…

Cole shoved his hands down against the pavement. *Get up.* His head turned. The vehicle was in position once more. Fuck.

The engine growled. The headlights hit Cole.

He knew he wasn't going to be able to move in time.

CHAPTER EIGHT

She wasn't going to sleep. After an hour of staring at the ceiling—broken by ever not-so-fun bouts of tossing and turning—Courtney admitted the truth to herself.

She was too wound up. Her blood seemed to boil in her veins. She felt as if she was about to jump out of her skin. And every time that she actually tried to close her eyes...

Stay away from him.

She threw off the covers. Climbed from the bed wearing her t-shirt and boy shorts. The t-shirt hit mid-thigh so Courtney figured it covered her well enough. And she finally did exactly what she'd wanted to do for the last hour—

She went to Ben. Courtney yanked open the guest room door, and she marched to his room. His door was partially ajar, and for a moment, she hesitated. How desperate did it look that she was running straight to him?

But then again...so what? She felt desperate, and he'd told her that if she needed him, all she had to do was call out.

Her fingers curled around the doorknob. The door opened with a squeak as she stepped inside. Darkness filled the bedroom, and it took her eyes a moment of straining intensity to adjust. The covers on his bed were a tousled heap. No sound whispered in the room—well, just her own breathing. Her breathing seemed way too loud. "Ben?" She inched toward the bed. "I…I wanted to come in here and—"

And what? Talk? *No.*

Not be alone? Again…*no.*

Have mind-blowing sex so I don't have to think about the creep after me? That was a very strong ye—

The bed was empty. She was right beside the mattress before she made that realization. She'd come tip-toeing into Ben's room, ready to throw away all her pride, but he wasn't even there. How very anticlimactic.

Her hand reached out, and she turned on the bedside lamp. Light immediately spilled onto the covers. The big, empty king-sized bed.

Where was he? Courtney spun around. Part of her wanted to run right back to the guest room. But, no, she'd crawled out of bed for a reason.

I want Ben.

She hurried out of his bedroom. Her gaze drifted over his home—everything was so still and quiet and…the balcony doors were open. Her head cocked. Moonlight spilled in from the open balcony, and she found herself hurrying forward. When she stepped outside, the night wind blew over her cheeks. His back was to her, but he turned instantly as if he'd sensed her approach when she knew that she hadn't made a sound. Courtney felt the impact of his gaze like a red-hot touch on her skin.

"Courtney?" His body tensed. She saw that he was holding a glass in his right hand. "What's wrong?"

About a million things. "I couldn't sleep."

Some of the tension eased from him. "Yeah." He lifted the glass to his lips. Drained it and set it down on a nearby table. "Know that feeling."

She stood there, the wind blowing lightly against her. But it was a hot wind. That happened a lot in Atlanta. When the humidity was like a weight against your skin, even the wind didn't help.

"You want a drink?" Ben asked her.

"No." She licked her lips. "I want you."

Silence. Not really the response she'd expected. Courtney rocked forward onto the balls of her feet. "Ben?"

"I thought we were one and done."

A wince.

"Didn't you work me out of your system?" His voice was rough as he took one step toward her.

Her shoulders straightened. "Turns out, I didn't."

"Huh. How about that…" Another step.

Was this what it felt like when a predator stalked prey? Goosebumps rose on her arms, even with the heat surrounding her.

"Guess what, sweetheart?" He was still advancing.

Her breath heaved out.

"I didn't work you out of my system, either."

She slipped away from the open doors. Not sure exactly where she was going, just suddenly feeling very, very nervous as she edged over a few feet and stood in front of the brick wall that made up the side of his home. Ben followed her, and he caged her with his arms. His hands flattened against the bricks behind her.

"In fact," Ben murmured, voice low and seductive, "if anything, now that I know just what sex with you is like…I want you even more than I did before."

Her heart pounded far too fast in her chest.

"So, how about we make a deal?"

"D-deal?" She'd just stuttered. She'd worked so hard to overcome the stutter that she'd had as a teen. But it still slipped out, especially when she was nervous. She was nervous as hell right then.

"Fight with me all you want in court. In public. Play the game."

This wasn't a game.

"But when we're alone together, we take what we want—and what we want is each other. When it's just you and me, you can rip my clothes off. You can scratch me with your nails. You can scream my name, and I guarantee, you will love every moment."

Her nipples thrust against the front of her t-shirt. His words were turning her on, so it seemed only fair that she should say… "When we're alone, you can strip me. You can touch every part of me. You can sink into me, and we can *both* get lost in the pleasure, and I guarantee, *you* will love every moment."

A dark, rich chuckle escaped him. "There is no one like you." His head lowered toward her. "You *are* the one, Courtney." His lips took hers. Not in some soft kiss. Soft kisses were for hesitant lovers. They weren't hesitant.

He touched her, and need exploded within Courtney. Her hands rose and pressed to his chest. He wasn't wearing a shirt. He'd been on the balcony clad in a pair of low-slung jeans and nothing else. She touched hot skin. Hard muscle. Lickable muscle.

She could taste the drink on his lips and tongue. Whiskey. As she kissed him, she could swear that she felt a little drunk—but not from the drink. From him. From the way he made her feel. Wild and uncontrolled. She didn't care where they were. She didn't care that she should be afraid of the creep out there in the dark.

She just cared—in that moment—about Ben.

She wanted Ben. In her. Right then. Right there.

He pulled his mouth from hers and began to kiss a blazing path down her throat. She tipped back her head as a moan pulled from her. She loved the way his lips felt against her. Stubble lined his jaw, and it was rough against her skin, but she liked the roughness. Her breath came faster as his hands eased down her body, and he shoved up the shirt. A moment later, his fingers were on her breasts. Teasing the nipples. Plucking them. Driving her crazy. Her hips rocked against him. His cock was long and hard, and she knew he was just as turned on as she was.

His fingers slid back down her body, every movement electrifying her. Down, down he went until he was at the top of her panties. "These have got to go," he muttered.

He shoved them down. She kicked them away.

"You are so fucking sexy." The moonlight fell on them, and his face was savage with need. "I could eat you right up."

Please do.

When Ben stroked her sex, she arched up onto her toes.

"You're wet and hot. God, *perfect.*" He pushed a finger into her. Another, then his hand eased back as his thumb pressed over her clit. Moved faster. Applied more pressure. Had her gasping as her nails raked over his back.

He pulled his hand away.

No!

But then he lifted her up. Locked his hands around her waist even as she curled her legs around his hips. His cock shoved against her.

They were outside. She should tell him to take her in. She didn't think anyone could see them from where they were. After all, she was close to the wall, they were up high, they were—

His cock pushed inside. "You feel like heaven."

She rocked against him, wanting more.

He sank deep. Drove all the way inside. Her head fell back as pleasure ripped through her. Oh, yes, this was—

"Fuck, *condom.*"

Her gaze met his. She'd realized he was bare when he pushed into her. Her inner muscles clamped tightly around him. Savored the feel of him right before he pulled back. Pulled *out.*

"I'm sorry, baby. I'm clean, I swear, but…I should always take care of you."

"I'm clean." Her breath came faster. She was on the brink, her body so tense and eager. "And I'm on birth control."

She felt him stiffen. Even in the dark, she swore his face became harder. Rougher.

"Are you saying…" Ben began in a voice that was little more than a growl.

She'd never gone without a condom with a lover before. But right then, she wanted Ben. Wanted him to drive deep inside and *finish* what he'd started. "I'm saying do *not* leave me hanging like this."

"Oh, sweetheart." He pressed a kiss to her lips. One that was oddly tender considering the need that ripped through them both. "I'm not that kind of guy. *Count* on it." But he didn't thrust back in. His head lifted. He stared at her with glittering eyes. "Do you want me this way? With nothing between us?"

She managed a nod.

"Say it, Courtney. I want it loud and clear."

She was about to go insane. "I want you to fuck me, right now. Nothing between us. Just you. Just me, just—"

He drove deep. *Yes!* Her sex clamped greedily around him. There was no holding back. There was only desperate desire. Her nails dug into him. She moaned. She choked out his name. She slammed her hips against him and came on an explosion of release that was *amazing.*

And he was with her. He pinned her to the wall, caged her between the bricks and his rock-hard body, and he took her. Plunged deep over and over, making her climax last so long that she couldn't catch a breath. But she felt Ben when he came in her, a hot eruption that she'd never experienced with another lover. Because she had always used a condom with her other lovers. Ben was the only one…and she'd wanted to be skin-to-skin with him.

She'd needed this.

Though she didn't want to push too hard and figure out *why* it was so. *Don't look too deeply. Don't try to find something that isn't there.*

This was simply sex. Casual. Basic. The act was filling a need. Keeping the monsters in her mind at bay. That was all. This wasn't forever. This wasn't some fairy-tale BS ending. She was a divorce attorney, for goodness' sake. If anyone knew that fairy-tale endings were pure Hollywood fantasy, it was her.

He withdrew from her, and Courtney couldn't help but tense. If she'd had her way, she would have instantly gone for another round. But he'd pulled away. So she should unwind her legs from his waist and make some casual comment. Or maybe she should tell him the sex had been awesome, because it truly had been.

Her legs slid down.

A shiver rolled over her. *Outside. I just had sex outside.* Sure, no one could see her, not from this angle, but she was so not an exhibitionist.

Wait, was she?

"What are you thinking?" He'd already adjusted his jeans.

"That I hope no one saw us." She let her shirt fall back down. Courtney squeezed her thighs together as she glanced around the balcony. Super awkward but…where were her panties?

"No one saw. I wouldn't let anyone watch, baby. You're for me alone."

A rough, possessive edge had entered his voice. Her gaze flew to him just as he bent down and picked up—yep, her panties.

His fingers curled around them. "I get that you think I'm a playboy."

"Um, aren't you?"

His head tilted back. "Let's be very clear. I am not *playing* with you."

The heartbeat that had just calmed down suddenly sped right back up. "Then what are you doing?"

"Wanting you more than I've ever wanted another woman."

He was so smooth. Always seemed to have the perfect response. That was why judges loved him. The guy was killer in court.

And in bed. She had to admit that. Totally killer in bed. "Can I, um, have those back?" With a wave of her hand, she motioned to her panties.

He didn't give them back. "Why? I thought the night was just getting started."

Her breath caught.

"Not one and done, remember? Not us. Enemies in court. Lovers when we're alone. That first round took the edge off for the night. Made it so I can go slower next time."

Courtney swallowed.

"I was out here, drinking so that I could try to stop obsessing over you, stop remembering how good your felt beneath my hands and my mouth, but the whiskey wasn't helping."

She didn't speak.

"Then you came to me, and, sweetheart, there was no way I could keep my hands off you."

It was her time to confess. Courtney took a step forward. "Just so we're clear, I like your hands on me. I like your hands, your mouth, your body."

He advanced. They stood barely a breath apart.

Another confession. "You're the first lover that I've ever been with…without a condom."

She saw his jaw clench.

After a moment, he rumbled, "You're my first, too, sweetheart."

Her tongue swiped over her lower lip. "The other men, with them, I just didn't want—"

"No." The word emerged as a growl.

"Ben?"

He lifted her into his arms, moving quickly and surprising her. She grabbed for him, holding on tightly. He kissed her as he carried her back into the apartment. Kissed her with a stark possession that she could feel in every cell of her body.

"Don't like hearing about others. Not the bastards who've had you," he rasped against her lips. "Let's not talk about them right now."

Courtney considered that. She didn't want to think about the other women who'd had Ben. Because if she thought of them, she might just want to hurt someone. She wrapped her arm behind his neck. "No one else is here. It's you and me. And that's it." No ghosts from the past. This time, she was the one to kiss him, and she felt her own possessive edge.

He eased her down so he could shut and lock the balcony doors. Did he still have her panties? Did she even care? Did she—

A long ringing pierced the quiet of his home.

Ben swore at the sound. A knot of dread formed in her stomach. It was after midnight. A call at this hour was never a good sign.

"Stay right here," he ordered.

He stalked away. Grabbed his phone from a nearby table and put it to his ear. "Yeah, bro, do you have any idea what time—"

He stopped.

Tension and fear snaked through Courtney's body.

"Is he going to make it?" Ben asked flatly.

Courtney inched forward. *Who?*

"Yeah, yeah, don't worry. I'll be down there. Meet you as fast as I can." He dropped the phone.

Her arms wrapped around her stomach. "Ben?"

He exhaled. "Cole Trevor was just the victim of a hit and run. SUV slammed into him right outside of your building. He's in the ER now, in critical condition."

"OhmyGod."

"Eric wants me at the hospital. He's not sure that Cole is going to make it. The driver—shit, a witness said the driver reversed and deliberately hit Cole *twice.*"

Shock held her rooted to the spot.

"If he survives, we have to make Cole talk to us. And if he doesn't…"

If he doesn't survive? Her hand covered her mouth.

"Then we have to find out who the hell ran him down. Because whoever went after him…it's possible that SOB is also after you."

CHAPTER NINE

"We are *not* supposed to be here," Courtney announced as she clutched his arm in a wee bit of a death grip. Her voice was prim and proper, but shaking a bit with nerves.

And, yes, as usual, Courtney was right. *Technically*, it was wrong to slip inside Cole Trevor's apartment. But Cole had been in surgery when Ben and Courtney had rushed to the hospital. The nurses at the hospital had been adamant that no one would see the man until he was in recovery.

Ben thought the attack on Cole was coincidental as hell, and he wasn't just going to return home with his tail between his legs. He was also not going to wait on Wilde Securities' agents to play by the rules as they dug into Cole's life. Especially not when he had a key to Cole's front door.

"No big deal," Ben assured her easily. "I'm the owner of the building. If the cops ask, I can say I needed to do some maintenance work in here."

"Or there was a gas leak," Simon Forrest offered with a shrug as he paced nearby. "That usually works when I'm, ahem, interrupted at the wrong time."

Courtney gaped at them. "Please tell me you two don't do this a lot."

Ben shrugged. He really didn't do this a lot. But as for Simon—he had no idea. Simon's idea of fun could be…different.

"Let's hurry this up," Simon urged as he glanced around. Ben had brought Simon to disable any security system that Cole might have in place, and Simon had done his job perfectly. Within about thirty seconds, the security system had been taken off line. "I don't want to be here too long," Simon added as he rubbed a hand over his jaw. "The longer we're here, the more attention we risk attracting. *And* Gwen is waiting at home for me. Trust me, she is not a woman who needs to be kept waiting."

Ben rolled his eyes. Simon was a lucky bastard to be with Gwen Soloman, and the guy knew it. Gwen was the celebrity of the moment, in every blockbuster flick, and Ben still couldn't believe Simon—quiet, intense, often *scary* Simon—had gotten the star to fall for him.

The world was full of wonder. And insanity.

The guy has way more game than I suspected.

"We need to start searching. If he's got a computer, we can take it to Eric. He'll have every secret off that thing in moments." Simon headed for a nearby desk.

"You're planning to *steal?*" Courtney sounded horrified.

Simon cast a glance back at her. "Is this your first B and E?"

Her eyes doubled.

That would be a yes.

"Stop teasing her," Ben muttered. Simon's sense of humor could leave much to be desired, but Ben knew the man would have his back to hell and beyond. That was how Simon was made. He gave all for his friends. Ben offered a quick, reassuring smile to Courtney. "It's not a B and E. I have a key, remember?"

"Oh, yeah," Simon said, voice encouraging. "Use the dimples on her. That usually works, right?"

Such an ass.

Courtney crept forward. "I don't want to get arrested."

He tried a wink. "It's okay. I know a good lawyer."

Her lips parted.

"No laptop here. Let's check the bedroom." Simon had pulled on gloves. He'd tossed Ben a pair, too.

Because, obviously, it was *not* his first B and E.

"Don't touch anything, Courtney," Simon directed her. "No gloves for you, and we don't want you getting your prints—"

"I've been here before," Courtney cut in as she squared her shoulders. "I'm sure my prints are all over the place."

They'd better not be in the bedroom. Unbidden, jealousy stirred within Ben. A very unusual feeling because he didn't usually get jealous of anyone. Didn't get possessive. But…

Even back in law school, she was different.

Thus, the punch to Gavin Donally's jaw.

"Let's try to leave things undisturbed." Simon was opening the bedroom door. "Things are easier that way. And…uh, this *isn't* the bedroom."

Ben hurried toward him. There was something about the tone of Simon's voice—

"That's his work room," Courtney called out from behind them. "He's an artist, and he told me that he liked to keep his work private."

Simon hadn't moved into the room, but he *had* turned on the lights. "Private." No emotion in his voice now. "So that means you never saw what was in here?"

"No, he didn't want me to go inside when I came by to—"

"I can see why." Simon stepped over the threshold. "Yeah, you're both gonna want to get your asses in here."

Ben went in first, and fury burned through him. "What in the actual fuck?"

Behind him, Courtney sucked in a sharp breath.

One wall was like a freaking murder board—one of those boards that you'd see on an episode of *Castle* or *Criminal Minds.* Photos were taped to the big, bulletin-like board. At least a dozen photos, and most of them were images of Courtney.

"If he's an artist," Simon drawled, "then the man has one very specific muse."

Courtney pushed past Ben and rushed toward the pictures. "That's me going into the courthouse." She pointed. "At work." A deep inhale. "Jogging in the park. And that coat—I wore that in January. That was before he moved in here. He was watching me..." She spun to face Ben, with her eyes huge. "Back then?"

Before Ben could respond, Simon noted, "I'd wager the bastard moved in here because he wanted to be closer to you. This apartment is right under yours. For all we know, he could have surveillance set up in your place that allowed him to watch you."

Fuck, fuck, fuck. "I let him in." Rage and guilt twisted in Ben. "I'm so damn sorry, Courtney. I *let* that bastard move right in with you." He should have checked the guy's background more. Should have made absolutely certain that Courtney was safe. She was too important to risk this kind of shit.

If you weren't in the friggin' hospital, Cole Trevor, I'd be putting you there right now.

"You're in some of the photos, too," Simon noted quietly.

Ben saw his image staring back at him. His eyes narrowed because that photo—"Shit, that was from Friday night." It was at the bar. He stood beside Courtney, his body leaning toward hers, his gaze on hers.

"Who are the other guys?" Simon asked.

Courtney didn't answer. She'd turned back to stare at the photos.

"Courtney?" Simon prompted carefully.

She gave a little flinch. "This guy…" She pointed to a tall, African American man who stood with her as they entered a diner. "That's Cedric Davis. He's a new attorney at my firm." Her hand moved toward a man who stood close to her height—in the picture—a guy with bright, red hair and pale skin. "Kevin Haddix. He's an old friend from high school. He moved here a few weeks back, and I was just trying to make him feel welcome in the city. And the last man—that's one of my clients, Hayden Laslow."

Cole had been watching her. Stalking her…*and* the guys she'd been with? There were no pictures of her with women. Just the men.

"Why would he take these pictures? Why print them up? I mean…" She threw a glance over her shoulder at Ben. "Who does this?"

Someone who was obsessed.

Simon lifted up a notebook from the table. "He has your schedule here. When you leave in the mornings, how long you go for your runs, how long it takes you to get to work." He flipped through the notebook. Whistled. "Uh, yeah, this shit is personal."

Courtney grabbed for the notebook.

Simon held it just out of her reach. "You don't have on gloves, remember, and—"

"*Screw* the gloves." She snatched the notebook. Her eyes widened as she peered down at one of the pages. "He has the date and time that he saw us in the elevator." Her wild stare came back to Ben. "Like, he wrote that shit down." She flipped through the notebook. "He wrote down any time I went out with a man. How long I was with him. When I came home."

In case there was any question...Ben planned to rip apart the sonofabitch.

"*Why?*" Courtney asked, voice choked. "Why the hell is he doing this to me?"

Ben's phone beeped. He yanked out the phone and narrowed his eyes as he read the text from Eric. "Cole is in ICU. A nurse said he could have visitors soon." He looked back up at Courtney. Her face was too pale. Her lower lip trembled, and she still clutched the notebook.

Cole Trevor had been stalking her. The bastard had been watching Courtney for months. That shit was ending. She would not be put at risk again.

Oh, hell, no.

Cole would tell him *everything*. And then they'd make sure the bastard never got near Courtney again.

***

"I get that you're furious," Eric stated as they hurried down the hospital corridor. "But try to show some restraint. I had to bribe the head nurse to get us access back here, and if you cause a scene — if you *attack* the dude who is in ICU — security will be called on us."

Let them come. Ben wasn't in control. He knew it. Rage burned and spread inside of him, and every time that he saw the fear on Courtney's face, he wanted to attack. She should never have been afraid. She should never have been threatened.

I let the bastard get close to her. This is my fault.

Eric grabbed his arm, stopping Ben before he could shove open the door to ICU. "Get yourself under control," Eric ordered, voice nearly whisper-soft. That was the thing with his brother. The angrier Eric became, the lower his voice dropped. He became quiet and intense.

Ben was the opposite. When rage fueled him, he didn't go soft and lethal. He attacked. Loud, hard, fierce.

Right then, he wanted to *destroy* anyone who threatened Courtney. He wanted to —

She took his hand. Threaded her fingers with his.

His gaze shot to her. Her delicate shoulders straightened, and she lifted her chin. "We're doing this together," she told him. "And if he lies to us, we'll both forget restraint."

She was afraid. He saw that. But she was also furious, and she damn well had that right. Wilde agents were going over every square inch of her apartment under Simon's direction. Simon was afraid that Cole hadn't stopped with just taking photos of Courtney. He was afraid that Cole had put surveillance *in her home.*

Shit.

Fucking hell.

She squeezed his hand.

A nurse bustled out of the ICU. Her wide, green gaze went first to Eric, then it swept down the hallway. "Three can't go in," she mumbled, voice a little nervous. "ICU rules—normal rules—are for two family members at a time. I'm *telling* the others I think you're family in order to get you in, but only two people can enter. Only two."

"We're going," Courtney responded at once, pulling on Ben's hand. "And we're going now."

The nurse exhaled. "He's going to be groggy. That poor man is on a great deal of pain medication—"

Poor man, my ass.

"He sustained several broken bones and internal injuries and he—"

"He's going to live?" Courtney cut in, voice tight.

The nurse nodded, her blonde hair gleaming under the light. An *I love my patients* button had been pinned to her left breast pocket. "Absolutely, you do not need to worry about that—"

"We weren't worried," Ben told her. "Not even a little." *And if he doesn't tell me the truth, I just might kill the asshole myself.*

The woman bit her lower lip. "Five minutes."

That wasn't much. But it would have to work.

Soon, the cops would be there. They'd be questioning Cole. Eric was going to pull his strings and make sure all of the evidence at Cole's place was properly collected. *And* that the jerk found his way to a jail cell.

Ben and Courtney followed the nurse inside. The place was quiet, and the nurse's shoes squeaked over the floor. A nurses' station was in the center of the space. A collection of desks, monitors, files. Small rooms snaked out around the station. The nurse pointed to the room on the far left end. "He's in there. Please, don't stress him."

Can't make that promise.

"The poor man has been through a terrible ordeal, and he needs to recover. Five minutes," she said again. Then she hurried back to the station.

Courtney seemed to brace herself before she went in Cole's room. Ben made certain he was right at her side. As they neared the bed—*Jesus*. Cole looked like hell.

The skin on his face was red, torn. Probably because he'd slammed into the pavement and been run over *twice.* His left arm and right leg were both in casts. Bandages covered his upper arms and chest. Wires were connected to him, an IV fed into his arm and—

His eyes opened. "Court…ney?"

She was at the edge of the bed and still holding Ben's hand.

As far as he was concerned, she could hold his hand forever.

"What…happened?" Cole's voice was a weak rasp.

"You were hit by a car," Ben told him curtly. "Twice."

"Don't…remember."

Could be true. After accidents, Ben knew some people *did* forget. But they'd get back to talking about the hit-and-run in a moment. "Do you remember stalking Courtney? You remember *that?*"

The machines beeped faster.

Ah, yes, I think you do.

"I was in your apartment," Courtney said. "I saw the photos. What in the *hell* were you doing?"

Cole shook his head, moving it slowly against the stark white pillow behind him. "It's not…" But his voice trailed off.

"Not what?" Ben demanded. "Not proof that you've been stalking her? Because it sure as hell is. Just like the notebook is proof. You followed her on every date she took with a man. Documented how long she was with the guys. You watched her every move, you sonofabitch, and I want to know *why*."

Cole let out a low groan. "My body has been…wrecked to hell…can this wait?"

Was he fucking serious? Ben lunged for the bed, letting go of Courtney's hand. "You stalked her," he snarled.

The machines were beeping so fast now. Fast and loud, and he could hear the rush of footsteps heading toward them. Hell, the nurse must be coming for her patient.

He needed answers from Cole. "I'm going to turn your ass over to the cops. I'll make sure Wilde Securities gives the PD enough evidence to toss you into a cell. You will *never* hurt Courtney again, you understand?"

"Not…me…"

"You didn't take those pictures?" Courtney asked, voice shaking.

The nurse rushed into the small patient room. "I told you he couldn't be stressed! I told you—"

"I...took the pictures," Cole admitted.

Fuck not stressing him. "You bastard—" Ben began as his vision turned blood-red with fury. The machines screamed.

The nurse cried out, "You have to leave!"

And Courtney demanded, voice choked, "Why? Why would you do this to me? I thought we were friends."

She was hurt, and he was going to make Cole pay.

The nurse grabbed Ben's arm. "You're leaving, *now.*"

More footsteps were rushing toward them. More nurses? Or even security personnel? Ben didn't care. He wasn't done with Cole. "You tried to hurt Courtney."

Once more, Cole shook his head. Blood seeped through one of the bandages on his chest. "N-no."

"She was attacked in that parking garage! And *you* took a picture of her right before the attack happened. You were there. You were—"

More nurses burst in. Two women. One man.

"I was *protecting* her," Cole rasped.

"Bullshit! You attacked her. You left that message on her apartment wall, and I am going to make you wish you'd never been—"

Hands grabbed Ben and tried to haul him back.

"Ben." Courtney's voice. Quiet.

His head swung toward her. He stared into her eyes and his rage calmed, just for a moment. *I will not let anyone or anything ever hurt her again.*

"M-my job..." Cole managed to say, voice straining. "P-protect her...It's wh-what I was...doing...why...watching..."

Ben's attention snapped right back to the man in the bed. "What? Don't you dare lie to me—"

"No...lie." Each word was a struggle. And the circle of red on that bandage was spreading. "My job...protect *her*. Was h-hired...b-bodyguard..."

What in the hell?

"You have to leave, *now*." The nurse who'd originally let them in—she was now glaring and sweating.

And the others were swarming the patient.

Ben and Courtney backed away. They got out of the ICU as quickly as they could and found Eric pacing in the hallway.

"Well?" Eric stared at them. "What did you find out?"

"First, you're gonna need to pay that nurse more money." Ben winced. "And maybe make a small donation to the hospital." Or not-so-small.

"Ben..." Eric seethed.

Courtney stepped in front of him. "Cole said he wasn't stalking me." She dragged a hand through her heavy mane of hair. "He said that he was protecting me. That he was my bodyguard."

"Total bullshit." Ben's fingers clenched into fists. "*Has* to be bullshit."

The way Ben figured it, Cole was trying to cover his ass, but it wasn't going to work. The jerk was going down.

CHAPTER TEN

"It's not bullshit." Eric spun his laptop around so that Ben and Courtney could see the screen. "First of all, the guy's real name is Cole Vincent, not Cole Trevor. And, yes, he is former military, Delta Force to be exact. He's a lethal SOB, and he's been working in the private sector for the last year."

Courtney stared at the screen, her gaze flying over the material there. Cole Vincent? Her temples throbbed. They were back at Wilde Securities after an excruciating night that had seemed to never end. Good thing she'd already had the next few days scheduled off from work. Everything was straight-up chaos, and she didn't know how she would have dealt with a court case, too.

She'd actually scheduled the time off *before* all of this madness had started. She'd thought she might get some time off and head down to the beach. Those plans were screwed, along with most things in her life.

"From what I can determine, Cole is a freelance guy, one who offers his services out to the highest bidder," Eric continued. "Very hush, hush, very elite."

"He said he was an ex-con." Courtney ignored the increasing ache in her temples. "I didn't think you could get in the military with a criminal record."

"His crimes were committed when he was a minor. His record was sealed. A deal was made with someone in power along the way, and, presto, the guy was suddenly being all he could be for Uncle Sam."

Ben glowered at the computer screen. He'd been especially quiet—he was *never* quiet—since they'd left the hospital last night. He'd taken her back to his place, walked her to the guest room, and told her to get some sleep.

She'd thought he would come in with her. But…

He'd left her alone. She'd tossed and turned all night, and dawn had not been able to come soon enough.

Then Eric's call had come a few hours later.

"His services aren't cheap." Eric tapped his fingers against the top of his desk. "Whoever his employer is…we're looking at someone with a very large bank account, especially if Cole has been playing bodyguard to Courtney for the last few months."

"This can't be real," she whispered. "Why would anyone hire a bodyguard for me?"

"A bodyguard who truly sucks at his job," Ben added, voice brisk. "'Cause I sure didn't see the jerk running to the rescue in that parking garage."

Eric hesitated. His expression was clearly troubled. "I'm afraid there is more."

She didn't want more, thank you very much. Could he just keep the more?

Eric inclined his head toward her. "Simon found two listening devices in your apartment, Courtney. Cole *was* monitoring you all the time."

She could only stare at the laptop screen. At the picture of Cole that must have been taken when he had been part of Delta Force. His hair was cut in a brutally short style. He was missing his tats, and his face…it looked softer. Kinder.

"I am going to break his other arm." Ben surged to his feet. "That jackass." He started to prowl around the office like a caged lion.

Courtney's hands shoved against the front of her jeans. "Why?" That was the question that was driving her crazy. "I'm nobody."

Ben spun around. "The hell you are."

She blinked. His eyes were blazing. His hair was mussed. Stubble covered his jaw.

Dangerous and sexy.

Courtney swallowed.

"You're someone important, Courtney. You always have been, always will be."

Her chest ached. "Ben, my mom died when I was five years old. We were in a car wreck together and…I had some injuries." This was so hard. "At the hospital, I needed a transfusion—and, well, somehow during the course of my treatment, my dad found out that I didn't…I wasn't his."

She didn't usually tell this story. Not to anyone. Because it fucking ripped her heart out.

"He left me." Her fingers rose to press to her chest, right above the spot that ached so badly. "I was in the hospital, and he didn't come back. He *never* came back. I didn't see him again. I had no other family, so I was put in foster care. I bounced around the system for years until I turned eighteen. There was no one looking for me. Not then, not during college or law school. There is *no one* who would want to hire some bodyguard to watch me. I'm not important enough for someone to—"

"Don't fucking say it again." He was right in front of her. He grabbed her arms and hauled Courtney to her feet. "Do not."

Eric cleared his throat. "I, um, think I heard Dennis call my name. I'd better go see what he wants."

Dennis hadn't called him—

"I heard him, too," Ben said flatly, not looking away from Courtney but instead keeping his blazing blue eyes on her. "Go check and keep checking for a good long while."

A few moments later, the door shut behind Eric.

Ben didn't let go of Courtney. "You are important."

"My dad abandoned me. My mom—even before the crash, she barely had time for me. *That* is the memory I have of her. This terrible memory of my mom screaming at me that I'd ruined her life. That I was in the way." A memory that had haunted

Courtney for *her* whole life. "This idea that some mystery person hired a bodyguard for me — it makes no sense. I'm not on anyone's radar. I'm — "

"You're on my radar, and you have been for years. You're important. You're smart. You're beautiful. You're kind. When I see you, you make my fucking day better." His eyes widened, as if those words had come out by surprise. "Don't talk anymore shit about this, okay? Your dad left — then he's a sonofabitch who didn't deserve you. Real men don't leave. You got that? If I had a daughter, you can bet I'd do everything I could to make her feel loved and happy, to know that she was safe and protected and — " He kind of froze.

Ben stared at her with a dazed look on his face.

"Um, Ben?" Courtney prompted.

He shook his head. Squeezed his eyes shut. Muttered something she didn't catch. Then his hands fell from her. He turned away.

She didn't know what to say.

"He shouldn't have left." Ben's voice was growling. "And your mother shouldn't have said that shit to you. You deserve better. You deserve everything."

She could only stare at his broad back. "You're being…kind."

He laughed and didn't glance at her. "I'm not kind. I'm an asshole. Ask anyone. Hell, just open the door and ask my brother. He'll tell you. I can be a selfish, controlling prick. When I see something I want, there is no stopping me. I'll do anything to get the thing I desire."

His words sounded like a warning.

She wasn't in the mood to be warned. *You are smart. You are beautiful. You are kind.* "You can't say sweet things one minute and then try to get me to believe you're a bastard the next."

He spun toward her. "I *am* a bastard. You know that better than most."

Once, she might have agreed with him. But now... "I think I'm starting to see you."

His brows lowered.

"Maybe you're more of a white knight." Just like she'd believed when he'd come racing to her side in the parking garage.

Ben shook his head. "Don't believe it."

"I'll believe what I want." Courtney leaned into him. "You can tell me that I'm important, and I can tell you that you aren't an ass. Let's both believe those words."

His lips curled. His dimples *almost* winked. "I never know what to expect with you."

She searched his eyes. "Is that a good thing? Or a bad thing?"

"I'm trying to figure that out." His gaze dropped to her mouth. "I want to kiss you."

"I'm not stopping you."

"If I kiss you, I'll want to fuck you on my brother's desk."

Automatically, she peered at the desk. And the laptop that still sat there, with Cole's background information displayed on the screen.

"Actually, I always want to fuck you, if you want the record to be very clear, but I'm trying to hold my control in place while we figure out why someone sent Cole after you." His voice was gruff and the roughness slid over her skin, making goose bumps rise. "There has to be a reason."

She tried to slow her racing heartbeat. "No one ever cared when I was younger. There was no one swooping in to find me."

His eyes narrowed. "Cole will tell us. With the right pressure, we'll get him to tell us everything."

She tucked a lock of hair behind her ear and didn't look back at the desk. She also tried very hard *not* to think about having sex on that desk. "You think…" Courtney cleared her throat because her voice sounded too husky. "You think whoever hired Cole believed I might be in danger?"

"For all we know, that guy *is* the freaking danger. Could be some obsessed jackass who didn't want anyone else close to you. The first attack on you happened right after you and I were together at the bar."

Yes…

"And then, after we spent the night together, the same bozo showed up at the park."

Her arms curled around her stomach. "And I got the friendly note on my wall saying to stay away—"

"From me," he finished flatly. "I think Cole reported to his boss that we were together, and the psycho lost his shit. We find out who hired Cole, and we eliminate the threat to you."

Okay. Sounded like a plan. A very good one. She wanted the threat gone, and she wanted her life back.

"Until then, though, I want you to consider staying with me."

Uh, oh. Her teeth sank into her lower lip.

His thumb rose. Pressed to her lips. "I fucking love your mouth, so don't hurt it."

Her breath eased out.

His thumb slid tenderly over her lower lip, then fell back to his side.

"You have a job, Ben. Clients—"

"My assistant has cleared my schedule for the next few days. Don't worry about my job. It's covered."

Okay, but... "You have a *life.* You don't want me and my problems busting in—"

"I want you." His gaze burned into hers. "Trust me on that. I. Want. You."

And I want you. Which was a major problem. Why not just admit it? "If I stay with you...we'll wind up in bed together again."

Ben flashed his toe-curling smile. "We didn't make it to the bed last time."

A sharp rap pounded at the door. "We clear?" Eric called out.

Ben ignored his brother's call. His gaze remained locked on Courtney. "Stay with me. The security team is still going over your place, trying to make sure there aren't any other surveillance devices. You need a haven, and I can offer you that."

Tempting, but… "We'll sleep together." *Even more tempting.*

"Only if that's what you want."

He was exactly what she wanted. Hadn't she proven that when she'd gone to him on the balcony? Ben had told her it was a no-strings arrangement, but the problem was that every time she was with him, Courtney could *feel* the strings. Could feel the pull to him. When all of this was over, Ben might be able to walk away without looking back, but could she?

"I want you safe, Courtney. I will do *anything* to protect you, and I need you to trust me on that."

She did. "I'll stay with you. One more night." That would allow time for the team to finish up at her home, and hopefully, time for Cole to tell them exactly who they were after.

Another rap at the door. "It's my damn office!" Eric announced. "Did you forget that *again?*"

"Come in." Ben finally stepped away from Courtney. He headed to the window and stared out at the busy Atlanta street below them.

Eric entered the room, his eyes narrowed and suspicious. "You two get everything all cleared up?"

Ben's body was tense. "Courtney knows she's important, and she won't make the mistake of ever saying otherwise."

Courtney rolled her eyes. "And Ben knows he's got serious control issues that *he* has to work on."

Soft laughter came from Ben. "You really think I'm the one in control here, sweetheart?"

"This is going to end so badly," Eric muttered.

Courtney frowned at him.

Eric gave her what she suspected to be a fake smile. "It's time for you to start the interview process."

Okay, what?

Her confusion must have shown because Eric explained, "Standard procedure for a security case, I assure you. You'll meet with Agent Julia Slate, and she'll get basic background info. We'll want to do research on close friends and former lovers. Make sure nothing suspicious pops at us."

She was supposed to give up a list of lovers? That sounded awkward as hell.

"Simon is at the hospital. He'll call us as soon as we're clear to see Cole again. So, you can work with Julia, and we'll let you know when we need to leave." Eric glanced at his watch. "Julia should be here any—"

Another knock at the door.

"Always right on time." He opened the door to reveal Julia—a small, almost delicate woman with dark caramel eyes and a wide smile.

She looked friendly, approachable, and totally the *opposite* of the giant, glowering guy behind her.

"This is Julia Slate," Eric motioned to Julia. "And her partner, Rick Williams."

Rick grunted. His hair had been buzzed down low, and his football field shoulders rolled back.

"This is Courtney McKenna," Eric continued with a wave of his hand toward her. "Our new client. If you two could take her down to the conference area and begin the preliminary questions…"

But Courtney looked back at Ben. "Are you coming?" *Why* did she want him close?

Because he makes me feel safe. I'm in a building full of bodyguards and security personnel, but it's the attorney who makes me feel better. What was up with that?

He turned away from the window, but shook his head. "Don't think you want me there while you're going over details about your past relationships." His hands flexed and clenched. "Trying to respect your privacy so you don't have to tell me about the lucky assholes who were your lovers."

"Ben," Eric's voice held a distinct edge.

Ben's expression softened a bit as he gazed at Courtney. "I'll be here when you're done."

Uncertainly, she headed toward Julia and Rick, but at the door, Courtney shot one more look back at Ben. He was still watching her.

"I'll be here," he assured her again. "I'm not going anywhere."

***

The door closed softly behind Courtney.

Eric's sigh was loud and long. "What in the hell are you doing?"

"Trying to keep a friend safe." Uh, what did it look like?

His brother marched toward him. Stopped right in front of Ben. Jabbed a finger in his chest. "I see the way you look at her."

"And how's that?"

The finger jabbed again. "Like she's the only thing you *can* see. Like you can't take your eyes off her."

"I can see plenty of other things." A pause. "Like your finger. So get it off my chest."

Eric yanked his finger — his whole hand — back and then crossed his arms. "Can you see that you are in *way* over your head? You're not a bodyguard. You're not a Wilde agent. You're not even an intern here! *You're an attorney.* You shouldn't even be involved in this thing! You brought her to me, and I can take care of the rest. I'll have Julia take point on Courtney's protection detail, and Rick can make sure that she has a secondary cover, just in case. You don't have to worry about Courtney. You can go back to your normal life, and I assure you, she'll be safe."

"Didn't you hear what I told Courtney?" Ben asked quietly. "I'm not going anywhere."

"Oh, fuck." Surprise — no, shock — flashed on Eric's face. "Just how *in* to this woman are you?"

Ben yanked at his collar, feeling as if the thing were too tight. "We're friends, I told you that."

"Friends with benefits."

He rather preferred...friends who fucked. But...no, even that wasn't right. Because it didn't just feel like fucking.

And, holy shit, did I really just have that thought?

"I don't want you hurt." Eric's voice was very, very serious.

Ben clamped a hand over Eric's shoulder. "Thanks, bro, but I doubt the woman is going to try anything particularly rough with me—"

Eric growled. "You could become a target." *He's using his Annoyed, Level Two voice.* "The message on her wall said, 'Stay away from him.' If she doesn't stay away, what do you think will happen?"

Nothing had better happen to Courtney. Not now. Not ever.

"Did you ever think that *you* could become a target? Huh? That you could be putting yourself at risk because you are getting involved in something that is way beyond your comfort zone?"

"Don't be too sure you know what makes me comfortable," he responded. "You don't know everything about me." Just like he hadn't known all the secrets his brother possessed.

Eric exhaled. His tight expression and fierce gaze showed his frustration. "I want you safe. You're my brother. You were hurt once before. When I saw you in that hospital room, *that* is the shit of nightmares."

Ben's scars seemed to burn. He hadn't talked much with Eric about that attack. Hadn't talked to anyone. But the nightmares would come sometimes. Nightmares, memories…of being helpless. Of feeling his blood pumping out of him.

Of feeling the hard slice of a blade cutting into skin and muscle.

"You don't need to be put at risk. Not for a *friend* that I didn't even know about until recently. Step back," Eric urged him. "Put some distance between the two of you before it's too late."

It's already too late.

"My team will keep her safe. Once we've closed the case, then you can swoop in again with Courtney."

Ben cocked his head as he studied his brother. "You got into the habit when we were kids."

Eric's brow furrowed. "What habit?"

"Protecting me. Always doing it. The same way you protected Piper her whole life."

Eric tensed.

"You rushed to the rescue, trying to fight all our battles for us. Then you just…" Ben waved his hand to indicate the office. "You went and made protection your whole business, didn't you? Man, you have to see that, if anyone is obsessed with control, it's you."

His brother lifted an eyebrow.

"I'm not backing off this. I'm not walking away. Not from her." Ben held Eric's gaze. "Whatever she needs, I'll give it to her."

"And if you get caught in the cross-fire? What then?"

"We have to find this jackass before that happens. We eliminate him, and we eliminate all the threats to Courtney."

"*Why* are you taking these risks for her?"

"Because she's worth it." That was all he would say. And it was the stark truth. He was quickly coming to realize that Courtney was worth…everything.

CHAPTER ELEVEN

"I don't have an ex who would want to stalk me." Courtney shifted a bit in the chair. Her feet were flat on the floor. Her spine perfectly straight. Her hands folded in her lap. "I can give you names, but when you check them out, you're going to see that there wasn't any giant emotional attachment. The relationships ended, and we all moved on."

Julia lifted an eyebrow as she glanced at Rick.

He remained silent, but a faint smile curled his lips.

"What?" Courtney asked.

Julia sighed. "You're a divorce attorney, so I know you've seen just how ass-crazy people can get when emotions are involved. People cheat. People lust. They get obsessed. That crap happens constantly."

"Same shit, different day," Rick rumbled.

Courtney stiffened. "I know some relationships can certainly...deteriorate, but I don't think—"

"You don't think any ex harbors an attachment for you? That some guy might be jonesing to get you back? Or that some man is pissed as all hell that you walked away?" Julia nodded. "Maybe you're right. And in that case, the investigation will move quickly. But if you're wrong, it's *our* job to find out the truth for you."

What was she supposed to say? "The relationships didn't last long. The involvement was…" Light? Brief? Superficial? God, this was hard. "I have trouble letting people get close, all right?" Always had, always would. She'd once heard a social worker say that he feared Courtney couldn't properly attach to anyone. That her father's abandonment after the accident had made her "emotionally stunted."

Fuck him. Her nostrils flared. "I haven't been in love. No relationship lasted that long. Nothing progressed to that extent."

Julia and Rick shared another look. She didn't like their looks. Her gaze darted to the door. Ben had said he wanted to give her privacy, but…

I feel better when he's here.

"Just because you didn't feel a connection," Julia responded carefully, "it doesn't mean the men didn't. Sometimes, one person can love with her whole heart, but the other can feel absolutely nothing."

Julia's expression didn't waver. Her gaze remained direct. Yet Courtney caught the faintest hint of pain in the other woman's voice.

But then Julia cleared her throat and just straightened her shoulders. Her nostrils flared. "Let's start with the most recent guy and work back from him."

Okay. Most recent. "Ben."

Julia blinked. Twice.

"Ben's the most recent," Courtney added quickly. Super recent. *Current.* "After him, we'd need to go six months back. I dated an accountant named Kris Gregory. I think we were together for about a month."

Julia typed in something on her laptop.

"Before that, it was, um, a teacher named Kevin Clarke." He'd been sweet. The guy had loved kids. And—

"How long were you with Kevin?" Julia asked.

"About a month."

Julia's fingers stilled a minute, then she went back to typing.

"Ah, then it was…last year, I dated an architect named Antonio Flores." Antonio with his big dreams. He'd wanted to transform the city.

"How long were you with Antonio?"

Courtney swiped her tongue across her lower lip. "Does the length really matter?" Jeez, she could see the pattern here herself, and, yes, she'd known what she was doing but admitting it out loud…

"It gives us a sense of time. Lets us know how attached the man may or may not have gotten."

Frustration churned in her stomach. "I told you already. These relationships didn't end in some big, dramatic split. Antonio and I went our separate ways after about—"

"A month?" Rick asked, voice deep and quiet.

Courtney nodded.

Julia wasn't typing anything. Her head tilted to the left as she assessed Courtney. "That your rule?

You have a one-month rule with the guys you date?"

Courtney swallowed. Not a rule so much but… "A month gives you time to date. You have time to get to know the person. You can have fun." Courtney hoped her expression gave nothing away. "But after a month, things can start to get too serious. Too intense. You go from dating someone to being in a relationship. To having expectations…" Her words trailed away.

"And you didn't want that," Julia concluded. "You have a time limit, and the guys know it."

It wasn't like she told the dates about her rule. "It's just better for everyone that way," Courtney said, aware that her voice had gone too soft. "Too much of a commitment *would* lead to trouble. The kind of trouble I've seen in court. You'll start to trust the guy after too long, and if you trust the wrong person…" Her heart ached. "You're just let down."

Julia was staring at her with — with sympathy?

Courtney glanced away.

"Easier not to get hurt that way, huh?" Julia murmured. "If you don't stay with them long enough to care, then it is easy to walk away."

"Easy for us *both* to walk away," Courtney corrected quickly. "That's why I said that no one would be harboring some crazy obsession for me. The relationships just didn't last that long."

Julia shook her head. "They didn't last long for you. But maybe when you walked, one of the guys wasn't ready to let go."

BEFORE BEN

"They were ready," Courtney insisted. No one was playing for keeps. It wasn't that deep. It wasn't love. It had *never* been love.

Julia started typing again. "Let's continue."

***

Ben glared down at the city below. Courtney still wasn't back. It had been over an hour. Just how many exes were there to talk about? And, hell, no, he hadn't wanted to hear her discuss them. Any dumbass who'd been foolish enough to have her and let her go…

She's mine now.

The thought was surprisingly savage and possessive, and he wasn't usually possessive about many things in this world. Eric was the possessive one. Eric was the intense one. While Ben…

He was supposed to be all about fun. Living life to the fullest. Seizing the moment and loving the hell out of every second. There were plenty of amazing women in the world, and he hadn't wanted to settle down at this point.

I mean, I'm not settling down. He and Courtney — they were…

The door opened behind him. He glanced back, expecting to see his brother because, after all, this *was* Eric's office. But his brother wasn't there. Instead, Ben's best friend — and his brother's wife — poked her head inside.

"He's not here, right?" Piper loud-whispered. Her blonde hair brushed over her cheek. "Dennis said he was meeting with some of his agents, but I want to be extra sure."

Ben shook his head. "He's not here."

"Thank goodness." She hurried inside, shut the door, and then bounded toward him. He could practically feel the energy pouring off her.

So, of course, Ben became immediately suspicious. After all, he'd known the woman since Pre-K. She'd been at his side for pretty much every bad — and good — moment in his life. That meant he could read her like a book. And when Piper got all excited like this, her body practically vibrating, her eyes wide, her lips trembling with a smile...it meant only one thing.

His head cocked as he studied her. "Piper, you have a secret."

"I do!"

He winced. Her voice had been *loud*. A Piper side-effect of excitement. Ben crossed his arms over his chest. "All right. You gonna tell me or are you gonna make me guess?"

She gave a mocking laugh. "As if you could. This one is so going to—"

"You're pregnant."

Her jaw dropped. "What?"

"That's the secret. You're pregnant, and you haven't told Eric yet, and you're trying to figure out how to share the news and you want *me* to help you."

"OhmyGod, how did you know?"

Shock rooted him to the spot. He'd just been *bullshitting* her. Saying that all just to get a reaction out of —

"Uh, Ben?"

He staggered a little. "You're...pregnant? Seriously?"

Her smile was huge. "I'm pregnant!"

He grabbed her and tackle-hugged her like only a best friend can. "I'm an uncle!"

***

"May I talk to you just a moment longer?"

Courtney paused at the conference room door. Rick had left a few moments before, and she'd been so eager to escape after him. Only it seemed the escaping would have to wait a bit longer. She pasted a smile on her lips as she turned back to Julia. "Of course." Her hand waved vaguely in the air. "More questions?"

"I don't want to get in your personal business."

Um, yes, the previous questions had been all about her personal business.

"But speaking from experience, you can't protect yourself from pain. You can try to wall yourself off from everyone else, try to keep your heart out of reach because you think it's safer that way, that it won't hurt as much that way, but you're wrong."

Courtney sucked in a breath. "I need to go find Ben—" Once more, she turned away.

"Does he know about the one-month rule?"

Courtney's fingers tightened around the doorknob. "You're right, this is very much personal business."

"Because he's a nice guy. Sure, he can play the dick sometimes, but once you get past the surface, you realize he's the kind of man who will be there when you need him, no questions asked."

He had been there for her that way. But... She glanced over her shoulder at Julia. "We aren't serious. Ben understands me. I understand him." *Enemies in the courtroom, but outside...*

"Are you sure about that? Because I was carefully watching your face each time you mentioned him."

Oh, crap. What did that mean? What had Courtney given away?

Julia's fingers lightly touched Courtney's arm. "Just...don't let pain that some asshole in the past caused you — don't let that stop you from having the chance at something really good. Okay? Because while you're trying to protect yourself by setting your one-month limit, you just might be missing out on something really special. You might miss out on life because you're too afraid to live it. The past will hold you down, and it will hold you back."

"I'm not *afraid* to live my life." Now she was getting pissed. Wasn't she? Not like she was afraid Julia was right. Or that, deep down, she might have felt the same way... "I happen to like my life as it is."

Julia nodded. Her hand fell away from Courtney's arm. "And will you like it if Ben walks away in a month and hooks up with someone else?"

Hell, no. The thought shoved through Courtney's mind, but all she said was... "Ben and I have an understanding. He's helping me right now. You don't need to worry about what's happening between us."

"I like Ben. He's a good friend. And Eric is the best boss I've ever had. They were both there for me when I was going through a pretty dark time." Her lips curled down.

Even as she felt sympathy, a tendril of jealousy stirred in Courtney. "Are you... interested in Ben?"

Julia's eyebrows rose. "That's what I'm talking about." A satisfied tone filled her voice.

Courtney blinked. She had no idea what the woman was talking about.

"You're territorial where he's concerned. You might think this isn't serious, you might be trying to stop yourself from letting it become serious, but a part of you wants more—and you want that more with him."

***

Ben let Piper go so that he could smile down at her. "Oh, God, I hope it's a girl. A baby girl would wreck Eric. He'd be tied so tightly around her little finger. Guy would be one of those dads who wears a tiara and meets her for tea, and it would be *awesome*."

Piper laughed. "Like *you* wouldn't be showing up for tea, too?"

Well, of course, he would. He'd do anything for his niece.

"I don't know how to tell Eric." Her words rushed out. "You're the only person who knows about it so far. Me, you, and my little stick with the plus mark on it. I want it to be special. I want him to be so excited. And I want this memory to last *forever —* "

"Piper," Ben sighed her name as his fingers stayed curled around her shoulders. "This is you. This is Eric. He worships the ground you walk on, so when you tell him that you're having his baby, you will instantly make him ecstatically happy." She should have understood this by now. "You don't need to do some elaborate surprise reveal. You just need to tell him, and it *will* be a memory that lasts forever for him."

Her eyes teared up. Oh, hell, he hated it when she cried. He pulled her in for a bear hug. "Piper…" Ben muttered.

He was looking over her shoulder so he saw the door swing open. Ben figured it was Eric coming back, and he prepared for a quick back away from Piper —

It wasn't Eric.

It was Courtney.

And she immediately stilled when she saw him hugging Piper. Stilled…and then her eyes narrowed. Her delicate jaw hardened.

One of her eyebrows went straight up.

BEFORE BEN

Oh, hello...that's interesting.

Ben stepped back and let Piper go. She followed his gaze and spun around. "Oh." Piper's hand flew up to cover her heart. "I was afraid you were my husband!"

The other eyebrow joined the first as it rose. "And you didn't want your husband to see you in Ben's arms?"

"Oh, no, I don't care about that," Piper said breezily. "Eric sees that stuff all the time. I just wasn't ready to talk with Eric yet. Trying to work my way through this." She headed toward Courtney, a spring still in her step because the woman was riding high. "You look so familiar." Piper offered her hand. "I think we've met before, but please accept my apologies because I can't quite place you." Her smile was big and friendly. "I'm Piper."

"We met but it was a long time ago." Courtney took the offered hand. "I'm Courtney McKenna."

"Courtney..." Piper seemed to taste the name. She tapped a finger to her chin. "*McKenna?*"

Uh, oh. He got a bad feeling in the pit of his stomach. *For the love of expensive whiskey, Piper, do not say —*

Piper glanced at him. Snapped her fingers together. "Right! Of course! Ben's Courtney. I have heard *so* much about you over the years."

Courtney blinked. "You have?"

"So much." A firm nod. "First started the day I had to patch up Ben's hand in law school because he'd punched some jerk who'd talked smack about you. Ben must have pounded the crap out of him, and, honestly, Ben doesn't fight that much. Thought you two might hook up after that, but then Ben got all weird and clammed up on *me* — "

"Piper!" Sweet Jesus, the woman over shared.

She blinked. Innocently. A total fake innocence. What in the hell did she think? That she was dealing with Eric? Ben could see right through her.

Ben crossed to the two women. "That's enough of a walk down memory lane." He motioned vaguely toward Piper. *I will totally make you pay later.* "Courtney, you've probably realized she's married to my brother."

Courtney's expression was completely closed down. "I know who Piper is. Remember, I've seen the scars?"

His lips parted...

"Ooooh..." From Piper. A whole world of understanding in that amused sound. "She's seen you without your clothes on, huh? Guess things finally progressed the way you wanted."

Fucking hell. She was going to pay so much the next time they were alone. Through clenched teeth, he gritted, "I'm sure my brother is looking for you."

"No." She gave a happy little rock of her body. "He doesn't know I'm here."

"But if you were to go *find* him — "

She put her hands on her hips. "This is his office. I'm sure he will *find* his way to me soon."

He grabbed for patience. A whole lot of it. And, once more through gritted teeth, he managed, "But you had something to *tell* him."

Piper gave Ben her sunniest smile. "And I will tell him…don't worry about me." Paint splatters lined her jeans and top. She must have been working in her studio before she'd taken her pregnancy test.

"Oh, but I do worry." He needed to talk with Courtney. Explore the whole moment when he could have sworn he saw jealousy on her face. "I worry so much…" He took Piper's elbow. "That I am going to give you a nudge so you can find—"

The door opened once more. Eric stood there. Glowered. Typical Eric. "What's going on?"

Piper sighed. "Ben was giving me a nudge."

Eric immediately pulled her away from his brother and led her across the room. "Stop nudging Piper." He eased out a chair. Made sure she was comfortably arranged. Frowned worriedly down at her.

And Ben frowned back at him. Yes, as a rule, Eric was *extremely*, almost *hyperly* protective of Piper. But this was something else.

Shit, he knows.

Ben laughed.

Eric pointed at him. "You need to get to the hospital. Just got a call from Simon. Cole is awake, but the guy is saying he will *only* talk to Courtney."

Ben immediately reached for Courtney's hand. Her fingers curled with his. Fit perfectly. He headed for the door.

"Simon is there, and he's going to report back to me what you find!" Eric called out. "He's lead on this—so don't do anything stupid!"

Ben growled. Stupid? What the fuck? "I'll do what it takes to get the information we need." Because he wasn't going to just let a threat to Courtney keep existing.

Eric was protective as hell about Piper.

And Ben…

When it comes to Courtney, I'm realizing I feel the exact same way.

***

"I didn't know that…" Piper's voice was halting. "Courtney's a client? Is everything okay?"

No, it was pretty much a cluster, but they would be finding out who was after Ben's lady. "Don't worry about them." Eric didn't want her worrying about anything. "My team is on it." He trusted his team completely. Eric hovered over her. "Do you…ah, are you thirsty? Do you want to put your feet up? You cold? Hot?"

Her gorgeous eyes narrowed on him. "You know."

"Ah…know that you're the best thing to ever happen to me? Absolutely." He leaned forward and put a careful kiss to her lips.

When Eric would've pulled back, her hands flew up and fisted in his shirt-front. "You know my secret."

He smiled at her. "I think I could be married to you for fifty years and never know all your secrets."

Her expression held pure suspicion.

"If you've got a secret you want to share with me, though," Eric added carefully, "please do. I'd love to hear it."

She bit her lip. That luscious lower lip. Then she dropped her hold on him. "I'm pregnant."

"I love you so much," his immediate response.

Her eyes gleamed. "You're excited?"

Excited didn't even cut it. He was the luckiest SOB on the planet, and he knew it. "Baby, you are my world." She was...and their baby.

Piper is having my baby! His hand was shaking as he reached out to touch her stomach.

CHAPTER TWELVE

"There's nothing going on between Piper and me. We're friends, have been since we were little, crazy kids terrorizing our Pre-K teacher, but we've never been together as *anything* more."

They were in the elevator when Ben made that announcement.

Her hands twisted in front of her. "I…didn't ask."

"Didn't you?"

Her gaze cut to him.

"I was celebrating with Piper when you came into the office. She's pregnant, and probably telling my lucky brother that news right now. I'm going to be an uncle." His smile was absolutely thrilled. His eyes gleamed. "And I can't wait."

Her heart was drumming too fast. She stared at him and realized — the baby that Piper carried was completely and totally wanted. She could already see the plans and dreams in Ben's eyes. Soccer games? Princess parties? Campouts? There was so much hope there.

And if Ben was this excited, she could only imagine how thrilled Eric must be.

"Congratulations." Courtney cleared her throat. "I'm happy for all of you."

His gaze raked her.

The elevator doors opened, and Courtney pretty much surged out. But he caught her before she'd gone too far. His fingers wrapped around her elbow, much like when he'd "nudged" Piper. Only when Ben touched her, Courtney felt a surge of heat pulse through her. Her breath came faster. Her skin seemed more sensitive. Her entire body reacted as she turned toward him.

"And that's why." He wasn't smiling now. He backed her up until he caged her between a nearby wall and his body. "*That's* why Piper and I were always just friends. Because when I touched her, I didn't feel the surge."

Wait, *he'd* felt a surge, too?

"I touch you, and it's like my whole body gets hyper tuned. I can feel *everything* more."

That was exactly how she felt.

Footsteps rushed toward them.

"There a problem here?" A gruff, male voice demanded.

She turned her head—managed to pry her eyes away from Ben—and saw a man in a security uniform side-eyeing them.

Ben stepped back. "No problem, Tommy. Just taking a minute to let my lady know something very important." He inclined his head to Courtney.

The security guard didn't back away. Courtney realized that while he may know Ben, the guard still wanted her reassurance. "I'm fine," she told him quickly. "Thank you."

The guard took his time backing away.

Ben wasn't touching her anymore. She missed his touch.

"Let's be very clear on something." Ben's stare didn't waver. "If I came into a room and found some jerk with his arms around you, I'd be jealous."

She shivered. "We're just…" Her words trailed away. *Friends?*

Friends with benefits? Friends who had amazing sex?

He waited.

"We're not serious. Or—or—I mean, we haven't even said if we're exclusive. We hooked up on *Friday* night." It had just been a few days. Things were moving so crazy fast.

"I'm not going to fuck anyone else while I'm with you." His voice was a rough rasp. "And if you are planning to fuck someone else—"

"I'm not." Had he *missed* her six-month dry spell? She was pretty sure she'd told him it had been *six* months.

"You were planning to meet someone in the bar on Friday."

Cole was waiting. They needed to get to him. And the guy she'd been planning to meet didn't matter. "He was no one, okay? Just a guy I met online. A man who never showed up." She hadn't even bothered to mention him to Julia. What was the point? They'd never met in person. He'd stood her up, and she'd…found Ben?

He had a half-smile playing on his lips. "Then I'm eternally grateful that he's a dumbass."

She could only shake her head. "I don't know what to do with you."

"Oh, baby, I am sure you will figure it out." Once more, his fingers took hers. "But for now, let's go see Cole. He *will* be talking, and I want to know exactly what other intel he has to give us."

She wanted to know, too. Wanted to know everything that she could.

They hurried outside the building, and the Atlanta heat hit them. She tried to ignore just how crazily right it felt to hold Ben's hand. His Benz was waiting out front, and he held the passenger door for her as she slid inside.

He was being the gentleman. A protector.

He hardly seemed like her enemy at all.

In fact, he seemed like he could be something so much more.

They drove in silence for a time. Because her guard was down, because he made her feel safe and comfortable…the question just slipped from her as she asked, "Do you want kids?"

"One day, absolutely."

Her gaze darted toward the window.

"What about you? Want a little girl with your eyes? Maybe a fierce little attorney-to-be? Or maybe a son?" His voice was teasing. Typical Ben. "Someone who'll play dirty on the baseball field while you scream your heart out for him in the stands?"

She had to blink. She'd never had anyone screaming for her in the stands. No one had ever been in the stands, and she hadn't been on any teams. She'd just been alone. But if she had a kid...

"One day, absolutely," she repeated his words in a slightly hollow tone.

Silence.

"And I *will* scream my heart out in the stands for him or her." A million times, over and over. She'd go to *every* game. Her kid could be the star player or sit on the bench. Didn't matter a single bit. She'd still cheer and scream and *love.* "And I won't care if she wants to be an attorney or a circus clown. As long as my kid is happy and knows that he or she is loved, that's all I want."

"Courtney..."

Her gaze slid to him. He was looking at her.

"Courtney, you deserve—"

A car was barreling toward them. She saw it coming. Saw it moving as if in slow motion and she screamed.

But it was too late. The vehicle plowed into them, hitting on Ben's side. Metal crunched. Glass exploded. The air bag deployed and it was a sea of white and she was *screaming* the entire time.

Every moment seemed to last forever...

As she kept screaming Ben's name.

***

He ran from the scene. Jumped out of the SUV and just ran as fast as he could. His whole body was shuddering. He'd slammed down the gas pedal as hard as he could and just floored the sonofabitch. The impact had been terrifying. Metal had screamed—or maybe that had been the woman. Glass had blown everywhere. The vehicles had become friggin' sardines.

And he was bleeding! Some of the glass had cut him above his right eye. He swiped at the blood as he ran.

Someone yelled, "Stop him! He just hit that couple!"

When some fool tried to get in his way, he just slammed a shoulder into him. It had been an old guy who tried to stop him. Gasping for air, the jerk fell onto the pavement.

No one else tried to get in his way. His feet thundered over the pavement. He had a motorcycle waiting up in the garage. He'd get on it and get the hell out of there.

His payment would come that night. He'd be riding high then.

But as he rounded the corner, he couldn't help but glance back. The two vehicles were a crumpled mess. Glass was everywhere. The woman had gotten out of the Benz. There was blood on the side of her face. She was screaming the driver's name...

"Ben!"

Over and over.

From what he could tell, Ben didn't seem to be moving.

For an instant, he stumbled. And he remembered the other poor bastard. The one who'd tried to crawl out of the road...

I didn't kill him, though. Not that guy — and, and…maybe not this one, either. *Maybe —*

The woman turned toward him, her long, thick hair flying over her shoulders. For just a moment, their stares seemed to meet.

I'm fucking sorry. He mouthed those words.

Then he ran.

CHAPTER THIRTEEN

"I am fine," Ben muttered for what had to be the tenth time.

But Eric glared at him. And grilled the ER doc more. "You're sure there are no internal injuries?"

"The airbag cushioned him on impact—"

"But he had to be cut out of the car. The firefighters on scene were using the jaws of life!"

Ben winced. That wasn't a memory that he particularly enjoyed. The vehicle had crumpled around him, and for a bit there, he'd blacked out. When he'd come back, Courtney had been yelling his name and fighting fiercely to get him out of the car. He'd smelled gasoline—or thought he had—and he'd tried to make her leave. He'd told her to get the hell away.

Instead, she'd grabbed his hand and held tight until the firefighters arrived.

They'd worried that his right leg was broken. It wasn't, luckily. And, yeah, he knew precisely how fortunate he had been. Every time he closed his eyes, he felt the slam of the impact once again. He hadn't even seen the other car coming. He'd just seen the terror on Courtney's face right before impact.

"He blacked out." Eric pointed a finger at Ben. "Does he have a concussion—"

"Yes," the doctor's response was quick. Light gleamed off his glasses. "We'll need to watch him for the next twenty-four hours. Make sure that he doesn't exhibit confusion, slurred speech—"

"Oh, for shit's sake." Ben stood up. His gaping hospital gown brought a chill to his bare ass. "I'm not confused. My speech isn't slurred. And I just want to see Courtney."

Eric frowned.

"*Now.*" He'd been checked out. Poked. Prodded. Screw all of that. *She* mattered.

Without waiting for anyone to say more, he marched for the door and yanked it open. He stepped into the hallway. Looked left. Looked right—

There she is.

She shot up from one extremely uncomfortable-looking waiting room chair. There was a bandage on her cheek. What the hell? No one had told him that she'd been hurt. He hurried toward her, aware that the paper gown was flapping and not giving a shit. It wasn't the first time he'd walked through a hospital and given folks a show. Probably wouldn't be his last, either. Not at the rate he was going.

"They wouldn't let me back." She staggered to a stop near him. But she didn't touch him. "They said only family could go back, and I'm not family."

He grabbed her. Pulled her against him. And took her mouth with his.

Behind him, Ben heard a cough and then the doc's voice as the man noted a bit wryly, "Doesn't seem too confused. Looks like he knows what he wants. But we should still exercise caution…"

Fuck off, buddy.

He was tasting Courtney. Savoring her. His arms were around her, and he was holding her tight. No, he wasn't confused, and he had *exactly* what he wanted.

But her hands slid between them and pushed against his chest.

Reluctantly, his head lifted.

She stared up at him with eyes that seemed so beautifully dark and deep. "I was scared." Her voice was quiet, small. "That driver headed straight for your side of the vehicle. Some of the witnesses swore that he deliberately ran the light, that he sped *up* before he hit us. You were trapped, and I didn't know how badly you were hurt, and you kept telling me to leave."

He kissed her again. Had to do it. "I wanted you safe." His hand lifted, and his fingers slid tenderly along her cheek, making sure not to press against the bandage. "How bad?"

She gave him a wan smile. "Just a scratch. Don't know why they put the bandage on. It had already stopped bleeding when I got here."

He backed up so his gaze could sweep over her. "Anything else?" He wanted to make certain she was okay.

Eric cleared his throat. "You can get dressed and *then* have this conversation."

Or he could have the conversation right the hell then because *it* was more important than putting on jeans. "Anything else?" Ben asked Courtney as he ignored his brother.

"Just some bruises. Nothing to worry about." One shoulder moved in a shrug. The top of her blouse slid to the side with the small movement, and his gaze immediately fell to the exposed curve of her shoulder.

And the livid red mark already there.

A savage hiss burst from him. He had a similar mark, but he didn't give a flying shit about his. *She* mattered. The fact that she'd been hurt mattered.

And he wanted to kick someone's ass.

His hand reached for her shirt. He unbuttoned the top button.

She immediately swatted at his hand as red stained her cheeks. "What are you doing?"

"Maybe he *is* exhibiting confusion," Eric drawled. "Ben, stop right now and get your clothes on!"

His fingers feathered over her shoulder, and his head bent. He pressed a soft kiss to her reddened skin. "I'm sorry, sweetheart." Another kiss. "I should have done a better job of watching out for you." He started to back away.

Her hand flew out and curled around his wrist. "*You* were the driver." Her expression was stark. Fear still lurked in her eyes, and he didn't like that. He never wanted Courtney to be afraid. "You were the one he hit. The one who took the full impact. And we both know that vehicle barreling at us couldn't have been some coincidence. Witnesses said he was parked there, almost *waiting*. When he saw us coming, that's when he shot forward. He was waiting to attack *me,* but you were the one in his way. You were the one who could have—" But she broke off and looked away. "I don't want you hurt. Not because you happen to be next to me."

He'd gladly stand *between* her and any threat—seven days a week. She should understand that.

Before he could say something else, Eric touched his arm. "Get dressed. We still need to talk to Cole, more now than ever before." Eric's voice was soft, subdued.

He'd get dressed, but Courtney would be coming with him. He reached for her hand. Pulled her with him. Brushed by the doctor and Eric. Before the exam room door closed, though, he glanced back at Eric. He wanted to make sure one thing was crystal clear. "If anything else ever happens—"

Eric's eyes narrowed. "It had better *not.*"

Protective older bro, to the extreme. Ben almost smiled, but didn't because this point was too damn important for humor. "She's never left in a hallway again, you got me? Where I am, she goes. You make sure of it if I can't."

He saw the flash of surprise on Eric's face. "You know what you're saying?"

Yes, he did. "It's sure as hell not the concussion talking. So make certain it happens. She's never left alone again." She'd been alone for too much of her life. The girl without a family—only to be told she couldn't go in with him because she *wasn't* his family? Oh, hell, no. That wouldn't happen again. "She goes with me. Always."

He shut the door.

And found Courtney staring up at him. Maybe he should explain. He didn't want her to think that he was—

She stepped toward him. She stretched onto her tip-toes, and her arms wrapped around his neck. She kissed him, an open-mouthed, sensual, but oddly sweet kiss. One that seemed to slide through his whole body, chasing away a chill he hadn't even realized he felt.

"Thank you," she whispered against his lips.

"For what?" He hadn't done anything. He'd failed to keep her safe. He should have been more vigilant. Hell, his brother would have been constantly on guard. Simon would have been watching for a threat from every angle. When the other driver had run through the light and plowed into them, Ben had been looking at Courtney. He hadn't even seen the threat coming.

Easing back, Courtney said, "Because, for the first time in my life, you make me feel like I belong."

You do, sweetheart. You belong with me. To me.

Courtney turned away before those words could slide from his lips. She crossed the small exam room and picked up his jeans. "Here." She offered them to him with a small smile. "I think the hospital staff would appreciate you covering up."

He strode toward her. Reached out for the jeans. Their fingers touched.

"Personally," she told him as some of the fear *finally* left her dark gaze, "I love the view."

***

His breath sawed in and out. He sat on the motorcycle, his legs straddling the vehicle as he waited for the payment to arrive. Unease slithered through him as he glanced around the dark parking garage. He didn't normally handle jobs like this one. B and E's were more his style. He'd done plenty of smash and grabs back in the day, even managed to hotwire some cars.

No one had ever gotten hurt before he'd started working for the new boss. This had been the first time that he'd taken a job *knowing* that he was supposed to mess someone up. First, it had been the guy he'd been ordered to run down in the road, and, shit, he could still hear the *thud* of impact when he closed his eyes. His hands had gripped the steering wheel so tightly, and he'd driven right for the guy.

Job one for the new boss.

He'd vomited after that hit and run. Even called the hospital and been damn relieved to find out the man was still alive. *Never killed anyone.*

Then the order for the second job had come through. He'd balked, but the boss had offered more money. A lot more.

And he'd thought…maybe it wouldn't be a big deal. Hurting someone. He could get used to it. He'd certainly gotten his ass kicked plenty of times. When you grew up poor and on the streets, it wasn't like you were gonna have a lot of options. Until he'd become big enough to fight back, he'd been the punching bag for every punk around.

So he'd thought he could handle it. Shit, the money had been too good to pass up. Ten thousand dollars to smash the SUV into someone else?

Should have been easy.

Only…

He didn't feel right. He kept seeing that woman as she struggled to get the guy out of the wreck. She'd been so upset. And he—he'd wanted to go back. Wanted to help. Wanted to say he was fucking sorry.

An engine growled, and he tensed. Night was coming. He'd been hiding, laying low as the sun set. He and the boss were supposed to meet under the cover of darkness, that had been one of the rules. This old garage wasn't used by anyone—it was too far away from Atlanta's busy streets. On the outskirts of town, all but forgotten, it had seemed like the perfect place for a pay-off. No one would be around to watch. But…

Why am I scared? He hadn't been scared, not since he was sixteen and big enough to fight back.

Headlights hit him, momentarily blinding him, and he lifted his hand to shield his gaze. He peeked around his fingers to see a big car, long, but sleek.

And the driver's side door opened even as the engine kept growling and the lights glared at him.

The driver put one foot down on the pavement. "Ken Smith?"

It was as good a name as any, he figured. He hadn't used his real name in ages, sure as hell not for a job like this one. "Yeah." His hand dropped. He squinted at the light.

"You did a good job smashing into that Benz."

His stomach was in knots. "Uh, the driver got out, didn't he? He's okay?" He hadn't been told to kill the guy. Just hit the car. Not so bad really...

So why does it feel bad?

"Does it matter?" The boss was standing behind the open car door, body partially blocked.

"Ken" swallowed and admitted the truth, "Yeah, it does."

The boss glanced around the empty garage. "You're going to grow a fucking conscience on me? Are you serious? You're nothing but trash. Some cheap thug who breaks windows and steals jewelry or whatever crap he can find."

He stiffened. He wasn't trash. He *wasn't*.

"That's okay." The boss's shoulders straightened. "I can deal with this. I *will* deal with this."

The knots in his stomach were worse. "I want my money."

"Right." The boss ducked back into the car.

A sliver of relief pierced his heart.

Right before the boss raised a hand—and the gun that had just been retrieved from the car. "Ken" didn't even have the chance to move before the first shot was fired. It was strange because the blast seemed to echo around him, an echo that lasted for so long…he didn't even realize he'd been shot, not at first.

Not until he looked down and saw the blood on his shirt. After he saw the blood and as the thundering echo died away, *that* was when he felt the pain. A white-hot pain that burned into his chest.

"A conscience will get me in trouble. I'm not about to let you ruin things for me."

Another shot. This time, "Ken" fell off his motorcycle. He tried to curl his body in, tried to protect himself—

The pain was getting worse. His whole body was on fire.

"Consider that your payment, asshole."

A car door slammed. Tires squealed.

And he realized that he was in a pool of his own blood. So much blood. He tried to crawl back to the bike, but could barely move at all.

He knew that he'd been left to die. The bullets were in his chest, and he couldn't draw in a breath. Was he choking? His heart pounded so hard, and tears leaked down his face.

The money was supposed to help him start a new life. A down payment.

His fingers fumbled…managed to shove into his pocket. He had his phone. A two-bit piece of shit that he'd—*dammit, yes*—stolen earlier that day.

When you had nothing, sometimes stealing was the only way to get anything.

I stole the phone.

I stole the jacket I'm wearing.

I stole the fucking motorcycle.

Because he'd just wanted something. He'd wanted a life like everyone else.

His fingers slid over the screen. His hand was shaking. He was shaking. The fire in his chest was changing, almost numbing now. Like…like ice.

Why was he getting cold? His quivering fingers pressed to the phone. He just had to dial three numbers. Just the nine. The one…

And…

The…one…

CHAPTER FOURTEEN

"What the fuck happened to you two?" Cole was partially sitting up in bed, and a glower hardened his face. "I've been trapped in this room with that bozo—" He pointed toward a silent Simon. "All day. And now you come in looking like hell—" He winced. "Well, not you, Courtney. You always look good, but that creep..." He waved toward Ben. "He's seen better days."

Ben's hands fisted. "You're going to see a whole lot of *worse* days if you don't tell me what I need to know."

Cole's gaze swept over them. "Tell me what happened to you two first."

Courtney headed for the bed. Her fear had faded—for the moment—and rage had taken its place. When she thought of what could've happened to Ben...how badly he could've been hurt... "Some jerk in an SUV plowed into us. Drove straight through a red light and hit Ben's side of the car."

Cole's face went slack with what looked like shock. Then worry had his eyes turning to slits as his jaw hardened.

"The driver jumped from the vehicle and ran from the scene, but the cops are looking for him now."

The machines around Cole beeped—fast and hard. "Shit." He swiped his hand over his face. His right hand since the left arm was immobile in a cast. "Shit."

"You *look* like you know something about this." Simon stalked forward, abandoning his position near the window. "You've got that guilty-as-hell expression that I really don't like."

Cole did have that expression. Courtney fought a surge of fury. "I thought you were my friend."

"I *am* your friend!"

"Bullshit," Ben called. "You're the guy who was spying on her. You think we didn't find the devices at her place?"

Cole flushed. *Guilty.*

If he weren't in a hospital bed, she'd be tempted to take a swing at him. "You put listening devices in my *home?*"

"I was protecting you! I swear, that's why I was hired." His voice was stronger, and he looked slightly better than death today. Not much, but some. "I needed to be able to hear what was going on in your place in case there were any kind of attacks. It was for your *safety!*"

She felt violated to her core. "How often did you listen?" Horrified, her gaze whipped to Ben. Oh, no, had Cole been listening when—

Ben's expression showed his rage. "When you're out of the hospital bed, you and I are going to work this little situation out."

"I'll help you," Simon offered.

Ben nodded.

Her gaze darted back to Cole. *So the hell will I.*

"Dammit, it was a *job*." Cole squeezed his eyes shut. "I was protecting her. And, look, no, when you two started your—hell, no, I didn't listen, okay? I don't need to hear that shit. I just turned the surveillance on long enough to make sure there wasn't any threat. That is what I was supposed to do. My employer was worried about her. He put me on her trail so she could stay safe. And the car wreck today—"

"That was no accident," Ben cut in.

"No, it was deliberate. It was an attack! That is exactly what my employer feared would happen."

"*Who* is your employer?" Courtney asked.

He seemed to falter. "I don't know. The money arrived in my account every month. I was emailed instructions about what to do. I was given a name for my employer, but a quick search let me know the name was BS."

Simon blew out a frustrated breath. "And that crap didn't raise like a million red flags for you?"

"Yes!" Fast and hard beeps sounded from the machines near Cole. "But I needed the cash so I took the job, and then when I met Courtney…" His gaze locked on hers. "I liked you."

"You know what?" Ben announced. "Maybe I shouldn't let the fact that you're in a hospital bed stop me from kicking your ass. Why put off for tomorrow what you can do today—"

Cole seethed, "Listen! I *liked* her as a person. She's sweet. She's kind. She helps people carry up their deliveries, and she always makes time to ask the kids in the building how school is going." He huffed out a breath. "She was a *nice* lady, and I didn't want anything bad to happen to her, so I stayed around, especially when—" He clamped his lips together.

"No." Courtney's voice was very definite. "You don't get to do that. You don't get to stop talking and to hold back. This is my life, so if you have something to say, you tell me, right now. Ben could have been hurt or killed today. Someone broke into my home and wrote, '*Stay away from him,*' on my wall. When I didn't stay away, this happened. It's *not* happening again. I want to know everything, and I want to know it now." Her breath was coming too fast. "I can press charges against you. You put listening devices in my house. I can have you thrown in jail. I don't care that you think you were my bodyguard or that you were protecting me. *I* think you were stalking me. I think you should be—"

"He wanted something with your DNA on it."

She blinked. "What?"

"I got freaking creeped out." Cole ran his right hand over the stubble on his jaw. Considering all the casts and bandages on him, he was probably lucky to be moving *that* hand so well. "He wanted your DNA. A toothbrush. Hair samples. Started asking a month ago. Got more demanding. That shit was weird, so it put me on high alert."

Her DNA? Now she faltered. "I...I did one of those home DNA kits..." Her gaze darted to Ben. "I did that about six months ago." The timeline slammed in place for her. "God, I just — I wanted to know where I'd come from." Was that so crazy? She'd grown up with no family, so when an ad for one of those ancestry services had come up on a social media site, she'd clicked it. She'd done the sample, sent it in, and hoped against crazy hope that it would come back and she'd get a hit. That she'd find her long-lost father. Her *real* father. Instead, she'd found fourth and fifth cousins, all on her *mother's* side. And she'd found out that her distant family members had been Italian, French, Asian, and Spanish.

"Six months ago?" Ben spared a hard glance toward Simon. "And then you just coincidentally get this asshole," a nod in Cole's direction, "as your shadow shortly after that?"

Yes, she was connecting the dots, too. Especially because Cole's employer wanted her DNA.

"Your employer has money to burn." Ben rolled back his shoulders. "And you say he wanted you to *protect her?*"

"Yes."

Ben rubbed the back of his neck. "Then maybe we are looking at this wrong. Maybe...maybe the employer is the one with the enemies." His gaze sharpened on her. "And *his* enemies are after you, Courtney."

"No." Her immediate denial. "That doesn't explain why *your* side of the car was hit today—"

"Maybe I was just in the way." She could see the wheels spinning in his mind even as his words sent chill bumps rushing over her skin.

Maybe I was just in the way. And he'd been hurt because he'd been with her.

"My boss…" Cole cleared his throat. "He wanted to know who she was dating. How long she was with her partners. If anything became serious. He was almost fanatical about that stuff."

"And *none* of this shit made you realize you needed to pull out of this job?" Simon burst out. "Seriously? You're former Delta Force! You're supposed to help people, to protect them, to—"

"My best friend fucking died in my arms. I didn't protect him, so I know what a failure I am." Cole's right hand balled up the sheet near his hip. "I spiraled, all right? I got back to civilian life, and I took the most dangerous jobs I could find. When I nearly got my ass blown to hell on my last assignment, I knew things needed to change. Guarding a beautiful lady seemed like a no-brainer, and, yes, when the red flags started flying, I was worried. *That's why I stayed.* I didn't trust my boss. I was trying to track down his real identity. I was trying to keep Courtney safe. And then I found my ass run down by a driver who didn't stop." He shook his head. Glared at Ben. "What kind of car hit you? Because I remember a black SUV hurtling toward me."

Courtney pushed back on her heels. "A black SUV. It was abandoned at the scene."

"Eric already connected the dots on that," Ben said with a grim nod. "He's making sure the crime scene teams check the vehicle thoroughly. If it's the same car that hit you, and odds are pretty friggin' high in my mind that it *is* the same one—"

"We don't believe in coincidence," Simon added darkly.

Another nod from Ben. "Then your blood is probably on it."

Cole's blood. And Ben's blood. Because they'd both been hurt.

"I *don't* think my boss did this," Cole spoke carefully. "He wanted her safe. He *knows* the threat is out there, so it's possible that he knows who is targeting her."

"Then we have to find out who your boss is." The determination in Ben's voice was clear. "And we make him tell us where the threat is coming from."

***

"We're going to use him as bait."

Courtney's fingers tightened around the glass in her hand when Ben made that announcement. They'd returned to his place, and they both should have crashed after the truly hellish day they'd had. Her body was exhausted, but Courtney's mind couldn't seem to turn off.

He'd given her a splash of whiskey. She hadn't tasted a drop. Ben wasn't drinking—*because he has a concussion.* He prowled near the windows while she watched from the couch, her feet curled beneath her.

"We'll get Cole to email his so-called boss. Tell him there's an emergency with you. That you were targeted today."

All true…

"Cole might not have been able to trace the guy, but Wilde Securities will. We'll find him, we'll draw him out."

Using Cole—the guy had sworn to cooperate with them. Was that because he feared being tossed into a jail cell? Or because he truly wanted to help her, as he'd claimed in his hospital room?

Ben gazed out at the city. Tension rolled off his body.

She put down the glass. "You think it's someone related to my real father."

He didn't look back. "Isn't that what you think?"

It was what she feared. "The man who raised me until I was five…" She couldn't call him her father. Wouldn't. They hadn't been connected by blood, and he'd run as fast as he could when he'd learned that truth. "I looked him up when I was eighteen."

Ben glanced back at her. One look at his face and she knew—

Courtney sucked in a breath. "Wilde Securities looked him up, too."

"As part of your security investigation," he told her softly. "Family has to be checked out."

"He *wasn't* family."

"No, Francis Green—"

"*Frank,*" she cut in with more heat than she'd intended. But he'd never been a Francis. *Hey, Frankie!* She could remember the voices of his friends when they'd show up at the apartment. *How's Frank's little girl doin'?* Only she hadn't been his. And he hadn't cared a damn about how she was doing.

Ben's features were shadowed. "He died the year after he left you. Police report said he was drunk—that he walked right into oncoming traffic and never slowed down."

Her lips pressed together. "I don't want to talk about him tonight."

"You took that DNA test because you wanted to know where you came from. I think the test was a trigger for all of this."

"I *only* got results on my mother's side! There was nothing—"

"Maybe that's what the person was looking for. Someone with enough money and power can access those systems. Maybe this guy—maybe he was looking for someone who had a connection to your mother. Maybe he did the math and figured out your age. Maybe he *thought* you were the one, and that's why he wanted the toothbrush and the hair so that he could be sure."

Because Ben believed this all went back to her biological father. And, truth be told, wasn't she starting to think the same thing? "I always wondered what my real dad would be like. You kind of…" *Slow down. Your words are coming out too fast.* "When life is really sucking, you make an image in your head. A fantasy. That this wasn't the life you were supposed to have. That there'd been some kind of mistake." Her gaze dropped to her hands. "In my head, when I had nothing, I imagined my real dad. He had everything. Giant house. Fancy cars. And he was looking for me. He'd always been looking for me, and he wanted me to stay with him. He was never going to let me go. He wasn't going to walk away because I wasn't what he wanted. I was going to have the prefect life. I just had to wait on him to find me."

Ben slowly advanced toward her.

She swallowed. Lifted her gaze to his. "Then one day I woke up. Realized that he wasn't coming." You could only wait so many years before the hope faded away. "And I knew that if I wanted that perfect life, then I'd have to get it myself." She'd worked her ass off. "But just when I was close, when I was about to have all the things I wanted…this happens."

He stopped near the couch and stared down at her. "You are going to have everything that you want."

She could only shake her head, sending her hair sliding over her shoulder. "Maybe I'm not even sure what I truly want any longer."

The big house. A fancy car. Enough money so that she'd never be scared of where her next meal was coming from…

She *had* a nice apartment. She loved her car. And she hadn't been hungry — thank God — in a very long time. What else was there? More money?

Or…

Ben smiled at her. "Doesn't matter what you want. You'll get it. I think you can probably have anything you want."

I want you. Her breath caught as she looked at him. The thought that had just whispered through her mind was the absolute truth. She did want him. Sexy Ben. Strong Ben. She wanted him, and she didn't simply want him for a few nights.

But he'd almost been killed because he'd been in the same car with her. And the warning on her bedroom wall had been extremely clear.

Stay away from him.

While she wanted to stand up…wanted to put her arms around him and press her lips to his again, she didn't. Because as she gazed up at him, Courtney realized that the thing she actually wanted *most* in the world? It was for Ben to be safe.

He leaned toward her. The back of his hand slid over her cheek, being very careful not to brush against the bandage on her skin. His touch made her shiver. She was far too sensitive to him. Everything about him made her feel —

Someone pounded on his door. A hard, fierce rapping.

Ben jerked back.

Her heart surged in her chest as adrenaline pumped through her veins. The pounding had made her jump. She'd been so focused on Ben that the noise had scared the hell out of her.

The pounding came again.

"Are you expecting someone?" Courtney wasn't even sure what time it was. Late…had to be late.

"No." His jaw hardened even more as he whirled for the door.

She surged up from the couch and grabbed his hand. "Ben…" Alarm flared through her.

The pounding came again.

He gave her fingers a squeeze. "Don't worry. It's going to be okay." He advanced and glanced through the peephole.

Some of the tension left his body. Not all…but definitely some. His head turned as he glanced back at her. "It's Kadi Laslow."

It took a moment for the name to click. Then she blinked. In the midst of all the craziness going on… "Your client?" Her gaze darted to the clock on the wall. She'd been right. It was *very* late. And the woman was at his door. His home—not his office. "Why is she here?"

He yanked a hand through his hair as a fierce knock came again. "I have no idea. Give me just a minute with her, okay?"

Um, not okay.

Shit. Am I jealous again? She'd never been jealous before. But now, here she was, feeling green-eyed way too much where Ben was concerned.

He unlocked the door. Opened it, but then blocked that opening with his body. "Kadi." His voice was perfectly normal. Mild. "I don't think I had you listed for an appointment tonight."

What? What kind of response was that to the woman pounding on the door of his home? He needed to tell Kadi to just get her Botox-filled self back on home—

"*I need you.*" While Ben had been calm, Kadi's voice was shaking. Desperate. "I need you, and you're the only one who can help me." Then she threw herself against Ben.

Courtney cocked her head. Cleared her throat. "Ahem."

Kadi jumped.

Ben sighed.

And he finally opened the door a little bit more. When he did, Courtney got a good look at Kadi's face—and the long trails of black mascara that covered her cheeks.

"What's she doing here?" Kadi demanded. She pointed a finger at Courtney. "She's with him! With the bastard who *attacked* me tonight!"

Courtney sucked in a breath. She hadn't talked to Hayden Laslow since the meeting the other day. *Had other things on my mind.* She'd rescheduled all her appointments—

"You're defending him!" Kadi surged forward, her hands suddenly flying out like claws at Courtney. But before those claws could connect, Ben grabbed her around the stomach and hauled her back. "You're on his side!" Kadi accused. "Are you sleeping with him? Are you screwing Hayden?"

The day had already been *extra*. She didn't need this crap, too. "I'm your husband's attorney. Not his sex partner. You don't need to worry about that." Her chin lifted. "If he has physically attacked you, then we need to report the attack to the—"

"He fucking attacked my *character*! Don't you see? Don't you get it? He said I was cheating on him! That I'd been cheating since day one, and he'd found someone better!" She struggled in Ben's hold. "There *is* no one better than me. Sure as hell not your scrawny ass! So I am telling you—*stay the hell away from him!*"

The shouted words made Courtney stiffen.

Stay the hell away from him.

"She's *not* involved with Hayden, I promise you that," Ben's words were flat and hard. "Now calm the hell down, Kadi."

Kadi's mouth opened, closed. Then she squirmed in Ben's arms until she was facing him. "Why is she here so late?"

Why are you here so late? Courtney glared at the woman's back.

Ben just lifted a brow.

A sound of disgust tore from Kadi. "You're screwing *her*? The two of you are together?" She backed away from Ben. Tossed a wild glare from him to Courtney. "Isn't that like…some unethical shit?"

"We're not discussing your case, you don't have to worry about that," Courtney assured her crisply. "And I am removing myself from this situation right now. Ben, talk to your *client*. I'll be in the guest room."

She turned on her heel and marched away.

***

Courtney didn't slam the bedroom door. She didn't scream or rage. She quietly shut the door and didn't glance back.

"You can't screw her." Kadi glared up at him. "You're *my* lawyer."

Had she just told him what he could do? Ben was done. "Find a new lawyer then because my relationship with Courtney is non-negotiable."

"But, but—"

He curled an arm around her shoulder and steered her to the door. "You don't get to come to my place in the middle of the night, making demands. That's not how this works. You want to be a client, you make an appointment at my office just like everyone else." He thought about the nightmare going on in Courtney's life and anger burned in his gut. "And you don't get to cry wolf about an attack. If someone hurts you—then that shit is real. The world is full of victims who suffer every single day, and you coming to me, telling me you've been attacked—"

"I don't want to be left with nothing!" Tears pooled in Kadi's eyes. "I had that before! I spent two years of my life with that man, and he's not going to kick me out now. You were supposed to be the best! You were supposed to help me!"

"I always help my clients." He worked his ass off for them.

Her shoulders sagged. "Hayden has someone else." Her voice was small. Lost. "I went to him. I begged him to take me back, and he said...said I'd never be as good as her." Her gaze darted over his shoulder. "I...thought it was his lawyer?" Uncertainty there. Pain and worry.

Ben shook his head. "Courtney is his attorney, nothing more."

Her eyes squeezed closed. "I...was drinking."

Not a newsflash. He could smell the booze on her.

"I have messed up...so much, haven't I?"

"It's not your best night."

More tears.

"I'll walk you downstairs and get you a cab," he told her. "Then you go home. You sleep this off, and you do *not* go see your husband again, do you understand me? If you want a new lawyer, fine, get one. But he'll tell you the same thing...stay away from Hayden. The interactions you two are having now—the fights—it's only making the situation worse."

She swallowed. "How much worse can it be?"

He grabbed his phone and keys. Locked the door. As they stood in the hallway, Ben took in her mascara-covered cheeks and too pale lips.

"If I said her or me...you'd pick her, wouldn't you?" Kadi scrubbed at her cheek, smearing the mascara.

"There isn't a choice." He kept his voice soft. He never liked seeing any woman cry. "You're a client, Kadi. And Courtney—"

"What is she?"

Everything. "Non-negotiable," he said again. "That's what she is."

And he led Kadi to the elevator.

***

Kadi Laslow swiped over her cheeks as she climbed out of the cab. She'd made such a colossal ass of herself that night. Going to Hayden had been a desperate move, and when he'd thrown her out, when he'd said there was someone else, someone *better*...

Her ankle turned, and she almost fell. Stupid freaking high heels. Truth be told, she hated heels. And she hated tight dresses. And she hated the blonde of her hair. She'd always enjoyed being a brunette, but Hayden had wanted her blonde.

Just like Hayden had wanted her to have bigger breasts.

And Hayden had wanted her to be at his beck and call.

Hayden had driven her freaking insane. Was it any wonder that she'd cheated on him? *Take that, fucking Hayden.*

He said he'd give her nothing. At first, that had sounded like the end of the world to her. The worst nightmare on earth. And that was why she'd gone running to Ben. She'd wanted him to *fix* everything. But...

She kicked off her heels. Just left them on the sidewalk near her building. Or, technically, *Hayden'*s building. The condo she had there was his. Everything was his.

She'd had nothing before, and she'd moved straight into a mansion. She could do it again. She was still young. She was smart. Most men were idiots, and she could work with that.

Screw Hayden. She'd find someone richer, someone better. Someone—

"Grab the bitch."

Hands yanked at her shoulders even as some kind of black hood was shoved over her head. A scream broke from her as someone else lifted her legs. Her bag fell to the ground. She squirmed and twisted but was only held tighter. They threw her into a vehicle—she heard the engine growling and the tires squealing.

"He'll pay for her," a man grunted. "He'll pay the friggin' world to get her back."

Tears poured down her cheeks as they bound her hands and feet because these men—they were wrong. Her husband wouldn't pay a dime to get her back. Hayden…his business wasn't always legal. She'd *known* that going in. They'd even met—God, a lifetime ago—back when he'd still owned a few strip clubs. She'd been one of his dancers back in the day.

He had enemies. The kind that liked to break legs and arms.

"If he doesn't pay, she dies."

No. Hayden wouldn't pay! He wouldn't pay for her. He'd think getting rid of her this way was an easy out. He *wouldn't* pay and—
And I'll die.

CHAPTER FIFTEEN

She tip-toed out of the guest room again. This was becoming a habit. Slipping out of the room under the cover of darkness and going to look for Ben.

Only…this time, she wasn't looking for sex.

She was worried about him.

Courtney stilled in front of Ben's closed bedroom door. Just slipping inside while he slept seemed stalkerish, but the man had a concussion. She needed to make certain he was all right. If she checked on him and saw that he was okay, then Courtney was sure she'd be able to get back to sleep.

"He's not in there."

OhmyGod.

The voice—Ben's voice—came from the darkness and scared the ever-loving hell out of her. She whirled around.

He flipped on the lights. Ben was propped up against the kitchen bar. "I'm right here." Clad in an old t-shirt and jeans, he watched her with a hooded gaze.

"*Don't* scare me like that again. In case you missed it, I have some stalker after me, and scaring me in the dark is *not* something that is going to help me right now." Her heart was pounding frantically in her chest.

"Sorry." Ben inclined his head. "Just didn't want you going in and finding an empty bed. Not while I was right here."

Okay. He was there. He looked…good. Normal. Sexy. "How's your head?"

"Fine."

She took a step toward him. Faltered. "How's the concussion? I was worried about you, so I wanted to check and see how you were doing."

His fingers tapped on the bar. "Head's fine. I'm fine. You can go back to bed, no worries needed."

His voice was off, and his expression was too tight. Courtney took another step in his direction. "Is something wrong?"

"Kadi asked what I'd do if I had to choose between her and you."

Kadi was a pain in the ass. "I know we crossed, um, lines with our relationship—"

He straightened. Headed toward her with a slow, almost predatory stride. "Is that what we crossed? Lines?"

She had no idea what they'd crossed. "What did you tell your client?"

He stopped in front of her. Stared down at her. For the life of her, Courtney could not read his expression. "That she could find another lawyer." His hand cupped her cheek. "That's the thing, you see. She can find another lawyer. I can get another client." His lips pressed together. Then, after a moment, Ben rasped, "But I can't find another *you*."

Why couldn't she figure out his expression? "Ben?"

"Piper told you that I punched some dumbass back in law school because of you. But you didn't ask me why."

"Ah…why?" And where was this conversation going?

"Because the dumbass in question said you'd gone down on him. Gavin Donally told the whole fucking group of guys around him that lie."

"*What?*" Then, immediately, as rage fueled her, she exclaimed, "I didn't! That jerk asked me out, and I refused because—"

"Because a prick like him would never be worthy of a girl like you." His thumb brushed lightly over her chin. "I punched him because I was furious. Mad as hell at him for what he'd said about you. *No one* would talk about you that way." His hand fell away from her. "That was the first time I knew that I was in trouble."

She missed his touch. "You're not in trouble."

"Oh, I am." Soft laughter that rumbled and had her leaning toward him. "I tried to fight the truth for a while. Dated other women. Moved the hell on. But the thing is…the other women weren't you. And even when I supposedly moved on, I kept coming back to you."

"Ben?"

"I wanted you for years. What did you say to me the other day? 'One and done' I think?"

Her cheeks burned. "Don't throw that back at me. There is no way that 'one and done' would ever work with you." One time…and she'd wanted more. So much more.

"It would never work with you, either, sweetheart. I knew that as soon as I met you. I knew you were a forever-kind-of-girl. Or at least, you were for me."

He could *not* be saying—

"Sometimes you meet someone, and you know that person will change your life. You did that for me. I would look for you on campus, just because seeing you each day made me happy. After we graduated, I would look for you at court."

"You *fought* with me at court."

"And those fights are still helluva fun." His lips curled. His eyes gleamed. Then…His smile faded. "You would never be one and done for me. I knew you…*you* would be *the* one."

He couldn't be saying this. "No." She shook her head. "You just feel badly for me because I had a shitty day. Well, your day was worse. You were the one who was hit because of me, and you don't need to make me feel—"

He kissed her. Leaned down and pressed his lips to hers.

You make me a feel a million things, Ben. Need churned inside of her. Lust. Desire. And…tenderness. Her body softened as she curled her arms around his neck. As she pulled him closer. As she wanted so much more from him.

His mouth lifted. "I don't feel badly for you. I want you. More than I've wanted anyone else. And I will never want another woman this way. Because there is only one Courtney McKenna." A half-smile played at his lips as he looked down at her. "There's only one you."

Her heart squeezed. He was staring at her as if she were some kind of prize. Some gift he'd been fortunate enough to find. *No, he's staring at me…like I'm everything.*

No one had ever looked at her that way. "I'm scared." A hard truth from her. She was absolutely terrified of the way he made her feel. What if he changed his mind? Like Frank had done? What if he realized she wasn't what he really wanted?

If she let down her guard with him, if she let him in…

And he left…

Because relationships always end. Isn't that why you became a divorce attorney? One in two marriages end in divorce. You knew you'd have a steady client pool. Nothing lasts forever.

"You don't need to be scared with me, sweetheart. I'll protect you from every threat."

What if he was the threat? The biggest one that she'd ever face?

Julia had told her to grab life.

She was holding tight to Ben right then. Holding him as close as she could. The dimpled smile was on his face. The one that he used to charm so easily, but she didn't think he was trying to charm her. He wasn't playing her.

Ben lifted her into his arms.

"Wait! Stop! You're hurt—"

"No, I'm not."

Uh, yes, he was. "Concussion?"

He carried her to the wide bar in the kitchen. Put her on top of it. Slid between her spread legs as the long shirt she wore bunched around the top of her thighs. "The doc said not to exert myself too much." He leaned forward and pressed a kiss to her neck. "I'll just be nice and slow. Not rough and wild. No undue exertion."

Her hands were curled around his arms.

His head lifted. He stared into her eyes. "If this is what you want…"

"I want you." An absolute truth. She didn't know what would happen tomorrow or the next day—she just wanted him.

"Then you have me." He came in close. Pressed his lips to hers even as his hand slid down to her thighs. His slightly calloused fingertips trailed up her skin, making her tense as he went up, and up, and… "Oh, baby, did you forget something?"

"Maybe." *Maybe not.* She was wearing the oversized shirt and nothing else.

His fingers slid between her thighs. He kissed her as he stroked her. His tongue dipped into Courtney's mouth even as his fingers slid over her sex. His thumb worked her clit. Sliding slowly, giving just the right pressure.

She arched toward him.

He pushed a broad finger inside. Her breath caught.

His finger withdrew. His thumb pushed harder against her clit.

Her hips surged into his hand. Her mouth pulled from his. "This is…ah…so not sanitary, you know. People *eat* here."

A rough rumble of laughter. "*I* eat here."

Oh, no. *No.* No way, he was not—

He did.

He pushed her back on the bar. Pulled her legs forward. Leaned down and tasted her. Every lick, every slide of his tongue had her moaning. Her body was tight and eager, and his mouth was driving her insane. Pleasure waited just out of reach. She was so close to climax. It would just take a little—

Two fingers pushed into her as he licked the center of her need.

She came, gasping out his name.

"Hell, yes. Hell, *yes.*"

He positioned his cock at the entrance to her body.

Her hands reached for his. Their fingers threaded together. He drove into her, one long glide that filled her completely. Her body was still shuddering from her climax, and her sex rippled around him with the contractions from her release.

"I want to fuck you so hard," he whispered as he leaned over. "But I promised you slow…and nice."

He didn't make her feel nice. He made her feel out of control. Reckless. Made her dizzy with pleasure. *Nice* didn't fit into the equation.

Her legs wrapped around his hips. She stared up at him as she deliberately tightened her inner muscles around him. "Fuck nice." She'd been a nice girl all her life. She could be something else now. She could be anything.

He withdrew. Drove into her. Filled her with the heavy length of his cock, and she gave herself up to him completely—just as he gave himself to her. There was no holding back. There was no hesitation.

Their bodies surged together. He filled her. Deep. Total. Again, and again, and she came a second time, a hard surge of pleasure that swept through her entire body and stole her breath. Ben was with her. He drove deep, and his release surged into her. She held him tightly, stared into his eyes and saw his pleasure.

Saw him.

Ben. Ben Wilde. The man who'd been her enemy. Her protector.

Her friend.

Her lover.

And…the man that she very much feared…she might love.

***

Her hands were bound behind her. Kadi yanked at the rope, feeling it cut into her wrists. She'd screamed and screamed, but no one had helped her. Some asshole *had* punched her, and Kadi could taste blood in her mouth.

The hood was still over her, and she thought that was good, wasn't it? If the hood was over her, then they were planning to let her go. *I haven't seen their faces. There is still a chance they will let me go.* They didn't know yet that Hayden wouldn't pay a dime for her return. She could work this. She could work *them*.

The hood was yanked off her head.

I am fucked.

Kadi blinked against the bright light. It was a bare bulb that hung down from the ceiling, gleaming right in front of her face. Behind that bulb were shadows. Bulky forms that when she squinted, Kadi realized were the shapes of men.

"That's not her."

Kadi stiffened at the low voice.

"What are you talking about?" A higher voice. Still male, but had to be younger. His voice cracked, a sure sign of nerves. "I watched that lawyer's apartment. *She* came out with him. He put her in a cab. Sent her home. I waited until the cabbie left, and then I grabbed her."

"She's blonde."

Kadi sucked in a breath and tried to figure a way out of this.

"Uh…yeah?" The younger guy seemed confused.

"We're looking for a damn brunette."

A brunette at Ben's place? "Courtney," she said. Her voice cracked as much as the guy's had. She swallowed a few times and tried again. "You want Courtney." She didn't know why. Didn't care why.

All that mattered was that she had to distract these guys.

Silence.

I still haven't seen their faces. "I can get her for you. One phone call from me, and I can get Courtney to meet me any place you want. You want her, and I'll get her for you."

One of the bulky shadows moved forward. Into the light. He was big and round, with a face that showed her his life had been anything but easy. His nose was crooked, a long scar trailed down his cheek and hooked under his jaw. His hair was long and limp, and his wide neck sported a twisting tattoo — one that was punctuated by another long, thin scar. As if someone had once tried to slit the guy's throat.

And failed.

"Why the hell would you sell her out so easily?" He lifted his right hand and the knife he held gleamed beneath the light. He put the knife to her throat, and she felt it cut into her skin.

I'll have a scar like his if he digs any deeper.

Or she'd be dead. "Because I want to live." Truth. "I would sell out my own mother if it meant I lived." Another truth. In this world, you had to look out for yourself. No one else was going to do it. No one else would protect you or ever have your back. Not really.

He laughed. "I believe you."

He didn't move the knife away. And she was too afraid to breathe.

"Jimmy, get this woman a phone."

CHAPTER SIXTEEN

Ben's phone rang, jarring him from sleep. He'd carried Courtney into his bedroom and fallen asleep with her curled around him. He squinted at the clock, wondering who in the hell was calling him. Couldn't be the office—he'd given his assistant strict instructions that he wasn't to be disturbed. So—*had to be Eric.*

The phone rang again. His hand flew out as Ben grabbed the phone. His fingers swiped over the screen, and he squinted against the bright light. He recognized the caller's name, and a knot settled in his gut.

"Ben?" Courtney's fingers slid over his chest. "What is it?"

He put the phone to his ear. "Hello?"

"You need to get dressed and meet me at the police station," Eric told him flatly. "We've got a problem."

Yeah, he'd figured as much. "What is it?"

"Your hit and run? They found the driver."

"That's good." He gave Courtney a reassuring squeeze. "The guy can lead us—"

"He was a kid, Ben. Eighteen years old. And he's dead."

"What?"

"He was shot in some old parking garage. He managed to call nine-one-one, but by the time the paramedics got to him, it was too late."

Shit.

"The kid's prints were found in the SUV that plowed into your car." Eric's breath exhaled on a long sigh. "We already suspected the SUV that hit you and Cole would be the same one. We were right. The detective in charge has linked it to the hit and run on Cole."

Still he asked, "Is the detective sure?"

"Yes, it's Layla."

Layla Lopez. A detective they both knew and respected. And Layla was very rarely wrong.

"She's the one who tied the dead man to your hit and run. He fit the description given by Courtney and the other witnesses at the scene. Layla pushed for a fast check on the prints—that's how everything came together so quickly. I'm with Layla now and…" His voice became muffled. "I *am* telling him. Give me a minute." A sigh. "Layla wants you to bring Courtney down to the station." A pause. "Come to the station and then you'll go to the morgue. Layla wants Courtney to ID the body."

His gaze cut to Courtney.

"Ben? You there?"

"Yeah, yeah, I'm here. We'll be there as fast as we can." He put down the phone.

"I…heard the conversation."

"You ever identify a body?"

"No. Have you?"

"I had to go with Eric once." Shit. He pulled her closer. He wanted to shield her from every bad thing in the world.

"He was only eighteen? That's so young."

Too young. "I'll be with you." No way would he leave her side. He'd be with her every fucking step of the way.

***

"You good?" Detective Layla Lopez asked.

"No, not at all." Courtney sucked in a breath, swore she tasted bleach, and squared her shoulders. "I just want to get this over with."

The detective waved one perfectly manicured hand. Her dark hair trailed down her back in a long braid.

The ME—at least, that's who Courtney assumed the other woman was—lifted a sheet off the *body* that was on the table.

Immediately, Courtney's gaze flew to the man's face.

Man. Boy. He looks so young. She had to swallow three times before she could talk. Her gaze stayed on his face. The round jaw. The long, somewhat hawkish nose. The little bump in the middle of his nose, as if it had been broken before. His forehead was high. His dark hair fell back against the table.

"That him?"

Ben's hand pressed to the small of her back. Warm. Steady.

"That's the guy I saw running away, yes." The sheet covered him from the shoulders down. Had he really mouthed that he was sorry right before he'd vanished from the scene of the wreck? She could've sworn that he had. "What happened to him?"

"Shot twice. Bled out slowly." Another wave of the detective's hand, and the sheet was lifted to cover the boy's face. "Donnie Dwight. He's got a rap sheet. Mostly small-time stuff. Usually does B&Es, petty thefts. This is the first time…" Now her gaze moved to Ben. "The first time he graduated to attempted murder." She shook her head. "What is it with you Wilde boys? Does trouble always stalk you?"

"Only some days," Ben allowed.

On the ride over, Ben had told Courtney a bit about the detective. He'd said that she and his brother went way back, that she was smart and tough, and one of the best cops he'd ever met.

Layla's gaze darted back to the body on the table. Sadness drifted across her face as her lips pulled down. "No one should bleed out like that. No one should die alone." A sigh. "I will find his killer."

That was something else Ben had told her. Layla always got her killers.

Layla led the way to the door, and Courtney was only too eager to follow her. The morgue was icy cold, a cold that seemed to have settled into her very bones, and she couldn't get out of there fast enough.

In the hallway, Layla spun toward them. "The SUV he plowed into your Benz was the same vehicle used in the hit and run near Courtney's building." Her breath heaved out. "I had the techs and our lab do a rush job—we found blood and DNA on the SUV that matched up to Cole Vincent."

Cole Vincent. Because that was his real name. He'd been lying to Courtney, and she'd bought every line he'd fed her.

Dammit.

"Donnie wasn't a big-time player." Layla's lips tightened. "Getting involved in a hit and run? Trying to murder someone? That's next level stuff. It's—" She broke off, her gaze darting over Courtney's shoulder at the same moment that Courtney heard the quiet tread of footsteps.

She glanced back. A tall, handsome, African American man strode slowly toward them. His suit was impeccable, fitting his wide shoulders like a glove, and the crisp white shirt he wore had an easy elegance about it that told her his clothes were probably more expensive than a month of groceries for some families. Power clung to him, but...

So did sadness.

She knew the man by sight. They'd never met personally, but the guy's reputation proceeded him. Kendrick Shaw. *The* best defense attorney in the city—no, the state. Hands down. *Maybe the best one in the whole US.* As far as she knew, he'd never lost a case. And typically, he defended the people who made the big headlines. The rich, the powerful, and often, the very, very dangerous.

And he *always* got his client a not guilty verdict.

But why would Kendrick be there then? Why—

"He's in the morgue?" Kendrick's voice came out low and a little rough.

"Aw, hell." Ben moved forward and immediately locked a hand around the other man's shoulder. "Was he one of yours?"

Wait. That didn't make sense. Layla had just said that Donnie was more of a petty criminal. Or at least, he *had* been before he'd driven an SUV over Cole. Twice. *Not so petty any longer…*

And also, not so alive.

An eighteen-year-old kid…

Kendrick gave a slow nod. "I was representing Donnie." His gaze flickered to Ben, then to Layla. His stare lingered on the detective a moment. "Despite what people say about me, it's not all about the attention and headlines. Sometimes, I want to help the little guy." His jaw tightened. "I grew up in Donnie's neighborhood. I know how hard survival is there, and when I see a good kid making some very poor choices, I try to help him out."

Ben's hold tightened on him. "I'm sorry, man."

Kendrick cut him a glance. "I heard…Donnie came after you?" There was confusion in his words.

"He did," Layla responded, her voice crisp. "The criminal investigation is still on-going, but Courtney McKenna just ID'd Donnie as being the driver of the SUV who plowed into Ben's vehicle.

The *same* SUV was used in a recent hit and run. Luckily, that victim survived, but the obvious intention of that attack was for Cole Vincent to die."

Kendrick took a step back. Ben's hand dropped from his shoulder.

Kendrick seemed to gather his thoughts, and after a moment, he said, "Donnie wasn't a killer."

Layla shrugged one shoulder. "The evidence would say he was trying to *become* a killer."

Courtney's gaze darted to the morgue's closed doors. A shiver slid over her.

"*Courtney McKenna.*"

Her stare snapped to Kendrick. She found him staring at her with an intense focus.

"We haven't officially met, have we?" Kendrick squared his shoulders and offered his hand to her. "Kendrick Shaw."

She took his hand. Felt his easy strength. "I've heard of you."

He inclined his head to Ben. "And I've certainly heard of you. When Ben drinks, he talks a lot."

What?

"Not now," Ben muttered.

Kendrick nodded. He released Courtney's hand and eased out a long breath as he turned his attention back to Layla. "I want to see the body. Donnie doesn't have any family that's going to come looking for him. I'll be taking care of the kid. Everything—it's all going through me."

He'd cared about Donnie. It was obvious in his gruff words. Courtney's head cocked as she studied him. The court gossip mill said that Kendrick Shaw didn't have a heart. That he would defend a man who was guilty as all hell if it meant Kendrick got his name in the paper and a big check in his bank account.

But she'd never been one to believe gossip. After all, she'd been gossiped about plenty in her life. The stories had hurt, and they'd been bullshit. She decided not to play games, and to ask Kendrick for the truth. "Why were you helping him?"

"Because I got out." His lips thinned. "Donnie didn't. He was a smart kid, he just made some real dumbass choices. I'd warned him to keep his nose clean. Told him that he could turn everything around. He could have a chance, if he just…" Kendrick stopped and shook his head.

"This is beyond his normal work." Layla edged closer to Kendrick. "Why would Donnie have taken these jobs?"

"Money," an immediate response from Kendrick. "Kid wanted a new life more than anything else. I promised him that he'd get that life. I swore he would, but he had to follow the rules I'd set up."

Donnie didn't have a new life. He didn't have any life at all. "I'm sorry," Courtney told Kendrick.

Kendrick's stare jerked to her. Narrowed. "You're wanting to know why Donnie took the jobs…a better question would be…why did someone want Donnie to target *you*?"

"We're working to figure that out." Ben's response was flat. "If you want to shed some light on the situation, we'd appreciate it. If you want to tell us *who* Donnie used to work for or maybe the names of his acquaintances…?"

Layla nodded. "People who might have hooked Donnie up with a much more dangerous line of employment. Somebody who wanted Donnie to graduate from B&Es to murder."

Kendrick shoved his hand into his pocket. "Always got to be so careful with what you say. You make the wrong enemy, and you could find yourself dead in this town. I mean, what good is a criminal defense attorney, if he spills the secrets on his clients? His *very* dangerous clients."

He knows. He knows who hired Donnie, but he isn't saying.

Kendrick headed for the morgue's doors. Stopped. Looked back at her. "There's always a paper trail, though. One that the right people can follow. It's all about following procedures. The rule of law and order."

Courtney's lips parted.

Kendrick entered the morgue a moment later.

"I will never quite figure him out," Layla murmured. "Defends total scum, but Kendrick—"

"Kendrick is one of the good guys," Ben responded instantly. "And he told us exactly what we needed to know."

Yes, he had. He'd put the clues right in front of them. *Law and order.* Excitement surged through her. "We need to find out who posted bail the last time that Donnie was arrested."

Kendrick had told them *exactly* what they needed to know. Follow the trail. The paper trail left from court. The documents that *always* had to be maintained. If they got access to that information, then they could get the name they needed to know.

***

"I don't see Courtney McKenna."

Kadi flinched. The hood had been yanked off her head again, and that stupid bare light bulb was blinding her. She didn't even know why they'd bothered with the hood. Especially since the jerk leader had shoved his face in front of her earlier. She could identify him. The hood was just pointless now.

"Thought you said one phone call was all it would take," he leaned in close, his rather rancid breath blowing over her face. "You made the call, but we don't have *her*."

"You *will* okay? I don't have Courtney's direct number." Not like she and Courtney were besties, dammit. "But I left my husband a message saying that we *had* to meet. I told him when and I told him where. Said if he got his attorney at the meeting, I would agree to *all* of his divorce stipulations without any other arguments." She'd thought the plan was rather brilliant. Kadi felt like preening. She didn't, though, because she was tied to a freaking chair. "Now, you just need to let me go so I can make that meeting. You can follow me there. You'll see Courtney. You grab her. A done deal."

The plan had been *perfect* because setting up a meeting meant that these jerks would have to let her out of their stupid place. They would have to keep her alive long enough for her to show up so they could get Courtney.

The leader leaned ever closer to her, and her gaze dropped to that scar on his neck. Her neck had been bleeding because of him and his knife. Total jackass. He had no idea who he was dealing with. She was going to make him pay for hurting her.

"You try to screw us over…" Again, his breath blew against her. "And I will gut you."

Her eyes narrowed. "Follow me to the meeting," Kadi blasted right back at him. "And you'll get exactly what you want." Her soon-to-be *ex*-husband would jump at the chance to get her agreement for a no-contest divorce. He'd be there with his attorney. No doubt about it.

CHAPTER SEVENTEEN

"You have to be patient." Layla pointed at Ben. "I know you want this shit yesterday, but I have to work in the system here. We got the name of the guy who posted bail for Donnie at his last court appearance, but Jude Varga is just another petty crook, too. I have to keep making my way up the chain if I'm going to find out the truth. That means I go in the interrogation room with Jude, and I see what shakes loose."

"Let me come in, too," he urged her. Tension coursed through his body.

"No." Flat. Instant. "And you're not watching, either. We tried all of that before, didn't we? Been there and done that with you and your brother. It *never* ends well with you Wilde boys." She motioned toward her office door. "You and Courtney…you need to both leave now."

Courtney's shoulder brushed against Ben's. Her scent teased him, working to calm the savagery rising within Ben.

"When I have more evidence to give you, I'll call," Layla assured them. "Until then, lay low. It's time for the police to take over this case."

She was benching him? Not happening.

It was a good thing Ben already had a backup plan in place. A plan that might not be the most above-board, but, hey, desperate times called for desperate measures. *And I am desperate. I'm not going to sit around and wait for something to happen to Courtney.*

Layla could work within the confines of the law. And he could use every dirty trick he knew. Ben's fingers curled around Courtney's. "Let's go."

Layla's gaze turned suspicious. Obviously, she'd expected more of a fight because she knew him well. She was right to be suspicious, but she didn't stop him as Ben and Courtney fled her small office.

Courtney didn't talk until they were outside of the police station. His rental waited nearby. He led her to it, held open the passenger door, and his stare swept around as he looked for any threats that might be there. He'd be damned if he was caught off-guard again.

Behind him, he saw the dark sedan that waited just a few feet away. And in that sedan…

Julia and Rick.

Because he'd called and made sure that Courtney would now have twenty-four, seven protection. Julia and Rick would be shadowing her movements until the bastard out there was caught.

Ben hurried around the vehicle and slid into the driver's seat. The door slammed and—

"I have bodyguards now, huh?" Courtney's careful voice.

He pulled away from the curb. "I'm not going to have you put at risk."

She turned her head and gazed out the window. "And I'm not going to put you at risk, either."

Okay, he did *not* like the tone of her voice.

"I realized when I was staring at that poor boy in the morgue...you can die, too, Ben."

Everyone could fucking die.

"You were targeted *because of me*," she continued in a low voice.

"We're going to find out who is after you," Ben assured her. *Count on it.* "We're going to use Cole. Simon said that Cole sent his email to his mystery 'boss' already, and Wilde Securities will watch to make sure—"

"You've done enough," she cut in quietly. "Thank you."

Oh, no. Oh, *hell,* no. Ben whipped the car into the nearest parking lot.

Julia and Rick whipped in behind them. He swore when he saw Rick jump from the sedan and run toward them.

Ben rolled down his window. "We're fine! Stand down." *Just clearing some shit up.*

Not looking happy about it, Rick backed away.

Ben turned his body toward Courtney. "You need me." He had to cling to that. "I can go to Wilde Securities right now, I can get the hackers there to follow the money trail from Jude Varga back to his boss. I can find the truth much faster than the PD can. I'll get the boss's name. I'll go into his office. I'll *make* him tell me—"

"Stop." She reached for his hand. Squeezed. "This isn't you. Don't you see that?"

It *was* him. Who the hell else would it be?

"You don't live a dangerous life, Ben. You don't get into fights. You don't risk yourself—"

For her, he would.

"It's not safe." Her hair slid over her shoulders. "Don't you see that? It's not safe to be around me right now."

The only place he wanted to be was near her.

"The security system at my apartment has been upgraded." Her lips twisted in a smile that never reached her eyes. "I also now seem to have two bodyguards following me around. I'm good, Ben. I'm safe. It's time for you to go back to your life while I deal with this."

"Hell, no."

She blinked. "But I don't need—"

"You don't need me?" His voice was too rough. "Did you ever stop to think that *I* need you?"

Her eyes widened.

"I need you in my life, Courtney, because you've been a fucking bright spot for me for a very, very long time. I need you because you make the days better. Because you push me to be a better man. I need you because you are the best lover I've ever had, and truth be told, now that I've had a taste of you, you're the only lover that I can ever imagine having. I want you. Only you. I need you. You're the one, Courtney."

Her lower lip trembled. "But it's dangerous around me…"

"Screw it. You think I'm worried?" He was. He was freaking terrified, actually, but not of something happening to him. He was terrified something would happen to her. He had to stay close to her. Had to keep his eyes on Courtney because he was afraid that if he let her go, even for an instant…

I will lose her. Something bad will happen. I just got her — really got her — and I can't let some bastard rip her away from me now.

"I'm worried." Her voice was low. "I don't want anything to happen to you. I-I care about you, Ben." She stumbled over that last bit.

Care, huh? That was something he could work with. "For the record, I fucking *care* about you, too."

Her eyes widened.

Screw this. Not the best time or the right place but…his hand cupped her cheek. The bandage was gone, and a thin scratch slid over her silken skin. "You're not going to shove me aside because you're worried about putting me in danger. I don't care about danger. I don't care about any threat. You're what matters to me."

"You could be *hurt.*"

He nodded. "If I'm not there for you when you need me, hell, yes, I'll be hurt. I'll be gutted. Because you matter. You aren't facing this alone."

"I have the bodyguards out there—"

"You have me. I've always been there, but you didn't know it. I didn't let you know how important you are, and that is on me." He pulled in her scent. The strawberries that made him *crave* her. "I won't make the same mistake again." *All or nothing.* He planned to be all in with her. "I love you, Courtney, and I'm not leaving you. You can count on me to be there, no matter what happens. I will *always* be there."

Her lips parted. She searched his eyes. Shook her head.

"Yes. I love you." It felt good to say the words. To have them out there. "And no, I'm not waiting for you to say the words back to me. I might have loved you since the first day when you walked into my law class or when I saw you driving hell fast across campus ringing that little bell on your bike—"

She gave another shake of her head.

"But I get that you don't feel the same." Ben released a slow breath. "I'm going to show you that I can be a better man. I want to be better, for you. I want to give you everything that you want in this world." A ragged laugh. "Mostly, I want to keep you safe."

"Ben…"

He waited—

Her phone rang.

She ignored the phone and stared up at him. "If something happened to you…" Her tongue slid out and licked across her bottom lip. "It would wreck me."

His heart squeezed in his chest.

"I didn't want to get close to anyone." Her phone was ringing, but she was ignoring it. Staring up at him. Acting as if he was the only thing that mattered. "It was safer that way."

"Baby..."

"I think you got under my skin." Her words came faster. The phone stopped ringing. "I think you might have just slid into my heart."

Holy hell, was she saying—

Now his phone was ringing. No. He wanted to throw the phone through the window. He leaned forward and his lips took hers in a deep, hard kiss. Courtney was giving him the chance he wanted. The chance he needed. She was in his arms. She was saying that she—

And her phone was fucking ringing, too. *Shit*.

She pressed her hands to his chest. "We have to answer."

Yes, he knew they did. With all the chaos going on, they did. But... "We will finish this conversation."

Her head tilted toward him. "Count on it."

Courtney reached for her phone even as he yanked his own phone to his ear. He knew the ring tone. Simon. Answering with a growl, Ben demanded, "*Tell* me you've got something good—"

"Uh, and *tell* me you were doing something seriously important because you were ignoring my call—"

His eyes were on Courtney as she spoke quickly into her own phone. Ben swallowed and said, "I was dealing with the most important thing in my life."

"Yeah, well…" A sigh from Simon. "I've got news. News you are *not* going to like. The techs at Wilde Securities have been working their magic as they try to trace down the email that was used to send orders to Cole. And guess *where* that shit originated?"

"I don't want to guess. Just *tell* me—"

"Courtney's firm. The emails were coming from there. Someone at her firm *hired* Cole. She was right there, every single day, with the person who has been paying Cole to shadow her movements."

Courtney had put her phone down. A furrow lined her brow.

"Hold on, Simon," he snapped. "Courtney, what's happening?"

"That was my boss." She adjusted the seat belt that she still wore, her fingers sliding over it. "He told me that I had to come in, right now…or that he was firing me."

What?

"He said that Hayden Laslow has filed a complaint against me. That I'll be under review." She shook her head. "If I don't show up in the next five minutes, I should consider myself terminated."

Oh, really? They would just see about that shit.

***

The black hood was back in place, and Kadi was being transported in a car. The goons hadn't stuffed her in a trunk this time, so Kadi figured that had to be a plus. Maybe they'd put the hood over her head so she wouldn't be able to lead the cops back to their hide-out—or whatever they wanted to call their little hole-in-the-wall home.

Her body was tense. The leader had told her the time a little while ago, and she knew that there was about an hour until the big meeting. Courtney would be there. Hayden would be there. The goons would grab the attorney, and Kadi would be able to walk free.

Or will they kill me? Because that worry played through her mind. You always had to be ready for a double-cross. She'd learned that from watching her husband work. You thought one thing was happening, but really…something else was afoot. Hayden had been the master at having backup plans.

So maybe…maybe she needed to have another plan in place, just in case.

But what could she offer to the men who held her? Courtney's life? *Done and done.* She needed something else to sweeten the pot.

If you don't look out for yourself, no one else will do it…

CHAPTER EIGHTEEN

"I don't know what's going on." Courtney's assistant met her as soon as she entered the towering law office in the middle of downtown Atlanta. "I told Mr. Worthington that your clients had all been rescheduled. I mean, you were due this vacation time anyway. It was hardly a surprise. No one was inconvenienced, you already had this covered—"

"It's okay, Karen. I'll deal with this." Her employer's voice had been stone cold when she'd spoken to him on the phone.

Either come in to see me right now or do not come in at all. You will be done in this town.

Ross Worthington was going to threaten her? On top of all the crap she had going on in her life? She'd barely gotten off the phone with him before Ben had dropped his bombshell.

The email from Cole's so-called boss? It had come from Courtney's law office.

Everywhere she turned, it seemed like she was facing some kind of lie or betrayal. Everywhere except…with Ben.

They entered the elevator. The heavy doors closed soundlessly, and classical music filled the air. The music was supposed to be soothing. It just pissed her off even more.

"You don't need this place." Ben's voice. Low and steady. His blue gaze slid over her face. "They need you, sweetheart. You don't need them."

Easy to say when he had his own firm. When he already had all of his own clients lined up. But she…

Worthington, Waller, and Rain was *the* firm for launching in Atlanta. The firm handled all sorts of cases. Everything from civil and criminal suits to—

"We don't know who in this building was sending the messages to Cole," Ben added, still keeping his voice low. "Simon said Cole responded to the guy and is trying to draw him out."

"Draw him out—how?"

"Cole baited him deliberately, saying that he'd gotten proof of a relationship between his boss and you. If we're right and this whole case was related to your father, the guy is going to come running to find out exactly what Cole has."

Cole was in the hospital, incapable of doing his own running, while Simon stayed at his side as protection.

"My father isn't in this building." She wasn't buying that.

"Are you sure?"

Her gaze darted to the control panel. They were almost to the top floor. The floor where the major partners held court.

"Ross Worthington is the right age," Ben continued, and she sensed he was trying to be very careful with his words. "He also has enough power and money—"

"To basically put a stalker on me?" Yes, okay, he *did* have enough money for that. "But do you really believe Worthington would hire Donnie to try and kill Cole? You think Worthington is a murderer?"

The elevator doors opened.

They stepped onto the lush carpeting there. Every window on that level was floor to ceiling—and the city gleamed all around them. Ross's assistant—a young woman in black slacks and a low-cut top, with her blonde hair in a stylish twist—appeared and immediately led them to Worthington's office. Sharon Long had been working at Worthington, Waller, and Rain for as long as Courtney had been employed there. Though they'd hardly interacted much—when you were on the top floor, you didn't exactly mingle with the people below you.

"He's been waiting for you," Sharon whispered to Courtney. "And he seems pissed."

She was plenty pissed, too.

"Everything okay?" Sharon asked, eyes wide.

"Definitely not," Courtney told her.

Sharon's lips parted. Alarm flashed on her face.

They were at Ross Worthington's closed office door. Sharon was hesitating, so Courtney stepped forward and shoved open the heavy door. When they entered, Worthington was seated behind his massive desk. His suit coat was tossed to the side, his sleeves rolled up. His eyes were cold and steady behind the lenses of his glasses. Ross Worthington was in his late fifties, but the man worked out like a beast. He had a company gym installed on the third floor, and she knew it was his routine to arrive every morning at five a.m. for his workout. He didn't have a family. No wife. No kids. He had his work. As he'd said numerous times at office meetings, the firm was life. It *was* family.

Apparently, she was about to be kicked out of the family.

Sharon didn't follow them inside. She pulled the door shut, sealing them in with Worthington.

"Courtney." He rose to his feet. Then frowned when he caught sight of… "Ben Wilde? What the hell are you doing here?"

"Currently, I'm being a package deal with Courtney. Wherever she goes, I follow."

The words sent a lick of warmth through her. Ben's shoulder brushed her arm, and his touch was reassuring. A package deal? Ben…he'd said he would always be there for her. That he wouldn't walk away. Did she dare trust that?

"You weren't invited to this meeting, Wilde." Her boss glowered. "So why don't you—"

"Have a seat?" Ben finished. "Nah, I'm good standing, thanks."

Ross opened his mouth. Didn't speak.

Courtney decided to do the talking. "You threatened me today."

"I...I had a complaint about you." But he seemed confused, and his gaze kept darting to Ben. "I *gave* you the Hayden Laslow case as a favor—"

"No." They should stop right there. "You forced me to take Laslow even though I told you I already had a full case load at the time. I took the case as a favor to *you*. Don't act like you did any sort of service to me on this one."

Behind the lenses of his glasses, his gaze turned hard. "Hayden Laslow has a long history with this firm. He's one of our best clients and when it came to his divorce, I wanted a top attorney on his side." He inclined his head. "I gave you an opportunity. That's what I did, but then you squandered it." A rough exhale. "Hayden plans to formally file a complaint against you. He said that he believes you've been leaking confidential information to his wife, that you were working with her *and* her attorney..." Now his stare moved to Ben once again. "Her attorney, Ben Wilde. Hayden believes you have shared pertinent material with Ben because you're involved with him on a personal level."

Well, well... "Hayden believes a lot, doesn't he?"

"Do you *deny* it?"

Ben surged forward. She grabbed his arm. "I've got this." She'd busted ass at this firm. Worked nights and weekends. Taken the grunt cases forever. And now she'd found out that someone in *this office* had been behind the surveillance at her home. She was done. "I don't deny sleeping with

Ben. We're personally involved, and that's *our* business."

Ross jerked back. "You-you can't sleep with—"

"I can, and I did. However, I have not shared any privileged information about Hayden Laslow. Ben and I don't discuss our cases."

"We're too busy doing other fucking things," Ben threw out.

Ross frowned.

A sharp knock came at his door. Before Ross could call out, the door swung open.

Hayden Laslow stood there, breathing quickly, and with his cheeks flushed.

"He insisted on seeing you!" Sharon announced, voice vibrating with indignation. "I'm so sorry, Mr. Worthington!"

But Ross waved her away. Hayden's fingers brushed over Sharon's arm as he stalked inside. Then he slammed the door shut on the assistant.

Courtney's eyes narrowed. Typical jackass move. *Especially* with what she knew about Sharon and Hayden.

"Mr. Laslow..." Ross was oozing warmth. "I was addressing your concerns with Courtney, letting her know that her behavior would *not* be tolerated—"

"Watch your fucking words," Ben ordered. There was a dark, lethal intensity in his voice. "You don't own her, Worthington, so stop acting like you do."

No, Worthington didn't own her. He didn't appreciate her. And she was done. She could handle this battle on her own. A wide smile curved her lips as she stared at her boss. "I quit."

Ross blinked.

"You don't need to fire me. You don't need to investigate me. I'm done here." She wouldn't put up with bullshit. Not now. Not ever again.

"You're *firing* her?" Hayden asked, voice cracking.

"I—I was responding to your complaint—"

"That's what I was afraid of!" Hayden raked a hand through his hair. She realized then that the man looked a little…wild. Blood-shot eyes. Rumpled clothes. "It's over," Hayden breathed.

Yes, she'd said that she quit—

Hayden rushed toward her.

Before he could touch her, Ben was there, shoving a hand into Hayden's chest. "Back off."

Hayden froze. But his gaze flew over Courtney's face. "You did it. You worked a miracle. Kadi called me. She said—said she'd sign the divorce papers. She'll give up *everything* without a fight. I got more than I wanted. All because of you." He looked back at Ross. "Don't fire her. Don't ever let her go. It would be the dumbest move of your life."

"But, but you said—" Ross appeared lost.

"You want my business to continue?" Hayden demanded. "*Keep her here.* Don't let her go. Don't even think of it." He lifted his wrist and peered at his watch. "I have a meeting. I have to go but…" Again, his fierce gaze swung back to Courtney. "Thank you."

She had no clue what he was talking about.

He didn't offer more of an explanation. Instead, Hayden stormed from the office.

"I...I seem to owe you an apology." Subdued and uncertain, Ross peered at her. "You...ah...

"I still quit." She'd always planned to leave, anyway. Time to branch out on her own. Time to stop being afraid of risks. "But before I go..." She stalked forward and slammed her palms down on his desk. "I want to know why the hell you hired Cole Vincent to stalk me."

***

The car rolled to a stop, and the hood was ripped from Kadi's head. They were outside of her condo—the sleek little beauty that was *technically* owned by Hayden, but after they'd split, she'd moved into it. The man owned plenty of property around Atlanta, and this place that he'd kept for "entertainment purposes" with some of his clients? She'd liked it. So she'd moved her ass inside. Hayden was supposed to meet her there. She didn't see his car, but she was sure he'd arrive soon.

"When we go inside, you don't say a word to anyone, got me?"

She turned toward the leader. Pasted a smile on her face. "Got you."

He hauled her out of the car. Kept her locked to him and kept a knife pressed to her side. She thought the other jerks would follow, but they didn't. It was just her and the asshole with the knife. As they hurried up the sidewalk, she saw that her discarded shoes were still there. Her purse was long gone. Figured.

No one was out. Even if she'd wanted to call out a warning to someone, there wasn't anyone around to help her. Kadi kept her lips clamped together, but her mind was spinning. They rode the elevator in silence, and then...*My floor.* Each floor was a separate condo unit, and hers was on the top. When they reached the door of her condo, she typed in the code that would open the lock. Then they were inside and...

Hayden wasn't there. Fine, fine, she hadn't seen his car outside. He was just... "Running late," she murmured. "He'll be here. Courtney is *his* attorney and he'll—"

The leader got a text. She heard the little buzz and flinched. He pulled out his phone and when he did, the knife *finally* moved away from her side. He glowered down at the screen for a moment.

She looked for a weapon. If she went into the kitchen, she could get a knife of her own. If she went to the bedroom...

"Change of plans..."

Her head whipped toward him.

He was smiling.

Oh, God.

"Didn't realize who *you* were, lady. My mistake..." The knife gleamed. "This just got fun."

***

"I have no idea what you're talking about." Ross yanked at his tie. Sweat beaded his forehead. "Obviously, I made a mistake in the way I handled this situation, but Hayden is an important client, and I—"

"Cole Vincent." Her hands pressed harder against his desk. "He was hired by someone in this building. Hired to watch me. To monitor me. To collect my DNA."

Ross swiped a hand across his sweaty brow. "I-I don't know anything about that. We work with an array of investigators, you know—"

"I know when someone is lying." He was exhibiting classic signs. "I want to know why. I know that the higher ups here monitor *everything*, so if someone at this firm was sending the money transfers to Cole, then you had to know about it. Or *you* were the one doing it." Her suspicion.

He swallowed.

"This wouldn't get past you. You *are* Worthington, Waller, and Rain."

His gaze flickered to Ben. Then back to her. "We need to talk alone."

"No way," Ben replied instantly. "Whatever you want to say to Courtney, you can say with me right here. Maybe you missed the package deal part."

Ross shook his head. "This information is just for Courtney. I can't reveal what I know to anyone else. Either I only talk to her or I don't talk at all."

Ben laughed. "I bet you'll talk plenty when the cops get involved."

Ross's shoulders straightened, and steely determination entered his eyes. "You believe that? Don't. I've been in this game far longer than you can imagine. I know secrets that could destroy every judge in this town. And all the top cops? Plenty of them sit on a house of cards that could fall any moment. The cops don't scare me."

No, but *someone* was scaring him. She needed this information. Courtney turned to Ben. Hurried closer to him. Her hand rose and pressed to his chest. "Just wait outside for me."

"Courtney—"

"If I need you, all I have to do is call out."

He caught her hand. Lifted it to his lips. Pressed a kiss to her knuckles. "That's right, baby. That's all you have to do. I'll wait for you." He glared at Ross. "Watch your tone when you talk to her. Be a fucking *gentleman.*"

"Like I'm supposed to worry about what some smart-ass, upstart—"

"You are supposed to worry. Because *no one* hurts Courtney. Understand?"

Ross nodded.

Ben squeezed her fingers. Then he made his way out of the office. Took his time about it, and closed the door with a faint click.

Courtney braced herself as she faced off with her boss. Well, *ex*-boss as of about five minutes ago.

He stood behind his desk. His gaze swept over her.

"Confession time," Courtney said.

He didn't speak.

"We're alone. *Tell* me what I want to know." This was killing her. So she just got right to it. "Is this about my DNA? You're the one who told Cole to collect it?"

A jerky nod.

Oh, God. He had dark eyes, too. She'd just realized that. Dark brown eyes. And his hair had a tint of red. Her breath came faster. "Are you my father?"

He opened his mouth.

***

Ben frowned at Ross's assistant. The blonde was familiar to him, but he didn't remember meeting her. His head cocked as he studied her profile. She was working at her computer, typing quickly, as her fingers moved across the keyboard.

He closed in on her. Saw her shoulders stiffen.

"Is there something I can help you with?" Her head turned toward him.

Actually, yes… "As Mr. Worthington's assistant…I bet you have access to all his passwords and case files, don't you?"

She gazed up at him.

And as he stared at her…it clicked for him.

He knew exactly where he'd seen her before. *Hayden Laslow's lover.* She'd been the lover he'd slept with just one week after his wedding to Kadi. Ben's investigator had said the pictures had been anonymously emailed to him, and the investigator hadn't gotten the blonde's name. They'd been working on solving that mystery.

Mystery solved.

It also explained the tension he'd noticed between her and Hayden a few moments before.

"I have access to everything." She stood. "How about I take you to the lounge so you can relax while you wait on your friend?"

"Where did Hayden go?"

"Um...said he had an appointment with his wife. Something about papers to sign?"

They couldn't be signing papers. Unless Kadi had gotten a new lawyer, but damn, that would be fast work. He made no move to follow her, and the assistant stopped. She glanced back at him, a frown tightening her pretty face.

"I didn't get your full name," Ben spoke carefully.

"Sharon Long." She waved her hand. "And the lounge is this way."

"I'll wait here, thanks. You see, I told my friend that I would be right outside if she needed me. I believe in keeping my word to her."

Her gaze darted toward the hallway, and, presumably, the lounge. Then back to him. Without another word, she went back to her desk. Sat down. Started typing.

He turned away from her, his gaze sliding back to Ross Worthington's closed door. He wanted to be in that office with Courtney. He wanted—

He felt something hard press into the small of his back.

"That's a gun, asshole," Hayden Laslow muttered. "You say a word, and I'll put a bullet through your spine. And when Courtney comes running because she heard the thunder of gunfire, I'll put the second bullet in her heart."

CHAPTER NINETEEN

"I-I'm not your father." His Adam's apple bobbed. "But I know who is. *He's* the one who wanted protection put on you. The firm has used Cole Vincent before, I knew he could be discreet—that's why I hired him. Your father…he didn't want this ever being traced back to him, so the payments went through the firm."

Her heart was about to burst right out of her chest.

"He had his suspicions that you were his daughter. I told him that we needed *proof* because he could be wasting a lot of money on bullshit."

What? Her boss was such a tool.

"I was the one who told Cole to get the DNA samples. I was the one who wanted to be certain. And, hell, stop looking at me that way because I was doing it for *you*."

"I have no idea what you're talking about."

He rubbed a hand over the back of his neck. "I like you, Courtney. You're a damn good lawyer. A hard worker. And you—you have your whole life ahead of you. You don't want to be *his*."

A shiver worked its way down her body. She'd dreamed of her real father. His big house, his fancy cars...

But Ross shook his head. "You *don't* want to know him. There's a reason your mother ran from him and didn't look back. And you really think Frank McKenna's death was an accident? That he *walked* into oncoming traffic? No, no, he was punished. Punished because he *thought* he knew who your real father was. He was mowed down in the road, and the witnesses..." He laughed, but the sound was grating. "You know how easy it is to manipulate a witness. Happens all the time."

Her knees had locked. What he was saying...

"Your real father had Frank McKenna killed. Run down in the street. The *same* way that Cole Vincent was hit. I found out..." A nervous swipe of his tongue across his lower lip. "Cole had told him that he wasn't working the case any longer. But your father wasn't going to let Cole walk away. So he punished him."

Her skin was icy cold. "You're saying my real father is a murderer, but you've been...*helping* him?"

Ross's shoulders stiffened. "We have a lot of very important clients at this firm."

Their main cases...civil, *criminal*...

Her breath came faster.

"The DNA proved it," he whispered. "Cole wouldn't deliver the samples, so I found another way. *I* got them, and I paid for the additional testing. Shit, I did it because I didn't want it to be true. You're tied to a very dangerous man. A man with a lot of enemies. I'd hoped he was wrong. That you weren't *his*. But the proof I obtained sealed your fate. Anyone who wants to hurt him...they can hurt *you* now. You're his only weakness."

"*Tell* me his name." Her father wasn't some amazing guy who hadn't known she'd existed. He was a monster. A killer?

If her boss — former boss — was telling the truth. And she wasn't about to jump on that boat, not yet.

"He's the reason I hired you," Ross delivered yet another confession to her. "I mean, your resume was great, but *he* wanted you to have a job here. Said you deserved to work at this firm. Wanted you fast tracked to partner."

"I want a name." She wanted a name, and she'd go from there.

"Walk away," he whispered instead.

Courtney shook her head. "Not happening."

"I'm not going to tell him that you know. I *like* you. Just leave things, okay? He's not ever going to approach you. He's going to eliminate the threats to you. Sure, you'll have bodyguards like Cole shadowing you, but you won't know."

I will know.

"If I don't give you a name, then you can have some ignorance. People say *ignorance is bliss* for a reason. You can turn away. You can get a life. But if you find out...if you know, then it's going to eat at you. The truth will destroy you."

Because she was the daughter of some horrible monster?

"My team got him off on the crimes, but I know he was guilty as hell. He's not a good man. It's better to not know. Better to not have him in your head."

He was already in her head. He'd been there for years. "*Tell* me."

"Julian Rossi."

Julian the Jackal? No, no, that was wrong. She took a hard step back as she recoiled from the name. That couldn't be right. Julian Rossi wasn't just a criminal. He was a major mob boss. There had been movies made about him. He'd been one of the most powerful drug runners and arms dealers in the world. No, he'd been *suspected* of being those things. Never proven guilty. Never convicted.

Never…

"Wasn't it better not to know?"

She whirled for the door. "Fuck off." She needed to get to Ben. Right then. She had to tell him the truth. Now that they knew who'd been behind the surveillance, they could connect the dots. Rossi must have been the one who paid Donnie to attack Cole—and to come after her and Ben. Only…

Donnie aimed for Ben's side of the car. The attack hadn't been on her at all. It had been on Ben. *He'd* been the target.

Was Donnie the one who attacked me the first night in the parking garage? But…that didn't make sense. All of this was still not making sense!

She yanked open the office door.

Sharon glanced up at her, fingers poised over her keyboard.

Ben wasn't there. Courtney stumbled a little. "Where—"

"Oh, are you looking for your friend?" A light laugh. "He got a call from his client—Kadi, I believe it was? Said it was very important, and he had to go meet her right away."

He'd left. That didn't seem right. He'd said he would stay. Ben had promised to stay.

"He left an address for you." Kadi offered a slip of paper to her. And a wide smile. "I think he wants you to come there and meet him."

She took the paper. Frowned down at it.

Even as she stared at the paper, her phone rang. She pulled it up quickly, thinking it might be Ben, but no...

Unknown number.

She swiped her finger over the screen and put the phone to her ear.

"Courtney?"

Her breath rushed out.

"It's Julia. Rick and I are stationed right outside of your law office, and I've got to know...why in the hell did I just see Ben walking out without you?"

"He...has a meeting."

Sharon was watching her. A little too closely.

"And the guy who was with him? Sure looked chummy." Suspicion coated Julia's words.

The same suspicion that was swirling inside of Courtney.

Sharon kept smiling at her.

And Ross slipped from his office, coming after Courtney. A fast glance in his direction showed his expression was concerned. So worried.

Who in the hell was she supposed to trust? What was going on?

No, there's no question. I know who to trust. She knew exactly who to trust. "You go on without me," she said into her phone. "Of course, I can meet you for dinner later. You've got your priorities, and I have mine."

"I have no freaking clue what your priorities are," Julia told her bluntly. "But I'm guessing you're being watched right now? Do I need to come up with a full team?"

"No, absolutely not. Go where you're needed." *With Ben.*

Silence.

Sharon had turned back to her computer, but she wasn't typing.

Ross was practically breathing down Courtney's neck.

Julia waited a beat, then said, "You want full surveillance on Ben. If we follow him, we leave you unprotected."

"Exactly. Thanks so much."

"Dammit, you'd *better* be safe! I'm calling and getting backup to this building right away."

Not necessary because by the time backup arrived, she'd be gone. Her left hand fisted around the address. "I'm good. It was great to hear from you. You just take care of your business, and I'll take care of mine. Got to live your life, know what I mean?"

"I do." Julia's voice was low. "Be careful."

Courtney dropped the phone and stared over at Sharon. Beautiful Sharon. "You fucked him."

Sharon's shoulders stiffened. "I beg your pardon?"

"Ben showed me pictures of Hayden Laslow with one of his lovers — a lover he was with just one week after he married Kadi."

Sharon's eyes hardened.

"As soon as I saw the pictures, I recognized you."

Ross didn't speak. Probably because he knew his assistant had been screwing one of his biggest clients, and he hadn't cared.

He should care.

Her hand was still fisted around the slip of paper. "What's going to happen to me if I go to this address?"

"I have no idea," Sharon told her with a confused smile. "You'll...find your friend?"

Ross closed his hand around Courtney's shoulder. "You should leave — "

She shrugged him off. "Who did Ben leave with?" Courtney demanded.

"I don't know." Sharon blinked her long lashes. Those fake lashes looked like freaking spiders sitting on top of her eyes. "He was alone on this floor. Maybe he hooked up with someone in the lobby?"

Courtney gave her a cold smile. "Or maybe he left with Hayden."

Sharon blinked. "Mr. Laslow left a few minutes *before* your friend." Her lips pursed as she reached into one of the desk drawers. "I guess it's possible they could have connected in the lobby."

"And I guess it's possible you're lying to me right now." Courtney dropped the balled-up piece of paper on Sharon's desk. "This isn't Ben's writing. I've seen his writing on plenty of legal reports. You wrote down this address, not him."

"Because he *asked* me to do it…" Sharon explained with a nervous little laugh.

"No. Ben wouldn't just walk away. Not after he'd told me that he'd be waiting outside for me."

Sharon's gaze turned cruel. "Are you sure about that?" She leaned forward. "Maybe that's exactly what he'd do. You've been left before. You'll be left again. Because you aren't important. You simply *don't* matter."

That bitch. "I'm calling the cops. They can sort this out, and I'm sure they will have plenty of questions for you."

Sharon's hand lifted from behind her desk. Her fingers gripped the gun she held. "I don't think so."

Ross—who'd been so quiet and nervous the whole time—he sucked in a sharp breath of surprise. "Sharon? Sharon, what in the hell are you doing?"

"Taking what I'm owed." She aimed the gun at him and fired.

Courtney screamed as the bullet exploded. It tore through the air and slammed into Ross's chest. His blood spattered on her as she whirled toward him. His eyes were wide and shocked, terrified, and he toppled to the floor as he tried to grab for his chest—and the great, big, gaping hole that was there.

"Such a prick." Sharon rose to her feet.

Courtney dropped beside Ross. She put her hands to his chest. She had to try and stop the blood. *So much blood.*

"He's a dead man. It's just a matter of time. And he's going to bleed out fast, I can tell."

Courtney's head whipped toward Sharon.

"Don't worry. No one heard the shot. We're the only ones on this floor today, and let's just say that the walls here…totally thick. Soundproof." A cold smile. "You and I are going to leave now."

Courtney shook her head. Ross was still alive. She could help him.

"I'm assuming that little phone call you had was from one of the bodyguards who were parked outside the building, hmmm? Yes, I knew about them. And from what I could tell, you just told them to go rushing after Ben." Laughter as she slid from behind the desk. "That's exactly what I thought you'd do." She strode forward and put the gun to Courtney's temple. "Hayden is more than capable of handling them. He won't be alone at the condo, after all. I've got everything planned, you see. Every single moment."

Sharon wasn't going to warn Hayden about the bodyguards? She was that confident?

Or maybe she doesn't care if Hayden is caught and goes down for the crimes. Maybe the woman had a master plan in place. "And here I thought you were winging it."

Sharon smirked. "You wanted your dear old dad, didn't you? That why you came here today? Because you wanted him so badly?"

"I came here today because I wanted the attacks to stop." Because she'd wanted to know who was behind everything. Courtney knew she was staring straight at that person.

"Let's see what he'll do for you," Sharon murmured. "Let's see what your father will pay. Let's see what he'll sacrifice."

Courtney shook her head. "You're talking about a man I've never met. He won't do *anything* for me."

"You'd better hope you're wrong." Sharon leaned toward her. "Or I will put a bullet in your brain."

CHAPTER TWENTY

"Your condo?" Ben asked, voice flat. Hayden had made Ben drive over while the jerk had kept a gun pointed at Ben's side the whole time. "Your master plan is to take me to your condo?" He knew Kadi had been living there since the separation.

"Shut the fuck up," Hayden snapped. His breath came fast and hard. "Get out of the car and head inside. We're going to walk slow and easy, and if you try to get any help, I'll shoot whoever comes to your aid."

Ben glanced in his rearview mirror. He'd caught sight of the sedan trailing them. He didn't have to *get* help. Help had tailed him to the condo. Julia and Rick were keeping a careful distance, but he knew they'd spring into action as soon as they saw an opening.

But if they came after me, then who is with Courtney?

"Get out of the car!" Hayden yelled.

"Calm down. I'm moving. Take it easy." The last thing he wanted was for the SOB to get trigger happy.

Ben took his time strolling into the building. When they entered the elevator, he turned to the guy he'd pretty much always hated…and, apparently, with just cause. "What's the end game here?" Ben needed Hayden to talk. He had to make sure there weren't more players in this mad-ass game. "You get me to your condo, and then what?"

"You'll see." Hayden's nervous gaze jerked to the elevator doors.

Ben tensed. "Why are you doing this?"

Hayden's stare flew back to him.

"You've got plenty of money." Ben was trying to figure this out. "You don't need more money." Why did people commit murder? Three main reasons came to his mind.

Money? Hayden was rich as sin.

Sex? Considering that Hayden and Sharon were apparently working together, Ben was going to assume the two of them were still fucking, too. The woman had sure seemed to be more than a willing partner in this mess.

Revenge? Why would Hayden want—

Hell. "What did he do to you?"

A muscle flexed along Hayden's jaw.

"It's Courtney's father, isn't it? This whole mess is about him."

The elevator doors opened. With a wave of the gun, Hayden indicated that Ben should get out. Hands fisting, Ben moved forward—and immediately felt the gun shove into the base of his back again.

"He did something to you," Ben decided. "And now you want payback."

Hayden grunted. "Not to me."

Then who did her father hurt?

"Sharon," Hayden snarled. "He killed Sharon's fucking family, and now she is going to kill *his*."

Ice closed around Ben's heart. He'd left the law office because he'd believed that by going with Hayden…by going with Hayden, he was removing the threat. He'd thought Hayden was the one he needed to fear. The one pulling all the strings. The one who'd been after Courtney all along. He'd left to protect her.

Or, he'd thought that was what he was doing.

Instead, I left her with the biggest threat.

Hayden laughed. "You're such a dumbass. Didn't see that coming, did you? Of *course*, it was Sharon. She was always my girl. I was with her long before Kadi, and I'll be with her long after."

They were in front of the condo's door. With his left hand, Hayden reached around and typed in the key code. The lock disengaged.

More laughter from Hayden. "This is how it will work. Sharon has one of her guys in that room. She hired a team because she wanted those fellows to snatch Courtney from your place. I mean, it was obvious where she was hiding. But the idiots Sharon hired — those morons got the wrong woman. They took Kadi!"

Because Kadi had been at his place. He'd gotten a cab for her…

Hell.

"Kadi offered them a deal, of course. Because Kadi is always looking out for number one. Kadi promised she'd get Courtney here. She was ready to trade your girl for her own life."

The door was unlocked. The gun was at his back. And Hayden was a gloating piece of shit.

"Don't worry, though, if you're pissed at Kadi. If you're mad because she sold out Courtney so easily, don't be. Kadi got what she deserved. I took care of her." The nozzle of the gun nudged Ben's spine. "Told one of the guys who came here with her to cut Kadi up. She should be in pieces by now."

Fuck.

"That's how it will end. You'll be found with her body. Folks will think *you* and your client were lovers. That you went crazy and killed first her, then yourself. As for Courtney…no one will *ever* find her again. I mean, hell, not like anyone would look, huh? The woman is a loner. No close friends. No family other than the bastard Sharon is going to—"

"A bullet to the back won't look like suicide, jackass."

"I'm not going to shoot you in the back," Hayden snarled. He lifted the gun away from Ben's spine, just a few precious inches. "I'm gonna wait until we're inside and them I'm going to—"

Ben whirled and slammed into the SOB. They fell to the floor even as the gun exploded. The blast was loud and thundering, and Ben's ears rang. Hayden's lips were moving, but Ben couldn't hear a word he said. He didn't *care* what the guy had said. Rage fueled him as Ben plowed his fist into

Hayden's face again and again. Hayden tried to fight back. He tried to swing up his gun, but Ben snapped Hayden's wrist. He *felt* the bones break beneath his grip.

Then Ben went right back to pounding Hayden. Over and over. Blood spattered from Hayden's nose and mouth. This was the bastard who'd been plotting to hurt Courtney. This was the bastard who'd planned to kill Ben and—

"Ben!" A hand grabbed his shoulder and the sharp voice finally penetrated past the blaring bell in his ears. "Ben, we've got him!"

His head whipped up. Julia was there. Julia. Rick. They both had guns drawn and aimed at Hayden. A Hayden who wasn't fighting back. He didn't even seem to be conscious.

Ben blinked a moment, dazed, and then his gaze shot to the condo door. Hayden had unlocked that door, and he'd said—

God, Kadi!

Ben surged up and slammed his shoulder into the door. It flew open. "Kadi!"

She stood in the middle of the den. Blood covered her chest. Her neck. Her fingers...

And blood covered the knife that she gripped in her right hand. "He didn't think I would fight back." She stared down at the body in front of her.

A big bruiser of a guy who wasn't moving at all.

"His mistake," Kadi whispered. She dropped the knife. Her knees hit the floor a second later, and

Ben rushed toward her, trying to catch her before she tipped face-first into the dead man.

***

Half a dozen police cars were parked in front of Worthington, Waller, and Rain.

"Oh, Jesus, *no.*" Ben leapt out of Julia's car and ran forward.

"Ben!" Julia's yell followed him, but he didn't stop. He'd tried to get Courtney on the phone. Over and over again. But she hadn't answered. He knew that Layla Lopez and her team had swarmed the law office, and he knew—

That's a body being hauled out. He saw it, covered, and Ben lost it. "No!" His bellow tore through him as he surged toward—

Eric stepped into his path and grabbed Ben. "It's not her."

How the fuck was Eric even there?

"Julia ordered Wilde agents over here as soon as she left to tail you. I've already searched the building. Courtney is gone."

The words didn't make sense. He was staring at the covered body—

"That's Ross Worthington. He was shot in the heart. Courtney's phone was found right next to his body, but she wasn't anywhere in the building. Are you listening to me?" Eric's hold tightened on Ben. "Courtney isn't dead. She's not in the building. And neither is Sharon Long."

Ben sucked in a deep breath. "Where is Courtney?"

"We don't know, but we are working to find out. The downstairs guard didn't see anyone leave. Hell, he didn't even know the boss on the top floor had been killed so talk about being useless." Eric pulled Ben back toward the parking lot. "My people are digging into Sharon's background. I already have a group at her apartment, but they said there's no sign of her there. We'll try to figure out where she might go—"

"We need to check Hayden Laslow's properties. They are together—been that way for years, so she probably knows every place he owns." She'd know exactly where to stash Courtney. "Hayden has places both on and off the books. Sharon could have taken Courtney *anywhere*."

"What's the goal of taking Courtney?" Eric asked quietly. "That's what we need to focus on here. Because if we're going to find Sharon, we have to figure out what she wants."

Ben choked back his fear and rage. "She wants vengeance. Payback on Courtney's biological father." Sirens were wailing around him. *Have to find Courtney.* "Hayden said Courtney's father killed Sharon's family. That's what this has all been about."

Eric took a step back. "*Who* is Courtney's father?"

"I have no fucking clue." He pointed to the body in the bag. "He knew. Ross Worthington knew, and that's probably why he's dead."

"Hayden Laslow knows," Eric muttered. "If he was working with Sharon all along…*he* knows."

Yeah, about that... "Cops aren't gonna let me near him anytime soon." His hands flexed and clenched. The knuckles were scraped and raw, and he was about to go out of his damn mind. He had to get to Courtney. Had to save her. Had to find—

"Gentleman...Ahem..."

Ben whipped around.

Kendrick Shaw stood there, with his hands loose at his sides. He gave them a slow nod. "I believe that we need to talk."

***

"He's dead." Sharon paced along the empty stage, the gun in her hand, while Courtney was tied to a freaking chair.

Courtney glared at the crazy bitch. "Who's dead?"

Sharon whirled to point the gun at her. Back at the law office, they'd slipped out a private stairwell and exit, and Sharon's ride had been waiting. Only Sharon hadn't been alone. Two hulking men had been at her beck and call. They'd grabbed Courtney, shoved a hood over her head, and the next thing she'd known...she'd been in this place.

Looked like an old strip club. Complete with a pole in the middle of the stage.

Sharon threw her a wide grin. "Your *friend* Ben." She glanced at the slender, gold watch on her wrist, tilting the gun. "Should be dead by now."

The rope cut into Courtney's wrists as she lunged forward. "*No.*"

"Yes." A nod. "That was the plan, you see. Hayden was going to make it look like Ben and Kadi Laslow killed each other. Very bloody. Very painful. Very perfect."

"You are a fucking psychopath!" *Ben's not dead. He's not dead. He's not!*

Julia and Rick had been tailing him. They would make certain he was okay.

"I had an acquaintance waiting on Ben and Hayden." Sharon's smile could not have been more taunting. "He was going to make sure that Kadi was already dead by the time Ben joined the party." Her smile slipped a bit as her stare lingered on her watch. "Should've heard from him by now."

She swung around and pointed to one of the jackasses helping her. "Call Keegan. Find out what is taking his ass so long."

Keegan...that must be the man who'd had the order to kill Kadi? "I don't understand *why* you are doing this."

Sharon stalked closer to her. "Because your father is a bastard."

"I don't even *know* him!"

"I know him. He's the man who ordered the murder of my parents. I was twelve years old. *I* was in the house. I was supposed to be sleeping over at a friend's, but I'd gotten sick. I had to stay home." Tears slid down her cheeks. "I was *home* when your father's men arrived! My mom screamed for me to get under the bed, and I hid, and I heard *everything!*"

Twelve years old… "I'm sorry," Courtney said softly.

"I heard them say, 'No one betrays the Jackal.' Then the guns fired and my mom screamed, and I covered my mouth, and I didn't move. I didn't move until the smell got so bad that I had to crawl out from under the bed because I was going to vomit."

OhmyGod.

"Your father took my family from me." Sharon looked at the gun in her hand. "Now I'll take *his* family. He will have nothing."

"I am sorry for what happened to you and your family." Courtney lifted her chin. "But *I'm* not his family. I've never been in his life. He hasn't been in mine—"

Sharon leaned in close, putting her face close to Courtney's. "He's been in yours. Long before you did your stupid ancestry test to see where you came from. He *knew* the truth ever since Frank McKenna left you. He knew, and he's been pulling his strings all along. You think you magically got the plum job at the best law firm in Atlanta?"

"I *earned* that job. I graduated at the top—"

"You think you were given all the richest clients just because you were *lucky?*"

Courtney's breath froze in her lungs.

"And you had a bodyguard. Watching you always because your *father* became afraid in his old age. So afraid that someone like me…" Laughter. "Would want to make him suffer, too."

"Don't do this, Sharon."

"I already did it. I killed the man you loved..."

No, Ben isn't —

"Did you even realize you loved him? God, I used to laugh at you when I'd see you at the firm. Laugh at the way you tried to hold yourself back from everyone. So scared, weren't you? So scared to get hurt. But then you fell. I could *see* the way you looked at Ben today." She took a step back. "If it makes you feel better, I think he loved you, too. See, it was hard to get him to leave with Hayden. The only reason he finally did leave — well, Hayden said if Ben didn't leave right then, when you walked out of Ross's office, Hayden would fire a bullet into your heart."

Courtney shook her head.

"Want to know a secret?" Sharon put down the gun. Just put it on the stage floor. "We never planned to shoot you. That was just a lie Hayden told Ben. Shooting is too quick. Too easy for the Jackal's daughter. You're going to suffer. Messages are sent in this world. You'll be my message. When I carve you apart, your father will understand just what he's lost."

One of the men came forward and handed Sharon a long, wickedly sharp knife.

The other guy...he put down his phone. "Keegan isn't answering."

"Whatever." Sharon had taken the knife. "He'll be coming soon with Hayden. Just keep an eye out for them. Open the door when they arrive." She smiled. "I've got her."

She advanced on Courtney. The two men hurried toward the door.

When they were out of sight, Sharon said, "Maybe Keegan and Hayden won't ever show up. Maybe I don't have to worry about them anymore."

"That's why you didn't text or call Hayden and tell him that Ben was being tailed. You *wanted* him caught—"

"He was a means to an end. I'm at the end."

Courtney stared at the knife. Then at Sharon's smiling face.

***

"What in the hell are you doing here, Kendrick?" Eric asked before Ben could.

Kendrick inclined his head toward the chaos around him. "I have a new client."

Ben grabbed the guy, his *friend,* and his fingers clenched around Kendrick's shirt. "It had *better* not be Hayden Laslow."

"No." Kendrick's voice was controlled. Too calm. "I think we need to take this meeting away from the others. And we need to move *now.*"

Ben let him go and quickly followed Kendrick away from the cop cars and the sirens.

Kendrick paused next to his Mercedes. "Ross Worthington is dead, so his client came to me as soon as he heard the distressing news."

"The body isn't even cold yet," Eric muttered. "How the hell does news travel that fast?"

Kendrick smoothed his hands over his shirtfront. "For the right people, news can travel very,

very quickly indeed." He looked up at Ben. "I have an address for you."

Ben didn't move a muscle.

"You need to get there right away. If you don't arrive in time, I truly don't want to think about the consequences." A bead of sweat slid down Kendrick's temple. The guy *never* sweated. Never showed fear of any kind. But right then... "And I don't believe you want to think about those consequences, either."

"You know where Courtney is."

Kendrick gave him the address.

"Who is your client?" Eric demanded.

"You didn't hear this from me," Kendrick said. "You *never* heard this—"

Ben was already running away. He knew exactly who Kendrick's client was. *Courtney's father.* And he knew that if he didn't get to that address fast enough, Ben would lose his whole world.

CHAPTER TWENTY-ONE

"I'm sorry," Courtney said, voice choking out, "for what happened to you and your family."

The two goons were nowhere to be seen.

Sharon pricked her own finger on the blade of the knife, and her creepy smile stretched. "You're going beg me…"

"I'm sorry that your parents died. And I'm sorry…"

Sharon's eyes darted to Courtney's cheek. "Let's start here with the little cut that's already on you. I'll make it stretch from eyeball to chin. Won't that be nice?"

"I'm *sorry*," Courtney gritted out, "that you turned into such a psycho!" She kicked out with her legs. Because the dumbasses had only tied her hands together. Her hands were bound behind her back, but her legs were free. She kicked at Sharon, and the other woman screamed as she fell. The knife clattered across the stage, and Courtney rocked the chair hard. It went crashing down, and all of the breath was driven from her body as she hit the stage floor.

She blinked and saw that Sharon was scrambling for the knife. Shit. Courtney was still trapped. She'd hoped the stupid chair would break when she fell, but it hadn't. She kicked and jerked, moving with all of her strength. She twisted hard, her shoulders burning and —

Snap.

That hadn't been her shoulder. It had been the back of the chair. The old, wobbly chair. She rolled free, shimmying and heaving her body so that —

The knife sliced along her arm. Courtney screamed at the pain.

Sharon laughed. Then she stabbed Courtney in the shoulder. "You're going to die. You can join Ben. He's dead, dead, *dead* — "

She kicked Sharon in the kneecap. As hard as she could. Sharon's eyes flared with pain and shock because there had been a terrible crack.

Courtney kicked her other knee. Another crack.

Sharon fell, but she was still swiping out with the knife. It flew down Courtney's side, slicing her open, but she ignored the pain. Sharon yelled for the two men to come and help her. Sharon screamed for them as she rolled on the stage, unable to get up, the knife finally gone from her fingers.

The knife —

Courtney dove for it. She grabbed it — still with her hands behind her back — and started sawing at the rope that bound her.

Footsteps thundered from the front of the club.

The rope gave way. Courtney's breath left her in a wild sob as she brought the knife around to the front of her body.

"Shoot her!" Sharon screamed. "Shoot the bitch!"

"I-I thought we were gonna ransom her," one of the men called out. His gun was up and pointed at Courtney.

"*Shoot her now!*" Sharon ordered.

Courtney ran. Gun versus knife? Uh, she wasn't going to win.

A gun thundered, and she felt the bullet blaze across her hip, but she didn't stop running. Her hand clenched around the knife as she jumped for the side of the stage. There was a door there. Half-open. She shot through it and found herself in a long, dark hallway. She ran as fast as she could, ignoring the pain in her body. Desperate to get out. To find Ben. He had to be alive. She wouldn't consider any other possibility. Ben was alive. She'd get to him. She would survive.

They would be together.

She saw the glow of an exit sign in front of her. She slammed into the door beneath that sign, but…

It was jammed. The door wouldn't open.

She hit it again.

Again.

It wouldn't open.

Footsteps were running toward her. She slammed into the door again.

No fucking give.

The footsteps were too close. She whirled toward the man who'd chased her down the dark corridor. He was a big, hulking shadow, and cold laughter burst from him. "That door was nailed shut from the outside, lady. When the club closed, Hayden didn't want trash gettin' in…"

She gripped the knife and ignored the blood that covered her. He was going to lift that gun any moment and fire at her. There wasn't any place for her to run. She couldn't escape.

And I can't get to Ben. I can't tell him that I was afraid for too long. I should have grabbed tight to what he offered. I should have taken a chance.

Julia had warned her. Julia had told her the past would just hold her down.

My past is killing me.

She couldn't run any longer.

But she could attack.

It was dark, so he couldn't see her clearly. She couldn't see him that clearly, either. But he was a much bigger target.

Without a word, she lunged forward.

He fired.

***

Ben heard the sound of bullets as he raced toward the club. *No, no, no!* Not Courtney. Not her.

Eric and Simon were with him. More Wilde agents were supposed to be on the way. He wasn't waiting for that other backup to arrive. Gunshots were blasting, and Courtney was *in there.*

He ran for the front door, and some asshole shot at him. The bullet missed, and Simon fired the gun he carried. A grunt came from whoever the hell had just tried to kill Ben.

"Get back, Ben!" Simon blasted. "You don't have the training for this—"

The bastard who'd been waiting at the club's door was on the ground. His shoulder was bleeding and his gun—

Ben kicked it out of the way. "Where is she?" He had a weapon, one that Eric had given to him, and yeah, he knew exactly how to use it. He might not have the same training that Simon did but—

Ben heard another blast of gunfire from somewhere inside the club.

Ben didn't hesitate.

He ran into the darkness. "Courtney!" His heart thundered in his chest. Fear consumed him. Fear and rage. If Courtney had been hurt, if he got to her and—

A woman was on the stage. Crawling forward, with her body shuddering.

Ben staggered to a stop.

Sharon lifted her head. Smiled at him. "You're too late…p-payback…such…b-bitch…"

He bounded onto the stage. "Where is Courtney?"

"Dead. Exactly where…she's supposed to be…"

The gunfire had stopped. There was only silence. "*Courtney!*" Ben roared.

She had to be there. Had to be safe.

Sharon was laughing. Still trying to crawl. Getting *nowhere.*

And then Ben saw the blood on the wooden floor of the stage. Blood that made a trail as it led to the left — to a door down there...

He ran after that trail. Found himself in a long, dark hallway. His eyes strained to see. "*Courtney!*"

"Stop."

That wasn't Courtney's voice. A man's. Rough. Ragged.

Scared?

Ben heard someone running behind him. He stiffened.

"It's me," Eric rasped. A second later, Eric had a flashlight that he was shining in the dark.

Shining on the man who stood at the end of that corridor...and on the woman he held in his arms. Blood covered Courtney's shirt-front. Blood covered the bastard behind her.

But he gripped a gun. One that he had pressed to her temple.

"I'm not dying tonight," the guy shouted.

Ben lifted his gun. "If you don't let her go right now, I will kill you where you stand."

"No, no, you won't fire! You came for her! You won't hurt her!"

He would never hurt Courtney. She was the woman he loved. His fucking soul. He wouldn't hurt her, and he'd do *anything* to keep her safe.

"There is no way out of this," Eric called out. "We've got a team surrounding the building. You aren't getting away!"

"Shit, shit!" The gun jabbed into Courtney's temple. "I just wanted the ransom, you know? I-I didn't want murder..."

"Then let her go," Ben snarled. She was hurt so badly. He could see that. She was barely upright.

"Came running at me. Stabbed *me*..."

Ben took a slow step forward. His gaze remained on Courtney. "I love you."

Her lips trembled.

"You're the one for me, sweetheart. I want you to know that. The one I've been looking for my whole life." Another step. Eric kept his flashlight on the bastard who held her. Shining it straight into his eyes. Ben knew it was a deliberate distraction. *Another step. Another.* "You're the one, Courtney, that I want at my side for the rest of my life. The one I want to make happy. The one I want forever."

The fool with a death wish snapped, "*Stop, bastard! Stay away from her!*"

No. Never. "Courtney, you're the one I'd do anything for." Lie. Steal.

Kill.

And I'm close enough to touch her...now.

"*Now*," Ben shouted, knowing that Eric would completely understand what he wanted his brother to do. Just as he'd understood why Eric was shining the light for so long.

Eric turned off the light. The corridor was plunged into darkness. Courtney's attacker yelled as he was suddenly blinded.

Ben grabbed Courtney. He yanked her forward, shoving her behind his body even as he fired his gun. The bullet tore into its target and when the bastard who'd been holding Courtney screamed, Ben felt a savage satisfaction pour through him.

"Ben?"

The back door crashed in even as Ben pulled Courtney closer. Half a dozen Wilde agents swarmed inside, coming in with lights and weapons, and Ben saw that the jackass who'd threatened Courtney — he was on the floor, curled in a fetal position with his arms around his bleeding stomach.

"Ben?" Courtney's faint whisper.

He scooped her into his arms as her body seemed to go slack.

"Love you…" Courtney gasped.

"Baby?" His hold tightened. He could feel her blood against him, and terror clawed at Ben's insides. He ran with her, rushing outside, rushing past the Wilde agents. Rushing to the parking lot even as he saw the flash of lights in the distance.

Eric was shouting his name. Simon was trying to grab him.

While Ben was just holding tight to Courtney…because she was the only thing that mattered.

CHAPTER TWENTY-TWO

She didn't feel any pain. She remembered pain. Remembered a bullet slamming into her side when she'd been running at a man in the dark. She remembered a knife. A sharp blade. Remembered blood.

Fear.

But when her eyes cracked open, it seemed like a fog surrounded her. Everything was hazy. She felt numb as her head moved from side to side. She was looking for something. No, someone. Someone who needed to be there.

"I had to see you." A man's voice. Low. Rough. "So…sorry…"

That was the wrong voice. He was the wrong man. Not the one that she'd been looking for. Not the one she needed. Her head moved restlessly. She wanted him. Where was he? He wouldn't have left her. Not him. Not…

"Ben?" Courtney whispered.

***

"Why the hell am I not in the room with her?" Ben glowered at the doctor who blocked his path. "I'm her *family*. I should be back there with Courtney right now. You don't get to keep me from her."

The doctor glanced down at his notes. "One of the nurses said you caused trouble the last time you were in the ICU."

Ben surged forward. Eric grabbed one of his arms, and Simon grabbed the other as they fought to hold him back. It was a good thing they'd grabbed him. He might have decked the doc.

I still might.

"I'm not here to cause trouble," Ben gritted out as he was held back. "I'm here for her. I need to see Courtney. She is *my* family, and if you don't get out of the way right now—"

Ben saw movement down the hallway. Movement behind the doctor's back. Two big, steroid-raging dudes who hurried away from the wall and greeted a guy in a black suit as the fellow came stalking out of the ICU—

"Who the fuck is that?" Ben demanded. "And why is he leaving the ICU? I thought—" Now his wild gaze swung to Eric. "Courtney is in there. She's supposed to be guarded. Who is that guy?"

His brother looked confused, too. Eric's grip slackened, and so did Simon's. Ben tore free of them and barreled past the doctor. He raced toward the figure in black. "*Stop!*"

The goons whirled toward him. Their gazes were cold as death, but it was the man wearing the black suit—the man who stiffened before very, very slowly turning—it was that guy who held Ben's attention.

One look and Ben knew exactly who he was staring at. After all, it was hard to mistake one of the most infamous men in the United States.

Julian Rossi.

The murdering *Jackal.*

"The others don't come down this hallway. Understand?" Julian's voice was low. Polite.

At his words, his two men immediately sprang into action as they ran to intercept Eric and Simon. Ben glanced back at his brother. "They'd better not hurt—"

"Your brother and your friend won't be hurt. They'll be stopped. There's a difference."

Ben's gaze swung back to Julian Rossi.

He was tall. Almost...elegant in appearance. Faint lines spread from his eyes. His smile was chilling.

Ben's shoulders straightened. "I know who you are."

A nod. "Most of the world does."

"I know who you are to *her.*" Everything made dark sense.

Rossi's gaze drifted to the ICU. Lingered. Then it swung back to Ben. "No nurses are in there right now. No other patients. No one saw me enter, and when I leave this hospital, there will be no video footage that ever says I was here."

"Why *are* you here?"

"You know."

Because Julian's daughter had almost died.

Julian inclined his head toward Ben. "You say you know who I am...I know who *you* are to her, too."

"No, no, you have no clue—"

"You're the man my daughter called for when she opened her eyes."

What?

"You're the man she loves." Now Julian seemed to take Ben's measure. "Are you afraid of me?"

Smart people would be afraid. He wasn't feeling smart. He was feeling desperate. And crazy. "I almost lost the woman *I* love. Losing her is the only thing that scares me." He stepped forward, moving toe-to-toe with the killer. With Courtney's *father*. "So, no, I'm not particularly afraid of you. But I don't want you *ever* doing anything to hurt her, you understand?" His voice went low and lethal. "Courtney is the one for me. She's my fucking everything. I will destroy anyone or anything who ever tries to hurt her."

Julian's slow smile was the last thing he expected. "Good," Julian told him. "You'll do."

What. The. Hell?

Julian's smile vanished. "I'm everything they say and more. I never planned to have kids because I knew they'd be threatened. Everything I love is threatened in this world. *I* knew the truth from the time Courtney was five years old, but staying away from her..." Once more, his gaze slid to ICU. "It was the only way I could show her that I *did* care." He swallowed. "She won't understand that. And she'll hate what I am. The things I've done…" His jaw hardened. "I'm not a good man."

Uh, no. Serious freaking understatement.

"But my daughter…she is the *one* good thing that ever came from me." A low exhale. "Make her happy. Keep her safe." A shake of Julian's head. "I don't want my world to ever touch her again. I swear, I will make *sure* that it doesn't."

Julian snapped his fingers, and his two men hurried back to his side. Without another word, Julian turned and walked away.

"She's the best thing that ever happened to me." Ben's body was rock hard with tension. "I'll spend every day making her happy, and I'd give my life to keep her safe."

"I know." Julian glanced back at him. "That's why you're still breathing."

Ben's eyes narrowed.

Julian gave him a little smile. And then he was gone.

Footsteps thundered toward Ben. He whirled and saw both Simon and Eric closing in. Eric's face showed his shock. "Tell me that wasn't—"

"It wasn't," Ben told him flatly. "It wasn't anyone."

He shoved open the door to ICU and rushed inside. The place was deserted, just like Julian had said, and dammit, the nurses and doctors needed to get their asses in there. Courtney was hurt. She needed help. She needed—

He shoved aside a curtain and saw her in a hospital bed. Her skin was too pale. A tube fed into her arm. The doctor had told him that the bullet lodged in her side had been removed. The jackass in the dark corridor had shot her right before Ben had arrived. She'd been stitched up. She'd been *shot* and *stabbed*, and she'd survived. She'd kept fighting.

"There… you are." Her voice was weak, and it was so beautiful to him. Her hand lifted as she tried to reach for him.

Instantly, his fingers curled around hers.

"Knew you…wouldn't leave."

He leaned over her. Pressed a tender kiss to her cheek. "Not ever."

Her dark gaze was so tender. "I…love you."

"Baby, I will love you forever." It felt as if he'd already loved her his whole life but really…they were just getting started. He would be with her for everything. Every good moment. Every bad one. He'd be there to see her smiles. To watch her triumphs. To grow old with her.

Everything. Anything. He wanted it with her.

Her lashes flickered. "Was…someone else here?"

Ben tightened his hold on her. "He's gone."

She stared at him, and he realized that she knew exactly who'd been there. And who'd slipped away. Courtney nodded. "When I opened my eyes…" Her voice was still weak. "I wanted you."

And I will always want you.

"Don't…don't be my enemy any…more…"

"I never was." He pressed another kiss to her cheek. "Sweetheart, don't you see? I've always been the man in love with you."

Her lower lip trembled.

"And I will always be."

***

One week later…

"What are you doin' here?" Hayden Laslow jerked upright as he sat at the interrogation table. "You can't be here!"

Ben nodded toward the cop who waited a few feet away before focusing on his prey. "I have some friends in good places. They let me come in for this little talk. You know…seeing as how I *am* representing your wife in the divorce case…"

Hayden surged out of his chair.

The cop immediately shoved him right back down. Then he handcuffed Hayden to the table.

"Thanks for that," Ben told the cop. Daniel. They'd played cards a few times. Daniel was pretty good at bluffing.

Ben opened his briefcase and slid a stack of documents across the table. "As you'll see, you're getting nothing from the divorce. My client will be free of you, and you'll rot for the rest of your life."

Hayden snarled, "You—"

"I would be very, very careful if I were you," Ben told him softly.

Hayden stiffened.

"You targeted Courtney for a reason." Now he leaned across the table. The better for Hayden to fully understand him. "See, at first, I thought you were doing it for revenge. And Sharon, she *did* want revenge. But you…" He wagged a finger at Hayden. "You wanted power, too, didn't you?"

"You have no idea what you're talking about."

"My client is cooperating with the detectives in this station. Telling the cops *and* the feds everything that she knows about your business practices. *All* of your business practices."

Hayden's fingers were shaking as he reached for the pile of papers in front of him. "You gonna believe my bitch of an ex? *She* was willing to sell out your Courtney."

Kadi had confessed that truth, and she'd begged Courtney to forgive her. Kadi seemed like a different person, scared, lost, and she'd been visiting Courtney's hospital room over and over, pleading for forgiveness. She appeared genuine. Ben hadn't been ready to believe her, but it had been Courtney who told him things had to change. Courtney had said she didn't want to let bitterness and anger consume her.

Screw that, sweetheart.

Ben was still riding out his own rage. His gaze was on the current object of his fury. "*You* were looking to take over power, weren't you? What did you think would happen? That Courtney would be your leverage? That she'd draw your real target out? That you could take *him* out?"

"Like I said before, I don't know what you are talking about—"

"You failed," Ben said simply. "But you didn't think about failure when you started this, did you? Didn't think about the fact that the person you were trying to take down...if rumors are true, there are *plenty* of people in prison who owe him favors."

"I'll tell the world who she is!" Spittle flew from Hayden's mouth. "*I'm* the one who got her results from that stupid ancestry site. *I'm* the one who was monitoring her mother's family because I knew about her mother's past. *I'm* the one who pushed Worthington to get more DNA so we could get definitive proof." A smug smile. "Everyone will know, everyone—"

Ben walked around the table and bent to whisper in Hayden's ear, "There is nothing to tell. You need to worry less about who Courtney is...and more about the people you're going to be coming into contact with when you're locked away. You need to worry about who you can really trust in this world. And who might just be planning to kill you."

Hayden's head turned toward him.

The interrogation room door clicked closed.

Hayden jerked.

"Don't worry. That's just the cop leaving so we can have a minute alone."

"But, no, you—you can't—" Fear flashed in Hayden's eyes.

"I can," Ben said quietly. "I did. I can get to you anytime and anywhere. And so can *he*. You ever think of coming after Courtney, of sending *anyone* after her, and you're dead." He wanted the message received.

Hayden's breath heaved out. "You...you wouldn't hurt me."

"I would kill you in an instant."

Hayden choked.

Ben smiled. "Good to know we understand each other." He slapped Hayden's shoulder. "Don't forget to sign those papers for Kadi. She's looking forward to the single life." He picked up his bag and headed for the door.

"She's just like him!" Hayden yelled.

Ben stilled.

"I heard she *broke* both of Sharon's kneecaps. Like father, like daughter, right? How does it feel to know you'll be screwing a psychopath? She's never been close to anyone, has she? Because she *can't* form those attachments. He can't, either. They can't love. They can only kill and destroy. It's their nature."

His shoulders straightened as Ben turned. "It's *your* nature. You just described yourself. You didn't describe Courtney."

"'Cause you think she loves you! She doesn't! You're a fool! She'll kill you or her dad will kill—"

"Mention her father again, and let's see what happens."

Fear flashed in Hayden's eyes. His lips pressed together.

"You don't have any power now." They needed to be clear on this. "The money will be Kadi's. The businesses will be hers." *That* was why he was finishing her case. Because he wanted to take every single thing from Hayden Laslow. "You will have nothing, and you won't be able to get *anyone* to help you. You're going to be a target. So, if I were you, I'd start thinking of ways to save your ass."

Hayden's lower lip trembled.

"I think we understand each other now." With that, Ben was done. He exited, strolled into the hallway, and motioned for Daniel to head back inside. Ben exhaled before he rounded the corner, and…hell, he wasn't particularly surprised to find Kendrick waiting for him.

Kendrick lifted his brows. "Fancy seeing you here."

Ben strode toward him. "Thank you for the address." They hadn't talked since that night. He knew Kendrick had been avoiding him.

Voice low, Kendrick said, "You didn't get it from me."

"Are you in trouble, man? Do you need help?"

"I can handle my business, don't worry about that." He gave a nod. "And don't worry about Courtney. You didn't need to visit Hayden Laslow. No one will find out who her father is."

Ben was working to make sure of that fact. He'd be going to see Sharon next—

Kendrick glanced around. No one else was in the hallway. "For the record, Rossi didn't order the hit on Sharon Long's parents."

"How do you know that?"

"Because sometimes, my clients tell me the truth." Kendrick whistled. "He wanted Courtney to know that. Plenty of sins are at his door, but not that one."

Courtney had told him about Sharon's past. "If he didn't do it, who did?"

"Funny story." No humor was in his eyes. "According to my client, it was actually one of his underlings. A junior guy who wanted to steal power from the big boss. He was a much younger punk back then." One brow lifted. "Maybe you know him...Hayden Laslow."

What the hell?

"Sharon knows the truth. I was able to provide her with proof this morning when we had a very short but fruitful conversation." Kendrick's gaze glittered. "Believe me when I say that she will *never* be a problem for you or Courtney again. Of course, Sharon will also never be getting out of jail again, either. She will *die* in prison." A pause. "You know that she hired the men who abducted Kadi. Before she hired that crew, though, she employed Donnie Dwight."

Now the guy was spilling about Donnie?

"Donnie was supposed to abduct Courtney in the parking garage, and when he failed there, he was supposed to grab her in the park."

"Did Donnie break into Courtney's house?"

"No, that was all Sharon...from what I can gather." His shoulders rolled back. Sadness thickened his voice when he said, "Donnie ran down Cole Vincent, and Donnie was paid by Sharon to hit your side of the Benz. Sharon wanted you out of her way."

"Where'd you get all of this information?"

"My *client* wanted you to know all the facts."

"And *you* know that the cops have proven that Sharon's gun was the same one used to kill Donnie."

Kendrick nodded. "You understand why I am happy to tell you the full details about her actions. I will also make sure that any additional proof that I am given finds its way to the proper authorities. As I said, that woman will spend the rest of her life in prison."

So would Hayden Laslow. Though Ben wondered just how long of a life those two would have.

"Courtney will be safe," Kendrick assured him. "Always."

"Hell, yes, she will be." As far as Ben was concerned, one of the biggest threats to her was Courtney's father. "I will stand between her and any threat. I'm not afraid of him. Never will be. He *won't* hurt Courtney. He'd have to go through me first."

"Message received."

Ben hesitated. This was Kendrick. "Are you sure that you're okay?"

"He's not my enemy." Kendrick's lips twisted. "And he's not yours. It's the rest of the world that needs to fear him."

***

She was finally getting out of the hospital. Courtney didn't exactly have *stuff* that needed to go home with her. Ben had brought her a change of clothes, and she was dressed and sitting on the edge of the hospital bed. Her heart raced because she was so ready to get out of there. So ready for—

The hospital door opened. A nurse was there, pushing in a wheelchair. "Policy," she told Courtney with a nod. "You have to be wheeled to the front door."

What? Why?

"So you can't fall on the way out and sue the hospital. *Policy*," the nurse said again as if she'd just read Courtney's mind.

Courtney slid into the chair.

The door opened again. This time, Ben was there. He saw her, and his dimples flashed. "Ready to go, sweetheart?"

Her hands patted the wheelchair. "I, um, have to be wheeled out in the—"

He scooped her into his arms. "I've got you."

"No!" The nurse shook her head. "That is not the way—"

Ben carried Courtney into the hall. "Are you feeling okay?"

"The best." She stared into his eyes. Her arm had looped around his neck.

"You scared the hell out of me. I don't want you ever hurt again." He took her inside the elevator. People at the nurses' station gaped, but she didn't care.

"I'd rather you not be hurt, too." The elevator doors closed. They were alone. "Sharon told me that Hayden was going to kill you. I've never been as afraid as I was right then." She stared into his eyes. "I don't want anything to happen to you."

"Nothing will." He pressed a tender kiss to her lips. "Baby, nothing will take me away from you."

The doors opened. He carried her through the lobby and outside—to his new Benz. Carefully, tenderly, he seated her inside, then he hurried to the driver's side. He started the ignition—

Her hand flew out and touched his wrist. "My father is Julian Rossi."

"Yes, I know."

"He's...a killer."

"That's what I've heard."

Because they'd talked about it over and over. Yet she still had to say... "He has...enemies." Serious understatement. "People who might target me. I can't—I *won't* have you put at risk for me."

His head turned toward her. And once more, his dimples winked. "Having you is worth any risk, don't you know that?"

"Ben—"

"You're safe. We're safe. You don't need to be afraid." He leaned over and brushed a kiss to her lips.

Tears stung her eyes. Her fantasy of a father? It had turned into a real nightmare. "I'm a monster's daughter."

"No." He stared straight at her. "You're the woman I love. The woman I want to spend the rest of my life with. That's who you are. You're Courtney McKenna. Perfect, beautiful, strong, smart. You are my life."

"And you're mine," she whispered back. Fear gnawed at her. "But what if...what if I'm like him?"

Ben laughed. "You're not." He was so confident. His eyes seemed to shine with love as he stared at her.

"Ben..."

"Do you love me, Courtney?"

"With all of my heart."

"Good. Because you *own* my heart." His gaze turned even brighter. "You're not like him, baby. You will never be like him. You are everything that is good in my world." He spoke with such utter certainty.

When she'd been younger and the social worker had said that she couldn't attach...Courtney had feared that he was right. She'd feared that she'd always be alone. The one who would never fit in. The one who didn't *feel* like the others.

But with Ben, she was different. She loved him so much. With a depth that left her shaken. She wanted to laugh with him, talk with him, love with him—forever. She wanted to grab tight and never let go. "You're the good part of my world, too." An anchor that she'd always been looking for. One that had been closer than she realized.

His dimples winked. "Then let's get the hell out of here, huh? Because I want to take you home."

Home. The word pierced through her. As she stared in Ben's eyes, Courtney realized that she was home.

He was her home. The only one she'd ever need. She'd found her real family. She'd found him.

EPILOGUE

One year later.

"Wilde and Wilde…" Ben turned, his smile stretching and his blue eyes twinkling. "That is the *best* name for a law firm ever!"

Courtney laughed. They'd gotten married a week ago. One week—at a crazy, wonderful, unforgettable Vegas wedding. Instead of starting her own practice, she and Ben were creating *their* practice. Not enemies in court any longer. Partners.

In law.

In life.

She sat on the edge of the new desk that had just been brought in the office. A desk that they would totally have to christen. The last twelve months had been a blur. Hayden and Sharon had gone to prison. The men who'd helped them? Locked away, too.

She hadn't heard from her father, and Courtney knew, deep down, that she probably never would. She had a vague memory of him being at her hospital bed. He'd come to see her, come to make certain she was okay.

The world said he was a monster.

Everything she knew about him said the same thing. But...

I think I remember him saying he loved me.

All DNA evidence linking them had been destroyed. Kendrick Shaw had delivered that news. The ancestry company she'd used? Shut down.

Her father's power was stronger than she'd realized.

But her love for Ben?

It was stronger than anything in the world.

Ben lifted his hand, and his fingers stroked over her cheek. "Where did you go?"

She leaned into his touch. "Nowhere. I'm right where I want to be." The only place she wanted to be—with him.

Ben had told her about his talk with her father. By staying out of her life, Julian was trying to offer her the only thing he had to give...protection.

She'd always been afraid to give her heart to a man because she hadn't wanted to be cast aside again. But Courtney knew she didn't have to worry. Ben wasn't going anywhere. Neither was she. She would fight with all of her strength for their life together. And it would be a good life. No, an *amazing* life.

One that was filled with smiles, and laughter, and the law, and yes...

There would be bad times. Life was a mix of good and bad. But they'd face the bad times. Together, they could face anything.

***

Eric flattened his hands on his desk. "I'm giving you an opportunity here."

Cole Vincent straightened in his chair. "You aren't going to regret this."

"I sincerely hope not." Eric cast his gaze over his newest agent. Cole had been in physical therapy for months, and then he'd started busting ass to prove that he could be a better person…or rather, a better bodyguard. "I'm going to partner you up with Julia. She'll teach you the ropes. Do what she says and don't piss her off."

Cole nodded. "I think I can manage that."

The guy didn't know Julia. "Don't be too sure…" Eric murmured, but he waved his hand. "You'll find her waiting outside."

Cole scrambled to get out of the office. When the door shut behind him, Eric pulled out his phone. In moments, Piper's beautiful face filled his screen.

"I need to see her," he said. *And I always need to see you.*

Piper moved her phone, changing the angle, and his daughter's smile filled the screen.

The End

A NOTE FROM THE AUTHOR

Thanks so much for taking the time to read BEFORE BEN. I hope you enjoyed his story. After I wrote PROTECTING PIPER, I received so many notes from readers about Ben—I just had to give him a book of his own. It was time for Eric's younger brother to find his own happy ending. Everyone deserves a happy ending, right?

If you have a chance, please consider leaving a review for the story. Reviews help people to discover new books. (And authors love them!)

If you'd like to stay updated on my releases and sales, please join my newsletter list.

http://www.cynthiaeden.com/newsletter/

Again, thank you for reading BEFORE BEN.

Best,
Cynthia Eden
www.cynthiaeden.com

ABOUT THE AUTHOR

Award-winning author Cynthia Eden writes dark tales of paranormal romance and romantic suspense. She is a New York Times, USA Today, Digital Book World, and IndieReader best-seller. Cynthia is also a three-time finalist for the RITA® award. Since she began writing full-time in 2005, Cynthia has written over eighty novels and novellas.

For More Information

- *www.cynthiaeden.com*
- *http://www.facebook.com/cynthiaedenfanpage*
- *http://www.twitter.com/cynthiaeden*

HER OTHER WORKS

Romantic Suspense
- Secret Admirer

Wilde Ways
- Protecting Piper (Book One, Wilde Ways)
- Guarding Gwen (Book Two, Wilde Ways)
- Before Ben (Book Three, Wilde Ways)

Dark Sins
- Don't Trust A Killer (Book One, Dark Sins)
- Don't Love A Liar (Book Two, Dark Sins)

Lazarus Rising
- Never Let Go (Book One, Lazarus Rising)
- Keep Me Close (Book Two, Lazarus Rising)
- Stay With Me (Book Three, Lazarus Rising)
- Run To Me (Book Four, Lazarus Rising)

- Lie Close To Me (Book Five, Lazarus Rising)
- Hold On Tight (Book Six, Lazarus Rising)

Dark Obsession Series

- Watch Me (Dark Obsession, Book 1)
- Want Me (Dark Obsession, Book 2)
- Need Me (Dark Obsession, Book 3)
- Beware Of Me (Dark Obsession, Book 4)
- Only For Me (Dark Obsession, Books 1 to 4)

Mine Series

- Mine To Take (Mine, Book 1)
- Mine To Keep (Mine, Book 2)
- Mine To Hold (Mine, Book 3)
- Mine To Crave (Mine, Book 4)
- Mine To Have (Mine, Book 5)
- Mine To Protect (Mine, Book 6)
- Mine Series Box Set Volume 1 (Mine, Books 1-3)
- Mine Series Box Set Volume 2 (Mine, Books 4-6)

Other Romantic Suspense

- First Taste of Darkness
- Sinful Secrets
- Until Death
- Christmas With A Spy

Paranormal Romance
Bad Things

- The Devil In Disguise (Bad Things, Book 1)
- On The Prowl (Bad Things, Book 2)
- Undead Or Alive (Bad Things, Book 3)
- Broken Angel (Bad Things, Book 4)
- Heart Of Stone (Bad Things, Book 5)
- Tempted By Fate (Bad Things, Book 6)
- Bad Things Volume One (Books 1 to 3)
- Bad Things Volume Two (Books 4 to 6)
- Bad Things Deluxe Box Set (Books 1 to 6)
- Wicked And Wild (Bad Things, Book 7)
- Saint Or Sinner (Bad Things, Book 8)

Bite Series

- Forbidden Bite (Bite Book 1)
- Mating Bite (Bite Book 2)

Blood and Moonlight Series

- Bite The Dust (Blood and Moonlight, Book 1)
- Better Off Undead (Blood and Moonlight, Book 2)
- Bitter Blood (Blood and Moonlight, Book 3)
- Blood and Moonlight (The Complete Series)

Purgatory Series
- The Wolf Within (Purgatory, Book 1)
- Marked By The Vampire (Purgatory, Book 2)
- Charming The Beast (Purgatory, Book 3)
- Deal with the Devil (Purgatory, Book 4)
- The Beasts Inside (Purgatory, Books 1 to 4)

Bound Series
- Bound By Blood (Bound Book 1)
- Bound In Darkness (Bound Book 2)
- Bound In Sin (Bound Book 3)
- Bound By The Night (Bound Book 4)
- Forever Bound (Bound, Books 1 to 4)
- Bound in Death (Bound Book 5)

Made in the USA
Coppell, TX
16 March 2020